THE
VIGILANTE'S
Bride

THE VIGILANTE'S Bride

YVONNE HARRIS

BETHANY HOUSE PUBLISHERS

Minneapolis, Minnesota

Published by Bethany House Publishers
11400 Hampshire Avenue South
Bloomington, Minnesota 55438

Bethany House Publishers is a division of
Baker Publishing Group, Grand Rapids, Michigan.

Printed in the United States of America

Library of Congress Cataloging-in-Publication Data

Harris, Yvonne L.
     The vigilante's bride / Yvonne Harris.
          p.   cm.
     ISBN 978-0-7642-0804-1 (pbk.)
     1. Mail order brides – Fiction. 2. Cowboys – Fiction. 3. Montana – Fiction.
I. Title.
     PS3608.A78329V54   2010
     813'.6 – dc22

                                                                                2010007458

For Robert, again

CHAPTER
1

"Marry him? I most certainly will not. Why, I've never laid eyes on the man!"

Emily McCarthy jumped to her feet and threw the copy of the *Chicago Daily Tribune* on the desk. It was folded open to a page of bride advertisements, one of them circled in red.

"What kind of man advertises in the newspaper for a wife, anyway? Is he crazy?" With hands folded tight to hide their trembling, Emily stared across the desk at an unsmiling Elvira Beecham, director of Aldersgate Home for Girls.

"Indeed not. Sit down, dear. You're white as a sheet. Our solicitor checked his references and gave a most favorable recommendation to the board. Bartholomew Axel is a wealthy widower in Repton, Montana. I'm sorry, Emily, but the board has decided it's time for you to leave."

"But not to marry a total stranger. I won't do that. I'll go back east and look up my mother's family. Maybe I can live with them until I find something."

"I doubt you can find them," Miss Beecham said gently. She toyed with a round paperweight on her desk, rocking the glass ball back and forth in her palms. "We tried years ago to locate them, but no one knew your mother's maiden name, only that she was a shop girl in Richmond, Virginia, before she married your father and came to Chicago."

Emily gripped the edge of the desk, fighting a surge of panic. Aldersgate was the only home she'd ever known. She'd been brought there as an infant, found crying alongside her dead mother in a Chicago boardinghouse. She had no memories of any other life.

"On your behalf, I suggested we accept Mr. Axel's offer of matrimony." Miss Beecham paused, as though considering her words. "It's not unusual for a man to go this route. There are few available women out west, and I imagine the competition is very keen." She smiled. "Don't look so sad, dear. Marrying Mr. Axel is an opportunity for any woman. He's rich and he's respected. I did what I truly thought best for you."

Emily leaned forward and studied the older woman's face for some sign of compromise. Instead, she saw a tight mouth, seamed shut with resolve.

She'd known this day was coming, but she'd hoped it wouldn't. For the past two years she'd tried to find employment on her own. Miss Beecham had taught her to typewrite, and Emily had written dozens of letters and applications, looking for a teaching position or something in an office or a bank. Or perhaps as a governess.

But Chicago, like the rest of the country, was struggling

through the worst depression in the nation's history. Banks had failed, and unemployment lines stretched for blocks. Aldersgate had had seventy-five applicants one day last month when a rumor got out they needed a hired girl—and half of them were men.

"Miss Beecham, please don't make me leave. If you're dissatisfied with my work, tell me and I'll—"

"I've never been dissatisfied with you. You're a wonderful teacher. The children love you." She shook her head. "I'm sorry, Emily. None of this is your fault."

Miss Beecham folded her hands and looked across at Emily. "There's a new law passed about educating Indians, an experiment to 'civilize' them, teach them our ways. The government is sending hundreds of Indian girls to white boarding schools and orphanages, like ours, and they are paying handsomely for each Indian student we accept. We can sleep six more girls in your room. Frankly, Aldersgate needs the money. That's the main reason the board decided you have to leave."

"But—" Emily's voice caught. A slow, deep breath forced it steady. Eighteen-year-olds did not cry. When she trusted herself to speak, she straightened her shoulders. "This is not what I want to do."

"I know, dear. Unfortunately, it's what the board wants." Miss Beecham pushed her chair back and stood, signaling the discussion was over.

Emily clenched her hands together so tight her fingers hurt. A sick feeling dug at her stomach at the thought of marrying a stranger. Married? Why, she'd never even had a beau.

"What does he look like? How old is he?" she asked, her words stiff.

"I don't know. I didn't think to ask for a photograph," Miss Beecham said kindly. "Now go upstairs and begin to get your things together. Mr. Axel wants a Christmas wedding." A girlish smile lit Elvira Beecham's face. Her hand fluttered to her throat and fussed with the ruffled collar. "Isn't that romantic?"

Emily glared at her.

"He's taken care of everything. Mr. Phineas Martin, his banker, will meet you in Billings, Montana, and accompany you on the stagecoach to Mr. Axel's ranch in Repton. Mr. Martin promised me he'll see to it that you are properly married and settled in before he leaves the Axel ranch."

In spite of herself, a rush of hot tears filled Emily's eyes. Quickly, she looked at the floor to hide them. It was all decided.

The director sighed. "Be sensible, Emily. There's little a woman—a decent woman—can do here without a husband. Be a good wife to him, and I expect you'll be happy. He's provided the best of accommodations for you—even a ticket on the new Pullman car, not the coach."

With three quick steps she was around the desk. Smiling, she threw her arms around Emily and hugged her tight. "It's a blessing, dear. The Lord is giving you a chance to have a home and family of your own."

❧

DICKINSON, NORTH DAKOTA
DECEMBER 23, 1884

"B-o-o-o-a-r-d. All aboard!"

The conductor raised and lowered a red lantern, signaling

the engineer it was time to leave the station. Two short whistle toots answered. He swung up the metal steps of Pullman Car 67 and slammed the door. A banging cannonade ran the length of the train as steel couplings clanked together. Bell dinging, the locomotive pulled away.

Inside Car 67, Emily watched the darkened passenger depot glide past the window. She leaned back against the velvet seat and slumped with weariness. Would this trip never end? She'd left Chicago early yesterday morning. Already she'd traveled eight hundred miles, and she still had four hundred more to go before she reached Billings, Montana.

Her new home. She wrinkled her nose.

Montana Territory was a wilderness, a land full of outlaws and Indians and so uncivilized that horses were the only transportation. Horses! She rolled her eyes. Chicago had electric streetcars and a museum—a symphony, even.

Frowning, she stared out the window, trying to come to grips with the direction her life was taking. Her knees rocked gently with the rhythmic clicking of the wheels.

The car gleamed with mahogany panels and armrests, dark and rich-looking. The lush carpet, the upholstery, and the velvet curtains separating her private little cubicle from the aisle were of a paisley-figured burgundy. Below the arched ceiling of the sleeping car ran a foot-wide brass border that caught the light from the oil lamps overhead and glimmered, rosy and wine-colored.

Despite her fatigue, she looked nice and she knew it. Everything she wore was brand-new. More excited than she, Miss Beecham had taken her shopping with money the board had provided.

Emily smoothed the pleats of the midnight blue linen skirt over her knees. Miss Beecham had picked it out and also chose the tucked white waist with a ladylike collar so high it tickled her chin. She supposed she should feel very fashionable, very grown-up, but at that moment she was close to tears.

Ankles together, she stuck her feet out in front of her. Her first high heels, stylish Blucher-cut oxfords with black patent toes and a gray-kid vamp buttoned up the sides to just above her ankles—"low cut, very modern," Miss Beecham said. Emily made a face at the shoes.

Ugly old things.

She lowered her feet to the floor and went over in her head again the alternatives to marrying Bartholomew Axel. There weren't many. A job was what she needed, not a husband. She loved teaching, loved kids, and that was what Aldersgate had trained her to do. But there were no jobs in the middle of the school year, not unless some old maid teacher ran off to get married. Or died.

At this point she'd take any kind of work, even wash dishes to earn a living.

Leaning her cheek against the cool window glass, she scolded herself. *Be sensible. You need some way to support yourself—or else a husband.*

She wondered what Mr. Axel looked like. Not boyishly handsome, of course. He had to be a little older than she was to own and operate a successful ranch, but certainly elegant looking, a trifle dashing, perhaps. She hoped he wasn't tall. She was short, and big men made her nervous.

Her thoughts turned to her wedding and marrying a stranger. Not at all the way she'd dreamed it would be. The girls at school always giggled when they talked about it. Somehow, it'd never struck her the least bit funny. She wanted to be in love when she got married, totally, completely in love with a handsome man who adored her.

Mrs. Bartholomew Axel. Her throat tightened.

So much for love. She sent a quick prayer heavenward for the strength to get through this wedding—and possibly the rest of her life. She'd prayed a lot recently, had gone down on her knees every night since she'd read Mr. Axel's newspaper ad and begged Jesus to get her out of this. *Help me, help me . . .*

Nothing yet. Not a hint of an answer had come to her.

A white-jacketed Négro worked his way along the aisle with a basket and a big enameled coffeepot. Legs braced against the lurching of the train, he offered refreshments to the special Pullman passengers.

A few minutes later, she raised the cup to her lips, and her sense of humor bubbled up. She smiled and glanced around quickly, then extended her little finger out from the handle and sipped, imitating the society women she'd seen in Chicago. Why, in no time at all she'd be acting like a rich rancher's wife.

With a wobbly little sigh she set the cup in the saucer. She didn't *want* to be a rich rancher's wife.

The engine labored upgrade. Beyond the window, a cliffside, slicked with ice, glittered like diamonds in the moonlight. The silhouette of a stag bounded in graceful leaps down the embankment away from the tracks.

Up ahead, the locomotive belched black smoke. Sparks shot from the funnel as the engine snaked around a curve and out of sight. The train picked up speed, rushing down the other side, highballing it for Montana.

The car rocked. Lamp oil swirled in the ceiling globes. Faster and faster the landscape blurred past. Up ahead, the locomotive pistons pounded out his name.

AX-el AX-el AX-el AX-el AX-el AX-el AX-el . . .

The whistle shrieked.

Billings in the morning.

Billings in the morning.

LEWISTOWN, MONTANA

One month earlier, shortly before dark, the vigilance committee for the Montana Cattlemen's Association had caught eleven rustlers. They shot four and hanged the rest, left seven dead men swinging from the branches of two big oaks as a warning to other thieves.

A tall man holding a coil of rope rode a gray horse into the clearing. Erect, head up, he looked around, checking the preparations to hang the last rustler, a man named Willis.

He glanced at the thick tree limb overhead and nodded to the waiting ranchers. It would do.

Guarded by two men with rifles, Willis squinted up at him. "Ain't you Luke Sullivan?"

"So what if I am?"

"You the boss of these killers?"

Sullivan's mouth tightened. "You got something to say?"

He pulled several lengths of rope forward and began to form another noose.

"My name's Willis, and I knew your pa, that's what." He glanced at the group of fourteen silent, angry ranchers and licked his lips. "I got something you oughta know. Cut me a deal."

"No deals." Eight times Sullivan wound the rope around the top of the open loop and jerked each coil taut.

Willis stared at Sullivan's hands. "That's for me, ain't it?" he whispered.

Sullivan didn't answer.

Willis swallowed. "Your old man was cheated. That poker game was rigged. He never shoulda lost your ranch."

Sullivan's hands stilled, and he looked down at Willis. "That was twenty years ago and my pa was drunk."

"Not that drunk. Bart Axel stole the ranch and a thousand dollars from your pa, and that's a fact. I helped him do it." Willis talked fast, his voice thick and desperate. "I worked with Axel. We did it lots a times. Bart set them up, and I was the stranger who sat in at the last minute."

"Why?" Sullivan slid the coils together.

"Axel wanted your pa's place. He thought the railroad was coming through there."

"It didn't. They laid it ten miles west." Sullivan's voice rasped like steel files grating together. He'd been six years old then, and his little world had collapsed. His whole family had died because of that card game. Pa lost everything.

Two ranchers pulled Willis to his feet. Roughly, they bound his hands behind him, boosted him onto his big spotted mare, and led her under the oak tree. Sullivan rode alongside.

Willis looked over at Sullivan. "Let me go, and I'll help you get Axel. I swear I will."

Granville Stuart, owner of the giant D-S cattle outfit and leader of the vigilance committee, walked his horse next to Sullivan's and lowered his voice. "They were running off two hundred head today. We can't let him go."

"I know—didn't ask you to."

Stuart nodded and moved off to another group of men. Sullivan watched him swing down from the saddle to help collect their gear and rifles. The snow had started again, coming down hard, big wet flakes that clung to hat brims and coat sleeves. They were all anxious to leave. Some of the men had already mounted their horses.

Willis sobbed. His shoulders shook, and tears added to the wetness on his face. "Sullivan, I'm sorry 'bout your ranch and your family. I'm sorry . . . I'm sorry."

Sullivan stared at him. He rarely thought about his family. It'd been so long he couldn't remember their faces anymore.

He tossed the free end of the rope up to a worker straddling a tree limb overhead. The man hauled up the rope and fastened it tight. Another rancher stepped under the tree to hold Willis's horse.

The empty noose turned slowly in the air.

Sullivan caught it, settled it around Willis's neck, and slid the rope high under the left jaw. He snugged the knot tight behind Willis's ear to make certain the neck snapped clean and death was instant. That was the most he could do for him.

Sullivan backed his horse away. "May God have mercy on you. I don't."

He gave a curt nod to the waiting rancher beside Willis.

At the signal, the rancher threw his hand back and slapped the rump of Willis's mare, hard. She snorted and bolted from under the tree. Overhead, the branch sagged under the sudden weight.

Willis kicked once.

Snow sifted down and blanketed the ground in white silence.

Sullivan reined his horse around and galloped off alone.

He'd grown up with the harsh justice of range law, even believed in it. Frontier justice was better than no justice at all, he'd always thought. Until tonight.

When he got back to the D-S ranch that night, the biggest cattle spread in Montana, Luke Sullivan walked up the front steps of Granville Stuart's house and told his boss he quit.

"You're leaving on account of tonight, aren't you?" Stuart said.

Luke blew his breath out hard and nodded. "I know what we're doing is necessary, but I got no stomach for it anymore." He turned toward the door.

"Where you headed?" Stuart asked.

"Back to New Hope. Don't know after that."

Stuart stood up. "Luke, I hate to lose you. You're the best ranch foreman I ever had. Stay and I'll take you off the committee, if that's what you want."

"Thanks anyway."

Stuart slammed his hands on the desktop. "Willis could've been lying about Axel and your pa!"

Luke paused with his hand on the doorknob, not turning around. "I doubt it," he said slowly. "A man don't lie with a noose around his neck. Not even his kind."

"Willis deserved to die three times over," Stuart said, and leaned forward. "He was a killer as well as a thief. We got him for rustling, but he was wanted in three states for murder, convicted in Kansas for one. You know that?"

Luke nodded. "Yeah, I know that. And I still quit." He closed the door quietly behind him.

CHAPTER 2

Yellowstone Saloon
Billings, Montana
December 24, 1884

One month later, Luke sat at a corner table, a plate of beef stew in front of him, the first hot meal he'd had in two days. Eyes lowered, he turned his head and listened to the conversation at the bar.

A banker from Laurel, Montana, twelve miles west, was killing time with the bartender until the next stage left for Repton, the nearest town to Billings. Luke gazed across the rim of his coffee cup and studied the heavyset, fancy-dressed stranger with his stomach pushing over his belt.

Luke's jaw tightened. Two hard knots of muscle bunched below his ears as he mulled over who the fat gent had just said he was.

Martin. Phineas Martin.

Small world. The man in the yellow-flowered vest, sipping whiskey with his little pinkie raised, was Bart Axel's banker.

"You might say I'm making a"—Martin smacked his thigh and wheezed with laughter—"a delivery to Mr. Axel tonight."

Delivery? A corner of Luke's mouth dug in. Delivering money, no doubt, and Axel probably stole every dime of it.

Martin pulled a gold watch from his vest pocket and flicked the cover open with a flourish. He clucked his tongue. "I have to go. What's taking so long?"

"The horses, I reckon," the bartender said. "It's mighty cold out there tonight."

"Mr. Axel will not be pleased if I'm late. Should've been out there by now. He doesn't like to be kept waiting."

The bartender, polishing a glass, held it up to the light, then set it down, saying, "Never did."

"You know him?"

"Everybody round here knows him. Sells a lot of beef to the government."

Martin beamed. "Fine man."

The bartender pursed his lips and dried another glass.

Fine man? Luke snorted under his breath and scraped his chair back, his appetite gone. Axel was a thief and a killer.

Both men looked over as he rose to his feet, leaving the plate of stew unfinished. He shrugged on the heavy sheepskin coat hanging on his chair and pinched the buckles closed with sharp, metal pops. Black felt Stetson squared over his eyes, he strode across the room for the door, drawing a pair of leather gloves from a side pocket as he passed. The spring bell over the door jangled. Cold Canadian air rushed in.

"Stop in again, mister, you hear?" the bartender called. "And a Merry Christmas to you."

Head down, Luke stopped in the doorway and blinked in surprise. He'd completely forgotten tomorrow was Christmas. With a faint smile he touched a finger to his hat brim. "Right," he said. The door slammed shut behind him.

At the hitching rail in front of the saloon, his horse Bugle, a big sooty-gray with a black mane and tail, sawed his head and stamped in place as Luke approached. Luke chuckled, gave him an affectionate scrub between the ears, and led him down the street to a water trough in front of a closed dry-goods store. He pulled a Colt .45 Peacemaker from his right holster and used the gun butt to crack the thin crust of ice. He waited while the horse drank.

Across the street, two men led horses through the double doors of Stuncard's Livery and backed the animals into position, hitching up two fresh teams to the green and yellow Overland Stage and Express coach waiting out front.

Billings was nearly deserted. Down the street, the Northern Pacific train station was closed and dark. The clock on the depot tower said six o'clock, the last train from Chicago come and gone hours ago. The next one, an eastbound, wasn't due in until seven tomorrow morning, or whenever it got there.

Luke swung into the saddle and headed toward the end of town and the stage road that snaked across the frozen prairie to Repton, nearly twenty miles east. New Hope, his destination, wasn't that far, less than a two-hour ride. In the saloon he'd debated with himself about staying at the inn until morning, but decided against it. The road was good, and he didn't mind riding at night. Liked it, in fact. The moon was already up over the horizon, and the sky glittered with stars. With the heavy snowpack and a bright moon, visibility would be good, too.

A razor-edged wind flailed across the high prairie, spitting snow in his face. He pulled his hat lower on his forehead and tucked his chin out of the cold into the sheepskin storm collar, thinking again of the warm bed he could have had if he'd stayed in town. For four days he'd been riding south for New Hope. Ten more miles and he'd be there. Leaning forward, he patted the neck of the big gray. Bugle frisked his feet like a colt, as if he understood they were almost home.

About an hour outside Billings, he spied a squatter's sod hut, its domed roof outlined against the sky. A window shone with the oily yellow glow of a lantern. As he drew closer, a hound dog ran out partway and bayed at him, its tail stiff. After Pa lost the ranch, they'd lived in a sod house. Luke wrinkled his nose, remembering the damp stink of the place, the dirt floors, the mud walls. A dirt house for a dirt-poor family. He touched his heels to the horse and picked up the pace, anxious to pass by. The house had always smelled like worms to him.

And all because of a crooked poker game. Axel had cheated a good man and his family out of everything they owned. The anger he felt in the back of his mind flared into flame. The ranch and a thousand dollars—that was a lot of money.

Wheels and hooves rumbled behind him on the road from Billings.

The Overland Stage and Express driver cracked a whip out over the horses' backs. "Hiya-ha-ha! Ha!"

Luke turned toward the shout.

"Ha! Ha!" The whip split the air again. Rocking, swaying,

the stagecoach clattered around a bend—the horses' breath steaming in the frigid air.

Pa always said Axel rigged that card game, and nobody believed him. Not even his own son. But that rustler Willis had confirmed it. And though he'd been only a little boy then, Luke would regret that as long as he lived. He believed him now. Too late.

Guilt, cold and sour, backed into his throat.

Bart Axel's banker was on that stage.

Luke gripped the reins and set his jaw. It was time to even the score for Pa.

With a tug of the reins, Luke took the horse off the road into a thick stand of jack pines. From the protection of the trees he watched the stage approach. As he did, he loosened the red and white bandanna around his neck and pulled it up over his nose and mouth as a mask. What he was about to do was wrong, but he wasn't doing it for himself; he was doing it for Pa. He made a small squeak with his lips and gathered the reins. Instantly Bugle stepped closer to the road, poised like a statue, waiting. On command, he could break from a standstill into a full, flying gallop.

The moon slid out of the clouds again.

Chains jingling, four horses thundered past, the stagecoach a blur of wheels and spokes. Luke pressed two fingers against the gray's neck. The horse tensed, his heavy haunch muscles trembling with excitement.

"Go, boy," Luke said softly.

Bugle exploded from the trees. Neck stretching, he charged like a racehorse alongside the stagecoach. Luke pulled the Colt from his holster and fired once into the air.

"Pull up!" he shouted.

The driver fisted the reins, braced his feet, and stood in the boot, dragging the teams to a halt. Without a word he tossed his rifle over the side and snaked his hands into the air.

"I don't get paid enough to get shot, mister," he said. "I'm carrying no money."

"I know different." Luke held the gun steady.

"No money, and that's the truth. Passengers only tonight."

A curtain moved aside at the darkened coach window. A face peered out.

"You—inside the coach," Luke called. "Get out here and be quick about it."

Phineas Martin opened the door a few inches and called through the crack, "What do you want?" His voice quavered.

"The money."

"You heard the driver. There is no money."

Luke's voice dropped. "Hand it over, I said."

Up front, one of the horses blew its lips and stamped a hoof in the cold. Martin hesitated. Luke stared down at him and waited. A cloud of snow lifted, whirled into a small snow devil, and ghosted across the road. With a metallic *click-click*, Luke thumbed the hammer back, the unmistakable sound of a revolver cocking.

Martin threw the door of the stagecoach open and scrambled out. "Don't shoot! Don't shoot! I'm just a courier."

Luke pressed his lips together. He had no intention of shooting anyone.

Martin clutched a small leather satchel against his paunch. "You're gonna be sorry for this. You picked the wrong stage tonight. Mr. Axel will track you down for stealing this money – and for frightening his future wife."

Martin touched his hat to a small, dark-caped figure backing down from the coach. "Begging your pardon, ma'am, but you should stay inside."

Luke snapped his head up. He'd assumed Martin was alone. Instead, a petite form backed out of the stage and turned around. A lacy white fascinator draped her head and neck. In the moonlight, everything looked gray, shades of black and pearl.

Hands hidden inside her fur muff, she raised a startled face to Luke. As she did, the scarf slipped back and a mass of long, light-colored hair sprang free and framed her face, pale ivory in the dim light. His heart reacted with a funny little bump that surprised him. She was beautiful.

"What do you mean 'his future wife'?" Luke growled. "She's young enough to be his granddaughter."

Her mouth fell open. "His *granddaughter*?"

"If you missed that, lady, you're either blind or silly." Luke motioned her with his gun away from the stagecoach and out into the road where he could see her better.

With a prissy little walk she stepped away as he directed, then whirled around. Legs planted, she frowned up at him. "His *grand*daughter?"

Luke sniffed and frowned back, not knowing what to make of her. She seemed more concerned about Axel's age than having a gun pointed at her.

"What's your name—and how do you know Bart Axel?" he demanded. The bandanna hiding the lower half of his face muffled the words.

Her chin shot up. "My name is Emily McCarthy, and I

am neither blind nor silly, thank you. I simply haven't had the pleasure of meeting Mr. Axel yet."

Luke stared at her and shook his head. This night was just full of surprises. "What do you mean you haven't met him yet?"

"He advertised for a wife in the newspaper."

"And you answered it?" Disgust thickened his words. "A mail-order bride."

"It's quite common these days," she said primly.

"Not where I come from."

He edged the .45 away from her and stared down at Martin. "Give me the bag, man."

With a wary look, Martin handed the satchel up to him. Luke opened it, counted off a wad of bills, and stuffed them into an outside pocket.

One thousand dollars—close enough.

He swung his arm. The satchel, still full of most of the money, thudded into the snow at Martin's feet. Luke reeled the horse around and raced for a line of trees up the hillside, leaving the two passengers standing in the road beside the stagecoach.

For a hundred yards he rode hard. The image of a small, pretty woman trying to be brave streaked across his mind. She was on her way to marry Bart Axel without knowing what she was getting into. Not if Luke had any say in it.

He turned the horse. Bugle raced back down the hillside, slipping and sliding toward the road, toward the stage. In a cloud of snow, the deep-chested gray rushed out of the dark straight at the passengers. The stagecoach driver shot his hands into the air again.

Luke fastened his eyes on Emily McCarthy.

She snatched up her skirts and ran for the stage, her heavy cape billowing behind her.

Bugle pounded alongside. Leaning far out of the saddle, Luke swept her up easily and slung her across his shoulder.

"Yaaah yaaah!" He kicked the horse into a leaping run, heading for the woods with Emily. She dangled down his back like a rag doll, screaming as if he were slitting her throat.

At first he tried to ignore her, but she wouldn't stop. She hammered her fists into his back and shrieked and shrieked. Bugle snorted and tossed his head.

"Stop that racket!" Luke yelled. "You're making my horse nervous!" He gripped an armload of squirming woman with one hand and struggled to control fifteen hundred pounds of agitated horseflesh with the other.

So much for slipping silently through the woods, he thought. By now everyone in the territory knew something was going on.

"You put me down!" A bony knee jabbed him in the stomach.

"Ooooff!"

Then her other knee connected above his navel and nearly knocked the wind out of him. He had a wildcat in his hair! He clamped her calves tight with one arm and pinned her legs still against him. "Stop it! I won't put you down till you realize what you're doing."

"This instant—you put me down this instant, you hear? I know what I'm doing. I'm getting married tomorrow."

"To a man you've never seen?" He grunted. "You don't look stupid. How come you're marrying a thief and a murderer?"

"You're the thief and the murderer!"

"Listen, lady. I never stole a thing in my life that didn't belong to me, and every man I ever killed deserved to die."

"Oh," she said in a small voice and stopped hitting him.

"Now, you tell me how you got involved with a rat like Bart Axel."

"That is none of your business."

"Yeah, well, I just made it my business." He swung her off his shoulder and sat her sideways onto the saddle in front of him.

He turned the horse off the road and headed cross-country. They'd make better time on the road, but they'd be visible, and the risk of being seen—and chased—was too great. He cut into a woods of dense scrub oak and headed east until they were clear of the roadway.

As he took the horse up a small rise and into a clearing, he caught a glimpse of her face in the moonlight. Eyes closed, her lips were moving.

"You talking to yourself?" he asked, a smirk in his voice.

Her eyes snapped open. "I'm talking to the Lord. I pray when I'm scared."

Luke nodded. "He ever hear you?"

"Most of the time. Some of the time."

"Which is it?"

"It all depends."

"On whether He listens or not. Well, while you're at it, say one for me."

She gave an indignant little huff. "You're the reason I'm scared. Say your own."

No point in that. He'd learned a long time ago, the Lord went stone-deaf whenever Luke Sullivan started to talk.

They continued in silence. Guilt picked at him. Here he was, trying to help, and all he'd done was scare her to death.

"Come on, tell me why you're marrying an old man like Bart Axel." He kept his voice quiet so as not to frighten her anymore.

She let go a shaky little sigh, and he leaned forward, straining to listen as she told him about someplace called Aldersgate and the government sending Indian girls to white schools to learn to be civilized.

"So, you see, I have to marry him. But I'll be a good wife. He won't be sorry." Her voice cracked.

Though the words were confident, Luke heard tears just a swallow away.

"Please take me back to the stage."

His jaw set. "No."

Growing up in an orphanage made boys tough and self-sufficient, but maybe it didn't work that way for girls.

He concentrated on a snowy, chest-deep wash ahead of them and took Bugle around it. Trying to put more miles between him and the stagecoach, Luke cut across open country. Once Axel learned about the girl, he'd have every man on his place out hunting her.

With any luck at all, Luke figured he could outrun a posse, but he had to get her to New Hope while it was still dark. Maybe his friend Molly, who ran the place, could use her there. Her girls did all right for themselves. Molly would sure talk some sense into her, teach her a few things about men, too.

He headed across rolling hills and snow-covered rangeland, following a trail he sensed rather than saw, one hidden by the snow and underbrush, sometimes lost completely in the unbroken blanket of white. He'd grown up out here and knew every twist and turn of these trails. He slowed, debating with himself which way to go. North or east?

East would cut off five miles. His gaze pulled to the eastern sky and three ominous black buttes towering like sentinels—Crow Indian territory, a place he'd never stepped foot on. He headed the horse east, and, as cold as it was, he started to sweat.

Pryor Creek lay at the bottom of a coulee, the water a silver shimmer of moonlight through the trees. Loosening up on the reins, he let Bugle pick his own way down. Horses saw better than humans in the dark.

Time and again he hipped around in the saddle and checked the trail behind him, but no shadows slipped between the trees.

Sharp yips and a coyote's quavering howl slid through the silence. Seconds later, another answered. His scalp prickled. Indians? Those howls didn't always come from coyotes. Heart pounding, he peered into the dark and strained to listen. Nothing. Only the wet whisper of the water beside them. He drew in a slow, relieved breath. Normal night sounds. He took the horse across the creek and up the bank on the other side. There, he stopped to check the stars to get his bearings. Concentrating on the pinpoints of light, he relaxed his hold on her.

Emily ducked under his arm and slid down the side of the horse. Landing on her feet, she scooted up the embankment like a cat. Gone!

Luke came off the horse after her almost before her feet had hit the ground. He grabbed for her, came away with a fistful of air instead. In the dark he lost sight of her at once,

30

but he could hear the crunch of frozen snow as she scrambled up the hillside. He heard her cry out and fall, then get up and run again.

Clawing at bushes on the steep slope, he sprinted up after her. His boot slammed into something solid—probably the same log she'd tripped over. The next thing he knew, he was sprawled facedown in the snow, his hand stinging. He pulled himself to a crouch and listened.

She'd stopped. Hiding behind a tree, most likely.

A stone caromed past, cracking down the hillside—rock on rock—and then a faint watery *plop* into the creek. Carefully, he eased himself toward the source of the sound, working his boots sideways for a foothold. With each step, the snow packed and settled underfoot.

He stretched for a small sapling, closed his hand around it. Silently, he hauled himself up and waited. In the still, cold air he caught a faint whiff of lavender soap. She was close.

The moon broke out of a cloud. Clear ivory light wove through the treetops. If she'd remained still, he wouldn't have seen her, but she panicked at the moonlight and darted for the shadows. Luke lunged. His fingers locked like a vise around her wrist.

"You little fool." Anger made his voice harsh. "You'd freeze to death out here."

"Let me go!"

"I won't. For two reasons. First, I'm not about to swing for robbing that stagecoach."

"That's your problem."

"Well, the second one's yours, lady. We're in Indian territory.

31

I cut into the Crow reservation to save us an hour. No way would I leave a white woman out here."

Emily shuddered. Her shoulders sagged. "I'm afraid of you and your mean old horse. Why don't you just kill me and get it over with?"

"If I'd a mind to do that, I would have by now. And he is *not* mean."

"Where are you taking me?"

"To someone who'll talk some sense into you. She knows all about girls." Luke started down the slope, pulling Emily after him. "Come on, we're losing time."

Soon there'd be a posse of men with guns and ropes, bucketing across the countryside to rescue one Emily McCarthy.

She stumbled. He caught her. "Watch where you're going."

"I can't see," she whimpered.

His temper started to smoke. "You saw well enough to get up here."

"I didn't know about the Indians then."

He snatched her up around the waist and behind the knees. Carrying her, he began to work his way back down the hillside.

"And you kick me again, lady, so help me, I'll scalp you myself."

The words were scarcely out of his mouth when his boots shot out from under him. He fell hard on his behind and shoulder. Helpless, he clutched the girl on top of him, the two of them sledding down in the dark in a mess of stones and snow and frozen mud.

At the bottom, he picked himself up and set her on her feet in front of him. "You all right?"

Emily's mouth worked, but no words came out. A choked squeak was all he heard.

Hanging on to her with one hand, he brushed himself off with the other. He gave a soft whistle for the horse, then limped to it and boosted her into the saddle. Stiffly, he swung up behind her. For another mile they followed the creek in silence.

"I'm so co-cold. I got snow down my front when I fell." Her teeth chattered. She bunched the heavy woolen cape close around her neck.

Luke reached behind him and, with numb fingers, fumbled in the bedroll tied to the saddle and pulled out an old brown blanket that was mostly clean. He tucked it around her, muttering to himself. Tonight was not going well. He could hardly move his arm, and she—poor little snippy thing—was cold. He wasn't so great himself. Probably dislocated his shoulder falling down that ravine. His hip and leg stung like fire, he'd torn a glove, and his knuckles were bleeding. And she'd kneed him in the gut, not once but twice.

He eased his weight off his bruised backside and tried to get comfortable in the saddle.

"How much you weigh, Miss McCarthy?"

"Ninety-nine pounds."

Last time he was this sore, the man had topped two seventy and had fists like shovels. Yet she was just ninety-nine pounds and didn't have a scratch on her.

A few miles later, the sides of the gully flattened. Luke headed due north. Pryor Creek meandered away to the right. Almost there. He pushed Bugle into a slow gallop across open rangeland again. He guided the horse into a long lane curving around a low-lying hill. Along one side, a row of poplars thrust a black fringe against the sky, guarding a long approach to a big house with dark windows.

An iron picket fence surrounded the three-story structure. Gables jutted from a steep-pitched roof bristling with chimneys. Except for one window glowing in a dormer on the third floor, the house was dark. The window brightened as the curtain drew aside. A figure peered through the glass.

Emily pressed a hand to her heart and turned to him, wide-eyed. "It looks like a prison."

"It isn't."

Luke stopped before a scrolled iron gate set into brick pillars near the walk leading to the house. He swung himself off the horse again and lifted her to the ground in a courtyard, a large clearing surrounded with smaller buildings.

"Luke! Luke Sullivan! We been worried to death." Henry Bertel, a tall, thin man with a rifle, moved out of the shadows and broke into a run across the yard. He threw his arms around Luke and thumped him on the shoulder. "Am I glad to see you." Henry grabbed the reins of Luke's horse. "Man, you don't know what all's gone on here tonight."

"What happened?" Luke suspected he already knew.

"The stage was robbed! Old man Bolton and his boy from up the road just lit out of here, warning everybody to lock their doors. They're looking to get a posse together."

"Too bad we missed all the excitement." Luke shot Emily a *keep your mouth shut* look.

"Molly's been fretting all night, afraid you weren't gonna make it. Now she's scared to death you ran into the robbers. I'll take care of your horse—you go on inside and calm her down."

"Treat him good, Henry. He's had a hard night." Luke patted Bugle's neck.

Henry's bony face creased into a wide grin. "From the looks of it, so did you. What happened? You fall off a mountain or something?" He slapped his thigh and snickered.

Luke seamed his mouth shut, not trusting himself to answer.

Henry looked at Emily McCarthy and touched his cap. "Evening, ma'am." He turned back to Luke. "Got us another one, huh? Molly'll like that. We never get enough pretty girls out here."

She screwed her eyes shut. "Dear God in heaven, help me."

Henry frowned at Luke. "She sick or something?"

Luke glanced down at Emily and shook his head. "Naah, must be scared again."

Henry chuckled. "They always are when they first get here. Don't you worry, miss. Luke here will learn you the ropes in no time. She looks cold, Luke. Get her on inside and warm her up. I'll be in when I'm done with your horse and help you."

Her eyes flew open. "You animals!"

Henry's mouth fell open. Before she could say more, Luke spun Emily around and hauled her down the walk by her elbow, up the steps, and onto a columned porch. He shook her arm. "Don't you say another word—not one word, you hear? You let me do the talking." He scowled at her. "I haven't decided how to explain you yet."

The color drained from her face. Big saucer eyes stared at him. "I've never been in a place like this in my life," she quavered. "How dare you bring me here? I'm a decent, respectable Christian woman."

Luke stiffened and looked down at her, puzzled. "Never said you weren't."

Her voice rose. "I've heard about these sporting houses for men. I'm not that kind of woman. I will *not* stay here. The very first chance I get—"

Luke cranked the little handle on the door so hard it nearly flew off in his hand. The doorbell clamored. From inside came the sound of running feet.

Alongside him, Emily trembled, her jaw clamped.

"Miss McCarthy, can you read?" His lips barely moved with the words.

"Of course I can read!"

"Then, do it!"

He struck a match and held it over a small brass plate attached to the doorframe. In raised black letters, it said:

NEW HOPE FOUNDLING AND ORPHAN ASYLUM.

CHAPTER
3

CHRISTMAS MORNING, 1884

A long, thin cheroot smoking in his hand, Luke sipped a mug of coffee and leaned against the fireplace at the end of the dining room.

Earlier, in the room upstairs that still was his, he'd washed and shaved and changed into corduroy trousers and a checkered red and black buffalo shirt. Just before he came down to the dining room, he'd pulled a black string tie out of the wardrobe, telling himself he wanted to dress up a bit for the kids at Christmas.

Kids, nothing. The tie was for Emily McCarthy and he knew it. He'd knotted it around his neck and left the room quickly, avoiding his eyes mocking him in the mirror.

Breakfast was long finished. Now the cavernous dining room hung with the smell of roast goose and tangy mincemeat coming from the kitchen. And over everything floated the faint scent of balsam from the Christmas tree in the corner, its branches hung with paper chains and ropes of popcorn and cranberries strung by this year's crop of children. Christmas crowded in, always a little sad, a little poignant for him.

"Hey, Mr. Luke!" a voice called from overhead.

Luke looked up and grinned. Long wood beams, as thick as railroad ties, braced a ceiling vaulting to the second story. A boy about twelve had shinnied out on one of the crosspieces. Straddling it, he waggled his eyebrows at Luke. "Come on up, Mr. Luke."

"Get down from there, John. You know better than that. Molly'll skin you alive if she catches you."

"Naah, she won't."

Luke chuckled and stretched his hand up. "Trust me, she will, and I speak from experience. Come on down now before you get in trouble."

John waved the offer of help aside. Legs dangling, he boosted himself forward along the beam, scooting his bottom to the far wall. There he swung a leg over the side, hung by his hands, and dropped to the floor.

Years ago, Luke got stuck up there, climbing in forbidden territory, and no one had been allowed to help him down. All through supper he'd perched up there like a monkey, sullen and hungry and scared, watching the others eat. He'd learned a lot from that about obeying rules.

Down on his knees a few feet from Luke, a dark-haired little boy he didn't recognize struggled to untie the ribbon on a present, his forehead wrinkled in concentration.

Luke squatted, arms resting across his thighs. "Need some help with that?"

Solemn faced, the boy held the present out and watched as Luke used his pocketknife to cut the ribbon. Luke folded the ribbon, which could be used again to wrap another present. He ruffled the boy's hair and smiled as the youngster moved to a corner and sat on the floor, the present between his legs.

"I taught you well, I see," a voice behind Luke said.

Still smiling, he turned and handed Molly the folded ribbon.

Never a pretty woman, the years had not been kind to Molly Ebenezer. *Plain* was the first word that came to mind on meeting her. Her blue eyes were too pale to be considered striking, her figure too ample by anyone's standards, but humor and goodness lit her face with inner beauty. She was the nearest thing to a mother he could remember, and he loved her.

"Remind you of anyone?" she asked, looking at the boy unwrapping his present in the corner.

He looked at the little boy again. "Reminds me of me, I guess. But was I that serious?"

"Oh my, yes. Your first Christmas here, you nearly set your pants on fire. You backed your skinny little behind against the fireplace and frowned like it was the end of the world."

"For me, it was, I reckon." He gestured to the youngster ripping the paper off his gift. "How old is he?"

"Six. Same age you were when you came." Her face softened. "I miss you. How long can you stay this time?"

Luke palmed the coffee mug in both hands and looked at her, his gaze steady. "I'm not going back, Molly. I quit."

She nudged her spectacles up and blinked in surprise. "I thought you liked Mr. Stuart."

"I did. I do. Just had enough. I hired on with Stuart as his foreman, not his gun."

She reached over and squeezed his arm. "Vigilantism is an ugly business, and I'm glad you're out of it. I understand, though. With no sheriffs or marshals up there, decent folks have to be the law themselves, but I never liked your doing it. What brought all this on now, anyway?"

"Nothing new." He looked away. "I don't like what I'm turning into," he said quietly.

"What you're turning into is a fine man I'm proud of. Even down here, they brag about Lewistown and Stuart's vigilantes—"

"Vigilance committee—it's called a *committee*."

She nodded. "They say Lewistown is the safest town in the territory now because of them. They also say Stuart won't tell who belongs to the committee."

Luke took a long swallow of coffee and met her eyes. "People aren't dumb. They got a pretty good idea who we are."

"The preacher doesn't really belong, does he?"

"No, but I'd tell you that even if he did. Vigilance committees got no sanction under the law. What we're doing is necessary, but it's not legal." He put his arm around her and hugged her. "Seems to me, if a man goes gunning for rustlers, at least it ought to be for his own cows, not someone else's."

Eyes gleaming, she cocked her head at him. "Now, that sounds like a man who gets to church once in a while."

A smile played in the corners of his mouth. "Not often."

He dropped an arm around her shoulder. "God and me ain't exactly on speaking terms."

Molly sighed. "I hoped you were over that. You've been mad at God ever since your family died. Bad things happen to people, Luke, and it's not God's fault."

"I came to terms with that a long time ago, but by then I'd kind of drifted away. I gave up on Him, and He gave up on me."

Molly looked up, blue eyes serious. "I doubt that. In fact, I suspect He had a hand in your coming here last night. You wanted out of vigilantism and He arranged it. And I think He's got plans for her, as well. Nothing would stand in His way, even if it meant"—she looked around quickly and then lowered her voice—"that ridiculous business with you and the stagecoach. Makes me think He's also got a sense of humor."

She reached up and patted his hand. "We got law down here now. There's a sheriff in Repton. You wouldn't have to go after anyone ever again. That is, if you've a mind to stay."

He let out a small breath of relief. "I hoped all the way coming here you'd ask me again. You still want me to run New Hope's herd?"

"You know I do. I need you here." Her eyebrows pulled together. Across the room, Emily played with two of the little girls. She picked up a long string of cranberries and lifted the smaller girl up to place it back on the tree.

"She's good with children, I'll say that for her, but what am I supposed to do with her?"

"I wish I knew. I just couldn't leave her there to marry Axel."

Last night when he'd brought Emily into the house, she said little when he'd introduced her. Both hands stuffed into her little fur muff, she'd stood straight, her face stiff. She'd darted puzzled little glances first at Molly, then at Luke, and the excited children crowded around him and the little one hugging his leg.

But the minute he told Molly he found her standing in the road after the stage was robbed, Emily pulled a hand from her muff and held it up. "Stop right there." Yes, she'd said, that was the truth, but not the whole truth. Then she'd looked at the children and then at Molly. "I'd rather talk privately."

It had taken Molly less than two minutes to clear the children out, pin him down, and pry the whole story out of him last night.

Now Molly looked over at him. "What do I tell Bart when he comes after her?" Molly asked. "And you know he will. I can't keep her if she doesn't want to stay."

"Could you use her here? She sounds educated enough. Last night, she told me to keep my proboscis out of her business." He bent his head close to Molly's ear and asked softly, "What is my 'proboscis,' anyway?"

Reaching up, Molly tapped his nose gently, *tut-tut*ting at him and shaking her head.

"So I forgot." He grinned.

Lips pursed, Molly studied Emily across the room and turned back to him. "Maybe I could use a little help, if she can read and write, that is. I'm getting tired. The years are catching up with me. Two dozen children wears a body out."

Over the rim of his cup, Luke looked across the dining room at Emily. Her blue skirt hung smoothly to her ankles, and a long-sleeved white embroidered waist covered her throat and neck. She'd caught the thick mass of copper hair with a white ribbon on the back of her neck.

He'd had his first look at her in daylight at breakfast this morning. When she walked in with Molly and sat down across the table from him, he'd kept his face blank and tried not to stare. With all that red-gold hair and skin like new cream, she was the prettiest woman he'd ever seen in his life. And the snippiest.

He turned back to Molly. "She came out here to marry Axel because she has nowhere else to go. Aldersgate in Chicago only knew what he told them, and I'm sure he made himself sound like a regular pillar of the community." Sarcasm was thick in his tone.

"She's very pretty."

"Is she? I hadn't noticed."

Molly arched an eyebrow at him. "That'll be the day. I raised you, remember? There wasn't a girl in this territory you didn't check out."

His chest jumped with silent laughter. "I hope you kept that to yourself."

Her eyes crinkled. "This time I did."

He looked over at Emily and shook his head. "Bart's too old for her."

"I agree, but he's a wealthy man. She could do worse. A man gets lonely out here. He's been a widower for five years."

Luke's mouth set. "Have you forgotten why?"

Molly's hands fluttered a denial. "Rumors. Just ugly talk. There's no truth to that."

"Aw, Molly, everyone knows Elizabeth Axel wasn't dragged by her horse, not the way that woman could ride. No wonder he left town the next day."

"The same day. Said he was too upset to face people. He left right after the funeral."

Luke lowered his voice. "For Chicago. I was there with Stuart selling beef, and your grieving husband walked into the Stockmen's Club with a prostitute on each arm and both hands bandaged. Told Stuart he'd busted his knuckles in a fight back home. It was months before I heard about his wife and connected up the dates. He's always had a mean temper. My guess is he hit her one time too many. Emily McCarthy needs to know what she's getting into if she marries Axel. You have to tell her, Molly."

"I live next to him. I'd rather you told her."

Hands shoved into his pockets, Luke frowned across at Emily, then down at Molly. "I tried on the way here. She doesn't believe me."

Molly sighed and turned to leave. "Then she probably won't listen to me, either."

She crossed the room, said something to Emily, and they left the dining room together.

Ten minutes later, Molly returned alone. As soon as her gaze caught his, she shook her head. Grim faced, she beckoned Luke to a corner.

He followed, uneasy about what she must have learned.

"Her parents were from back east," Molly said. "Her father died in a mine explosion when she was an infant; her mother killed herself six months later. And you were right. She can read. She can also cipher, typewrite, play the piano, and speak a little French. She's been teaching at Aldersgate in Chicago, run by a big fancy church out there. The school has a hundred Cherokee girls signed up, funded by the government under this new law. The school let her go because they needed her room for new students."

"She told me about the Indian girls coming, but marrying Bart Axel—"

Molly gave him a sad little smile. "That was the kind director's attempt to help Emily start a life of her own. Emily could have turned it down, said she would have if she could have found any kind of job."

"So what does she plan to do?"

"Marry him."

"After what you told her?"

"Says she has no choice."

Luke scrubbed his fist up and down the back of his neck, spun around, and started for the kitchen.

She reached her hand out and held Luke's arm. "I'm as upset as you are. I talked till I was blue in there with her," Molly said quietly, her face solemn. "I'm not surprised at what you saw in Chicago. Elizabeth told me once that Bart had lady friends. She was also afraid of him." Molly's eyes filled. "Take Emily to the library, where you can talk alone. I'll back you up. Elizabeth was my friend."

Emily looked up a few minutes later when Luke finished talking. A wave of dizziness swirled behind her eyes, leaving her half sick at her stomach. "The Society would never send me to a man like that," she whispered.

"They didn't know," he said gently.

Emily sat at a long yellow oak table in the library, twisting her hands together and trying to pull her thoughts in line. There was a way. There was always a way. She'd postpone the wedding until she could telegraph Aldersgate for advice. In the end, however, it would still be her decision. Her mind was a jumble of thoughts stumbling around, bumping into each other.

She'd been stunned when Molly told her Luke had grown up here, that he and a little brother who later died had been the only survivors of an Indian attack on his family.

She never would've guessed it. He just oozed self-confidence. It showed in the way he moved, the way he talked. If she'd met him under other circumstances, she'd have taken him for a rancher. Not at all like a man who grew up the way he did, the way she did.

She looked up at him. "Why didn't you tell me you came from an orphanage like me? Instead, you deliberately let me think—"

"You were in no mood to listen last night." Arms folded, Luke sat in a chair tipped back against a wall.

"Because I thought you were an outlaw." Her cheeks heated with embarrassment. "If I hadn't told you I was marrying Mr. Axel, you'd have left me at the stagecoach. That's why you took me, isn't it? You felt sorry for me." She drew a shaky breath and looked at him.

Gray eyes met hers.

"Didn't you?"

Their gazes held. "So what if I did? Does it surprise you I did something decent?"

She rose from the chair, her back as stiff as a mop handle. "I don't need your pity. It wouldn't have changed anything anyway—"

"I knew that."

"What you did was wrong," she flared, a hand braced on her hip. "I don't care why you did it, it was wrong. For all I know, you're lying right now about Mr. Axel."

"You are the most muleheaded woman I ever met in my life." The chair legs came down with a thump. Luke stood, took a step around the table toward her.

She swallowed. The man was huge. He hadn't looked that big last night in the dark. And he looked angry. She backed up, careful to keep the table between them.

Luke raised his hands, then let them fall heavily to his sides. "It's Bart Axel you have to be afraid of. Not me."

Back and forth he paced the length of the room. His heavy boot heels rapped the wood floor alongside the bookcases. He muttered as much to himself as to her, "That's the thanks I get for trying to do you a favor—to keep you from making the biggest mistake of your life."

"And what kind of favor was that?" she snapped. "You ruined my wedding."

"I didn't have time to explain," he said with a wry smile.

"Because you were too busy shooting up the world."

He spun around, his face tight. "Once! I shot in the air one time to get their attention. I didn't plan on hurting anyone—and I didn't." He paced the length of the room again, wheeled around at the piano by the windows, and shook his index finger at her. "Bart Axel is dangerous."

She smacked her palm on the tabletop and flounced across her end of the room. "I'll tell you what's dangerous—anywhere you are." She glared at him.

He made an ominous little growling sound in his throat and glared right back.

"Still, I'm not a fool, not with both you and Molly telling me this. So I won't marry Mr. Axel until I determine for myself what kind of man he is. Me. I decide. Not you."

She jerked to a stop, as if remembering something, and looked up. "I have another problem. You see, Mr. Axel paid the Society a lot of money for me—"

"Slavery went out twenty years ago."

"Plus my railroad fare. Add that in." Her voice edged at the interruption. "If I don't marry him, I have to pay that back, and I don't have the money."

"Molly said—"

"Said I could work here for a little salary and room and board for a while." She looked down at her hands. "I can teach and I play the piano. I'll find work somewhere."

"Doing what? It's worse for women out here than in Chicago. There's no work anywhere. No jobs for men, except range work. Maybe you could get on as someone's hired girl, if you're lucky."

A thought streaked across her brain. "The piano! I read music. Maybe I can get a job in a saloon or a dance hall."

His jaw dropped. "You in a short skirt, kicking up your legs and showing your drawers? Don't be ridiculous."

Emily stiffened. "Don't be evil-minded. The other girls would dance. I'd just play the piano for them."

Those pale eyes now looked like wolf eyes, and they bored holes into her.

"Somehow, I believe you'd have other duties upstairs," he said. From her hair to her shoes, his eyes swept down her. "And you, Miss McCarthy, you wouldn't . . . last . . . an . . . hour." He threw his hands up. "You don't even know what I'm talking about."

"I do so. Girls talk. I know all about . . . such things."

He shot her a skeptical look.

"I'll lend you the money, and you can go back to Chicago." His tone of voice and fixed expression said the matter was settled.

"No, I am not going back there. I vowed never to set foot inside another orphanage." She let out a long, shaky breath. "I'll work at New Hope for a while if I have to, but only till I find a teaching job in a regular school."

"Now you're being sensible."

She pinched her eyes into little slits. "But as for you, Mr. Know-It-All-Sullivan, I'll thank you to stay out of my affairs in the future."

Luke stared at her; his face flushed an angry, dusky red. "Taking you off that stage was the dumbest thing I ever did."

He spun around, left the library, and slammed the door behind him.

Four miles away, at the X-Bar-L ranch, Clete Wade, ranch foreman, noted the nearly empty McBryan's whiskey bottle on Bart Axel's desk. He gave his boss a wary nod. When Bart tippled more whiskey into the glass, Clete shot a warning look to Wes Huggins, the wiry range rider he'd brought in with him. Boss was back on the booze. Bad sign.

Clete lifted his head at the whiff of roast chicken coming from the kitchen. Bart's Chinese cook had also baked a tall, spicy wedding cake. For the first time Clete could remember, the X-Bar-L was decorated for Christmas. A little tree, hung with a string of tinsel and a few colored balls, stood in the corner, and a pine wreath graced the wall. Fancy candles burned on all the tables, and a preacher napped in the spare room upstairs. On the sofa, red-eyed from a sleepless night, sat Axel's banker, Phineas Martin, whose duty was to give the bride away.

Only there was no bride.

"Got some news, boss. She's over to New Hope," Clete said.

"New Hope? How in blazes she wind up there?" Bart ran a hand through his gray hair.

Clete turned his hat around in his hands and shifted his feet. "It's a puzzle, that's for sure, but there's only one set of tracks out there," Clete said slowly, drawling the words out, his eyes slipping to the glass of whiskey in Axel's hand, then back to Axel's stormy expression. Bart had been drinking heavily ever since he'd learned of the stage holdup and the disappearance of Miss McCarthy. Every man on his ranch had spent the night combing the stage route from Billings to Repton, the closest town. They found nothing.

"Who told you she's at New Hope?" Bart demanded.

"We tracked them. Whoever robbed the stage cut down into the Crow reservation. We lost them when—"

Bart leaned forward and slapped his palm on the desk. "Not what I asked. Who told you she's at New Hope?"

"Wes knows a woman who works there," Clete rushed on. Sooner or later, the liquor would fire the fuse to Bart's temper, and he didn't want to be around when it did. "She said Sullivan rode in with a girl last night, said Miss Molly told the help that Sullivan found her standing in the road after the stage was robbed."

"Sullivan—Luke Sullivan?" Axel looked up. Quick anger flared in his eyes. "What's he doing back here? Last I heard, he was making good money managing Granville Stuart's place up at Lewistown."

Clete fell silent at Stuart's name.

Axel leaned back in his chair again and squared his legs, propping an ankle on the other knee. The silver spurs on his boots were Mexican and held oversized rowels, their spines honed to wicked points. He took no nonsense from a horse. Frowning, he twirled the little wheel with a finger. Well-oiled, the rowel spun with a faint clicking noise.

"What's the matter with you two? Don't tell me you believe the nonsense about him being one of Stuart's Stranglers?"

Clete frowned. "Maybe—maybe not. They never say if they are, but he does work for Stuart."

Bart flicked the rowel again and waited for it to stop spinning. When it did, he uncrossed his legs and sat up.

"Kind of a coincidence, wouldn't you say, Sullivan coming back the same night my girl is kidnapped, same night the stage is robbed?" He swiped the back of his hand down each side of a drooping salt-and-pepper mustache.

"Still, don't see how it could've been Sullivan. There's no

way in this world Luke Sullivan would ride into the Crow reservation, not the way that man hates Injuns. You're sure it was him who took Miss Emily to New Hope?"

Clete nodded. "Had to be. No other tracks out there."

"And those tracks went right through the reservation, not around it?"

Again, Clete nodded.

"Well, then, our Mr. Sullivan better have a mighty good reason for that," Bart said, slurring the words. "Otherwise, we just might stretch his neck a little. See how he likes it."

Wes Huggins spoke for the first time. "Not me. I ain't messing with him."

"Wes is right," Clete joined in. "He's trouble, boss. Fellow I know in Lewistown says Sullivan wears his guns to church. What kind of man does that?"

Wes broke in. "A vigilante, that's who!"

Bart snorted and waved a hand in dismissal. "Vigilantes don't go to church."

"This one does. He goes to funerals—funerals he's caused. Makes me squirm inside just to think it." Wes turned to Clete, forgetting Axel for a moment. "You ever see him draw?"

Clete shook his head.

Wes talked faster. "I did once, up in Miles City when he got jumped—and that's plenty for me. One minute he was just a-standing in the street, arms at his sides; the next minute, his gun's smoking, and the other man's down. And I swear, I never saw Sullivan move."

Axel waved a hand and snorted. "Watch yourselves and you won't have no trouble with him. Stuart and his gang go after horse thieves and rustlers."

"Maybe you better watch yourself, boss," Wesley blurted. "From what I hear, he's as fast with the ladies as he is with guns, and right now the lady he's got is yours."

"Shut up, Wes," Clete muttered.

Bart's face turned a deep, dark red. With a thin smile he said, "I hadn't looked at it quite like that, Wes." He picked up a nickel-plated revolver lying on his desk, a handsome Smith & Wesson Schofield with a carved ivory handle, monogrammed and engraved. Opening a desk drawer, he took out a box of .45 Schofield ammunition. Slowly, he thumbed cartridges into each empty chamber except the one under the hammer. He scraped his chair back and stood up, shoving the revolver into the empty holster as he did.

Adjusting the belt, he let it out a notch over his belly and worked the gun a shade lower on his hip. Spurs chinking, he crossed the room toward a rack of elk horns hanging on the wall.

He lifted off a black felt Stetson studded with a row of silver stars around the brim and turned to Clete. "Get some of the men together," he said, putting on the hat that cost more than some men's horses. "And bring the buggy around. We're going over to New Hope and get me my bride back."

CHAPTER
4

CHRISTMAS DAY, 1884

Four o'clock. Dark in half an hour. Emily reached for another oil lamp on the sideboard and lit it, trying to do something to be helpful, anything to keep her mind off what had happened with Luke in the library. Her face burned. She was fuming inside, and from the way he'd slammed the door, so was he.

She lit the wick, let the glass chimney clink down onto the base, then set the lamp on one of the long tables in the dining room. A little amazed, she stared at it. In Chicago, they had gaslights, not these old things.

As she reached for another kerosene lamp, her gaze held on the large painting hanging alongside the dish cupboard: *The Good Shepherd.* Jesus carrying a baby lamb. Molly Ebenezer must have chosen it. It was a perfect choice for children, much better than the one at Aldersgate.

There, a large painting of da Vinci's *The Last Supper* dominated the end of the dining room. Jesus and the apostles at their final meal together might be beautiful, but it was too adult for children and a little scary for some. Besides Jesus, she never could figure out who was who in the painting.

"Hi, Miss McCarthy." Wearing a Christmas red blouse and a swishy green skirt, a girl in her early teens carried a tray in from the kitchen and began collecting salt and pepper shakers from the four tables in the dining room.

Emily smiled. "You fit right in with Christmas," she said, and walked the length of her table, scooping up the shakers as she went. Setting them on the tray, she looked at the girl's green skirt again. If this were the dining room at Aldersgate, both of them would be wearing loose gray and white uniforms.

But at New Hope, not a uniform in sight. She'd hated those ugly gray things and didn't miss them a bit.

Everything here was different. Aldersgate had ninety-six residents, all girls; New Hope, only two dozen, boys and girls combined. And Molly knew every one of their names. She'd lined them up and introduced them to Miss McCarthy.

As Emily set the last shaker on the tray, the hard clatter of hooves and the rattle of wheels on brick sounded in the courtyard.

She hurried to the window and brushed the curtain aside. A man in a big black hat with stars on it climbed down from a big-wheeled green buggy. Five cowboys accompanying him swung off their horses. As a group they followed the barrel-chested buggy driver up the walk. Her stomach clenched and she struggled to suck in air. Without being told, she knew who he was: Mr. Axel. He'd come after her. She hurried to the dining room doorway and peeped into the hall.

Axel threw the front door open. "Molly! Miss Molly!"

Drying her hands on her apron, Molly appeared in the kitchen doorway at the far end of the long hall. "Evening, Bart. Guess I didn't hear the bell," she said, her voice crisp with sarcasm.

Emily shrank back, listening to the voices in the hall.

"You know why I'm here," Axel said, stripping off his hat and slapping it impatiently against his thigh. "I won't waste your time or mine. I've come for the girl. Where's Miss McCarthy?"

"In the back with the children, I believe. I'll go get her." Molly looked pointedly at a spot above Clete Wade's eyes. "Is your head cold, Mr. Wade?"

With a sheepish look, Clete swept his hat off.

Molly gestured to the assortment of roughly dressed men, every one of them with a gun on his hip. "There's no call for this, Bart. You tell these cowhands of yours to wait on the porch. And tell them the next time they come inside this house to knock first and to wipe their boots." With that, she turned and marched down the hall toward the dining room.

Behind her, Clete Wade waved the men outside with a smirk. "Downright chilly in here, ain't it?"

Lips pursed, Molly beckoned to Emily, then led her down the hall and into the parlor ahead of Bart Axel. Emily let out a relieved sigh. Luke was already there, down on one knee in front of the fireplace, adding another piece of wood to the fire. It was no accident he was in the parlor, she knew. However much she didn't like him, she was grateful he was there. Bad as he was, he was on her side.

"Emily McCarthy," Molly said, "this is our neighbor, Mr. Bartholomew Axel, the man you came from Chicago to meet. He owns the X-Bar-L ranch."

A broad smile split Axel's face. Both hands extended, he stepped forward. "Emily, my, my, my. I must say I'm pleased." He sounded breathless. Though he was nearly sixty, he had the build of a younger man, thick and stocky with shoulders as big as hams and a face that was nearly all jaw. His iron gray hair was parted neatly down the middle and slicked back, like a Spaniard's. "I had no idea you looked like this. Turn around, girl. Turn around. Let me see what I got to look forward to." He pointed at the floor and stirred his finger in the air.

A hot flush slid down her neck. He made her feel cheap. Humiliated, she stood still, making no move to do as he asked.

"I said turn around, girl."

Luke straightened, a piece of firewood dangling in his hand. "You think you're buying a heifer, Axel?" he said, a dangerous glitter in the back of his eyes.

Axel glanced at the wood in Luke's hand and bobbed his head to Emily. "No offense intended. Get your coat, girl, and let's go. I'm taking you home." There was authority in his voice, a kind of harnessed control that said he was used to being obeyed.

Disappointment swam through her. At Aldersgate they'd told her he was elegant looking. Why, he wasn't at all. His pants bagged in the seat, he was bowlegged, and he reeked of whiskey. Worse, there was a meanness in his voice that set off her alarm signals.

And he'd called her "girl."

Her mind reeled with thoughts shooting out in all directions. Not right. Her first meeting with her new husband-to-be, and he ordered her around like a servant. She wavered only an instant.

"Mr. Axel, I'm not going with you today. I think it's best if I stay at New Hope with Miss Molly for a while."

"What do you mean 'for a while'?" The tone of his voice dropped.

"Coming here, I got to thinking and decided it would be better for both of us if we . . . if we got to know each other first." Behind her, Luke let out a quiet hiss of relief. The heated flush in her cheeks slid down her neck. She felt foolish and embarrassed and eighteen years old.

"Nonsense. After the wedding you'll get to know me. Very well, I expect." Axel moved to stand in front of her, taking her hands in both of his. "Let me remind you, my dear, you are bought and paid for. Aldersgate has three hundred dollars of my money–"

"The cost of two horses," Luke cut in.

Bart's lip curled in a sneer. "For you, maybe. Not the kind I buy. And where do you fit into this, Sullivan?" Axel fingered his mustache and scowled at Emily. "Or maybe I should ask you that. How did you manage to take up with him, anyway?"

She pulled her hands from his and darted a glance at Luke, but his face was granite hard, his mouth unsmiling.

"After the stage was robbed, Mr. Sullivan brought me here," she said.

"And I'm thinking real hard about that," Bart said. "I'm also thinking I paid for a wife, and what I pay for, I get. Suppose you go put your coat on and come along. The preacher's waiting."

Emily swallowed and tried to speak, but words wouldn't come. Deep down, a piece of her had wanted so desperately to believe Sullivan was wrong, that Bart Axel was really a gentleman, a man who would make her a fine husband. He'd just crushed that hope himself.

"You hear me, girl?"

"I hear you," Luke said, "and you're downright insulting to the lady. Maybe you'd better leave. Come back when you find some manners."

The men's eyes locked, as if measuring each other. Although Luke was half a head taller and broad shouldered, Axel outweighed him. Warily, they faced each other. The silence stretched, tension crackling between them like a smoldering fuse.

"Now, now, Bart," Molly soothed, rushing in to snuff the fuse before it burst into flame. "Be reasonable. Emily hasn't said no. She just needs a little time to get used to the idea of getting married, I reckon. I said she can work here with me for a while until she does."

"I understood she *was* used to the idea. Who changed her mind? You, Molly?" He spun around to Luke and planted his legs apart. His mouth twisted. "Or have you been sniffin' around her skirt?"

Molly shot her hand out and grabbed Luke's forearm, restraining him. His hand had already balled into a fist.

Emily's chin tipped up. "Mr. Axel, I don't appreciate your remarks one bit," she said coldly. "These people have been kind to me. I think you owe them an apology."

Bart's eyes narrowed. "You sound downright disrespectful, girl."

Calmly, Molly continued. "No apologies needed, Emily. Bart, give her a little time. You're just a few miles away. Come visit whenever you like. Let her learn for herself what kind of gentleman you are. Or have you forgotten how to court?"

Emily folded her hands tightly together to hide their trembling. The thought of courting this man made her shudder. Kiss him? With those dry lips and that stringy mustache? Never!

Luke moved behind her and rested a hand on her shoulder. His fingers squeezed a warning. "Why don't you go back to the children, Miss McCarthy? I'll see Mr. Axel out."

Without a glance at anyone, Emily gathered her skirts and hurried from the parlor. Out in the hall, a rubbery weakness caught her behind the knees and she stumbled into the wall. Her breath broke on a quiet sob. Bart Axel was bad tempered and bad mannered, and she'd come *that* close to marrying him. If it hadn't been for Luke, she would have.

The moment Emily disappeared into the hall, Luke reached into his pants pocket and pulled out a roll of bills. Counting off three hundred dollars, he stuffed them into Axel's hand.

"She owes you nothing now. If she decides to marry you, it's because she wants to, not because she has to."

Axel's eyes jumped from the money in his palm to Sullivan's face and back to the money again. "This is my own money you're paying me with. You robbed the stage last night. And don't think I don't know why. You're like a dog with a bone. I told you years ago your pa lost to me fair and square. It's not my fault your old man couldn't play poker."

"Last month, just before we hanged him, your rustler friend, Clyde Willis, told me how you cheated my pa, said he helped you cheat a lot of men."

"Watch it, Sullivan. People get shot for remarks like that." Axel's hand moved toward his gun.

"Stop it," Molly cried, pushing between them. "I won't have this in my house. There are children here, and this is Christmas Day."

Bart stared pointedly at Luke's hip. "Where's your gun, Sullivan?"

The corners of Luke's mouth dug in. An hour before—much to his disgust—Molly had cornered him upstairs in his room, taken his guns, and locked them away until after Axel had come and gone. "Didn't figure I needed one in my own home," he drawled.

"This ain't your home."

"I decide that, and I say it is." Molly stepped forward. "Now, if you've finished your business, I'd be obliged if you'd leave. And don't you come back here till you've cooled off, either."

For a long minute, Axel didn't move, staring from Molly to Luke. Cramming his hat on his head, he turned and strode out of the room and down the hall. He was almost at the front door when he caught sight of two boys in buckskin shirts and long black braids chasing into the kitchen. He spun around, his face a splotchy red.

"Molly, what are they doing here? Months ago I told you to get rid of them Crow brats," Axel warned. "They ain't orphans. They don't belong here. New Hope is for whites."

"They're Chief Black Otter's boys," she said.

"I don't care who they are. They're still Injuns. And to think you're teaching the red scum to read and write."

"Bart, they're little boys, and it's the law now. It's right that we teach them."

"It's wrong, I tell you. Mark my words, they'll turn on you." He moved closer and shook a finger in her face. "They ain't fit to be around the rest of us. Chief or no chief, you get rid of them kids, or so help me I'll close this place like *that.*" He snapped his fingers with the word.

Luke brushed Molly aside and stepped between them. "You should've quit when you were ahead, Bart. Molly invited you back when you cooled off, but now I'm telling you different. Don't come back. You're not welcome at New Hope. Not as long as I'm here." He yanked the front door open. "Now get out before I throw you out."

For a long moment, Bart said nothing. Then, touching his index finger to the brim of his hat, he gave a curt nod to Molly, then turned to Luke. "Sooner or later, someone's going to shut you up, Sullivan. You're a walking dead man," he said, and went out the door.

"Bart—" Molly moved as if to go after him.

"He's drunk. Let him go." Luke held her arm.

Bart stormed down the walk to the empty buggy. He snatched the reins to Clete's horse from his hands. "Gimme your horse. I'm riding. You take the buggy back."

He toed the stirrup and sat himself hard in the saddle.

"But where's Miss Emily?" Clete blurted, then jumped out of the way as Bart gigged the spurs into the animal's hide. The horse snorted in pain and frogged a few steps sideways, then broke into a run, its mane and tail streaming.

Clete jumped up into the buggy. "We got trouble coming," he muttered to the waiting men. "Giddap!" With a hard slap of the reins, he sent the horse and its big-wheeled little carriage racing out of the courtyard after Axel.

Luke jammed his hands into his pockets and wondered what to say to Emily now. Her face was white, her lips trembling. The scene in the parlor with Axel had upset her. Maybe it did some good. She'd seen for herself what kind of man Bart was. And yet Luke sensed anything else he said about Axel would be unwelcome right then.

"What time is it, Mr. Sullivan?" Emily asked.

He glanced at the grandfather clock on the stair landing behind her. With a flash of intuition he knew why she asked. If he hadn't pulled her off the stage last night, she'd be married by now.

"Four thirty," he said quietly, and kept his face blank. He swallowed the surge of anger in his throat. Bart had wanted to slap her. Luke saw it and wondered if she did, too.

"I suppose you expect an apology from me?" Her mouth had pulled into a thin straight line.

The question surprised him. While he didn't expect her to throw her arms around him with gratitude, a thank-you would have been nice. "No. I took the money and I took you, though I had good reasons for doing both."

She looked up at him and said nothing.

"You've seen him – you still want to marry him?"

The blood drained from her face, leaving the creamy ivory skin with a chalky cast. Lips tight together, she shook her head and turned away.

Children clattered up and down the staircase, shouting and pushing each other, getting ready to put on a play. The two young Crow boys ran by, dressed in bathrobes as wise men now, dish towels wound around their heads for turbans. In the doorway, one of the cooks straightened a homemade halo on a little blond angel. A loud scraping of chairs and moving of furniture came from the dining room, signaling something important was about to happen.

"Miss McCarthy, the children have a Christmas pageant planned. Shall we go inside?"

She shook her head. "I don't feel like it now."

"Neither do I, but we're going to. These kids have practiced weeks for this. We're gonna watch and we're gonna clap." With a little bow he crooked his arm out to her. "Take it, or do I carry you in over my shoulder?"

She shot him a look full of knives, snatched his arm, and stamped down the hall beside him.

His lips twitched.

FRIDAY, DECEMBER 26, 1884

At two o'clock the next afternoon, Emily answered the doorbell and opened the front door. Feet planted, Sheriff Sam Tucker and his deputy stood on the porch.

Tucker, a tall, board-straight man who looked as if he never smiled, pinned her with a cold look. "And you must be Miss McCarthy from Chicago."

Emily nodded, her face stretched tight. "Come in, Sheriff. I'm Emily McCarthy. Molly and Luke are in the parlor. She told me you and Deputy Howard would be out today."

Molly had also warned her to watch every word she said. Sam Tucker was smart and knew the law better than some judges. He'd never met Luke. When Sam came to Repton, Luke was up in Lewistown working for Mr. Stuart.

In the parlor, Deputy Howard wrinkled his nose and pulled a small notebook and pencil from his shirt pocket.

Tucker looked hard at Luke. "So you're Luke Sullivan, are you? To my mind, you don't look like a man who'd hold up a stage and kidnap a woman passenger off it."

Luke kept his face blank. Not a hint of anger showed in his expression. He shoved his hands into his pockets. "Sheriff, I never took a thing in my life that wasn't mine. As for Miss McCarthy here, she was running down the road as fast as she could go when I came along."

"I see," Tucker said, in a tone which implied he did not. "Is that what happened, Miss McCarthy?"

When Emily hesitated and swallowed, Molly broke in quickly.

"I raised Luke Sullivan from a boy, and I don't raise outlaws," she said. "He's a fine man who does what's right, though *some people* might disagree."

Emily shifted, uncomfortably aware that Molly was looking at her when she said that.

"It's a puzzle all right, Miss McCarthy, why any holdup man would rob a stage, kidnap a woman, then set her down later on a cold, empty road and leave her out there. That don't make sense. How long were you waiting before Mr. Sullivan rode up?"

"Not very long."

"Did you ask him for a ride?"

"I didn't have to. He offered—sort of."

Deputy Howard tongued the pencil point, sniffed, and wrote something in his notebook.

The sheriff watched him write, then turned back to Emily. "And where exactly did you say Mr. Sullivan found you?"

"I was standing in the middle of the road."

"Thought you were running."

"I stopped when Mr. Sullivan rode up." Which was the truth. Surely they didn't put people in jail for telling the truth. She twisted her hands together and frowned at Luke.

Tucker narrowed his eyes and studied them both. "Was the stagecoach nearby?"

Quickly, she wet her lips. "It was dark. I couldn't see."

"The inside of a cat ain't that dark, Miss McCarthy," Tucker said softly. "A stagecoach is big and noisy, and that one had four horses. The man who kidnapped you—what did he look like?"

"I couldn't tell that, either. He had a mask on."

"And he never took it off—not once during the whole time?" Tucker's eyebrows flew up in pretended amazement. "Was he a big man, then? As big as Mr. Sullivan here, maybe?"

"It was too dark to see."

Tucker nodded. "Did he talk like he was from around here, or was it too dark for you to tell that, either?"

Sullivan's mouth twitched.

"Sheriff, I don't know how people sound around here. I'm from Chicago."

Tucker cleared his throat. "Begging your pardon, ma'am, but did he . . . did he harm you?"

A hot flush crept up her neck and into her cheeks. "No, he was a gentleman."

"Begging your pardon again, ma'am, he was a thief."

"Well, somebody raised him right," she snapped.

"I thought we was gonna arrest him," Deputy Howard said.

Sheriff Tucker looked over. "What for? Sullivan's got a ironclad alibi with both women backing his story, including his victim. Nobody was hurt in that robbery, and most of the money is still in the satchel—which strikes me as downright odd. A lawyer—even a dumb one – would make me look like a fool in court."

"He's a cool one all right," Howard said, and sniffed again.

"A little too cool, if you ask me. Ain't you got a handkerchief?"

Howard straightened a leg and pulled a rumpled handkerchief from his pocket. "He's polite and speaks good. Don't know as I believe he was with Stuart's Stranglers."

"Believe it," Tucker clipped. "I knew what he was — maybe still is — the minute I saw him. Stuart's group prides themselves on not looking like what they are."

The bare hedge of Caragana pea trees, crowded together on the other side of the road as a windbreak, rustled as they passed. Their frozen seedpods, hard as wood now, clacked together whenever the wind skirled. A gust of snow alongside rattled the Caraganas.

Howard rubbed his nose. "I hate these blasted pea trees."

"Let's get this over with." The sheriff touched his spurs to his horse and flicked the reins lightly. Howard did the same. At the gate to the main road, they turned left and headed toward Repton and the X-Bar-L ranch.

Tucker seamed his mouth shut. Axel wasn't going to like this.

CHAPTER
5

Chief Black Otter listened to his young son, sitting with him before a fire in his lodge. A ragged ribbon of scar slashed a crescent from eyebrow to chin, a souvenir from a war party many years before, when a tough old Sioux warrior split Black Otter's cheek open to the bone.

The soft white elk skin he wore was beaded with intricate designs, the leather fringe hanging from his sleeves nearly a foot long, a mark of status. Both moccasins and shirt glistened with embroidery of shiny red and yellow porcupine quills.

He'd been chief for twenty years, a fighting chief, and when he chose to wear it, his war bonnet hung below his hips. Black Otter stroked his upper lip thoughtfully, listening to Two Leggings telling him about the school, about Bart Axel's argument with Sullivan on Christmas Day, and his threat to close New Hope.

"Who this Light Eyes you call Sullivan?" Black Otter asked in Crow.

"He live at New Hope. Miss Molly likes him. He work all day. Where he came from, they say he was like law. He hang men who steal horses."

Black Otter stiffened. "He hang Indians?"

Two Leggings shook his head. "No, Father. He hang white men."

"Good."

Crow were the best horse thieves in the world. Or used to be. But times were changing for them. The buffalo were disappearing, the great herds cut in two by the railroad. The last time Black Otter took a hunting party out, they'd ridden for half a moon without seeing a single herd. Instead, they found piles of buffalo hides stacked high as a man beside the tracks, killed by white buffalo hunters. Sickened by the slaughter of the great herds – a slaughter undertaken to drive the Indians out – Black Otter ordered every pile they found set afire.

Fifteen years before, on the saddest day of his life, he'd made his mark on the treaty paper – a paper he could not read – and gave his solemn word the Crow would stay within boundaries drawn by the white man. But twice the blue soldiers came with their wagons and moved his people. Twice Black Otter had led a line of Crows that stretched behind him. Weeping women rode horses dragging travois loaded with tipis and household goods. Sullen braves and husbands rode silently alongside.

The government promised him the move to the Agency near Repton and bordering New Hope would be the last. They gave him another piece of paper. But from the very beginning, Black Otter knew the boundaries on the paper were wrong.

Part of the land the orphanage claimed as theirs belonged to the Crow Nation. Five square miles on New Hope's northern border was Crow land, a chimney-shaped tract, over three thousand acres of holy land.

Miss Molly read the treaty and said he was right. Twice she sent him with his paper to Fort Keogh. And each time he came back with promises that confused him and more papers with writing on it that meant nothing to him.

The morning after his last trip to Fort Keogh, the chief showed up at New Hope. Beside him stood his two little sons, Red Cloud and Two Leggings, all three of them wearing buckskins. Knowing not one word of English, both boys crowded next to their father, big eyed and silent.

"You teach them read and write you language?" Black Otter asked Miss Molly, his lips tight with embarrassment.

"Of course I will. And they are very welcome." Molly had smiled and taken the boys and their father inside.

Now, in Black Otter's lodge, Two Leggings continued speaking, pulling his father back to the present.

"Iron Hair no like Sullivan. No like Crow," Two Leggings said in English. "Iron Hair say we bad. He tell Miss Molly stop teaching us or he close school."

Two Leggings's small face clouded. His dark eyes met his father's. "What 'red scum' mean?"

A muscle flicked in Black Otter's cheek. "Iron Hair call you that?"

The boy nodded. "And Sullivan throw him out."

"What then?"

The boy shrugged. "Iron Hair say Sullivan is dead man. Why he say that? Sullivan not dead."

Not yet, Black Otter thought.

He rose and pulled a heavy buffalo robe around his shoulders. Ruffling his son's hair, he walked Two Leggings to the door of the lodge. With a faint smile he said, "Send Little Turtle to me."

The chief went back to the fire and waited for his best warrior.

DECEMBER 27, 1884

When Luke started out the next morning, the sky was a hazy, milky gray, deepening to a dirty lead color at the horizon. Cold air sifted in around his collar, around his wrists, and up his sleeves. Snow coming. He could smell it. The fullness in the air filled his nostrils and coated the back of his throat. Six to ten inches by morning, for sure.

Riding loose and free in the saddle, he headed out to the open range. He could ride like this for hours, then swing off easily without so much as a kink in a muscle and get on with whatever he'd come to do.

He wasn't more than a mile from the house when he caught a quick darting from the corner of his eye, like the flash of a deer in the woods, a blur of movement, there and gone almost before it registered in his mind. And then later, as he waded Bugle across a half-frozen stream, the soft crunch of a pinecone sounded behind him. He slipped his Winchester rifle from the saddle sling and cocked it. Tense, alert, he hipped around, scanning the line of cottonwoods and underbrush along the bank.

Fox? Bear?

Or Indian? The little hairs lifted on the back of his neck.

Luke sat motionless, scarcely breathing, straining to listen. Nothing but the quiet gurgle of water on the rocks at his feet. Yet the eerie feeling of watching eyes persisted. Whatever or whoever was out there was as still as he. A few minutes later, Luke clucked his tongue and took Bugle into the stream.

New Hope's range began a mile from the house, stretching south to the foothills of the Red Lion Mountains, the boundary they shared with the Crow reservation. To the west, toward Billings, the land was open pasture, a snowy, empty plain that stretched for miles. In the spring it would be belt-high with sweet blue grama grass, stretching as far as he could see, waving in the wind like a wheat field.

Half a dozen small streams crisscrossed it. As far back as he could remember, New Hope had got low on water only once. The other herds seemed to know it and kept drifting down. Years before, New Hope had fenced it off to keep out the other brands—mainly Axel's. If they hadn't, X-Bar-L steers would have grazed New Hope's grass to the roots.

Overhead, a couple of buzzards spiraled lazily. His eyes skimmed the empty pastures. New Hope's herd was smaller than he ever remembered, which meant he had to sit down with Molly and the books. In the summer, the herd ran around fifteen hundred head, she'd told him, and said they sold five hundred steers annually in good times. He'd thought he'd find maybe six or seven hundred cows being wintered, but he saw nothing like that many out here. Could be reasons for that, he told himself, like winter kill or disease. He hoped so, but deep down, something seemed wrong. It niggled at him, wouldn't let him alone—the same feeling he'd had in Lewistown when he discovered three percent of Granville Stuart's herd had been stolen.

Luke flicked the reins and rode forward slowly, his eyes soaking in every detail. Under Bugle's hooves, the frozen grass rustled like dry straw, and the farther he rode, the deeper the lines dug into his forehead. In several places, the fence was down, the wire trampled into the snow.

Near an outcropping of rock, Luke spotted another leaning post and a break in the wire. He wound the reins around the saddle horn and swung off. Squatting on his haunches, he picked up the strands of wire and shook his head. The fence wasn't broken. It was cut.

Two more hours of fence riding disclosed nothing new. Oddly, despite the cut fence, he found not one X-Bar-L cow on New Hope land. Was it possible Axel wasn't involved? He headed home, his brain calculating, sorting the facts. If there was a thread of logic tying it all together somewhere, he hadn't found it yet.

Before he was halfway home, snow began falling, big, thick flakes sticking immediately to everything they touched. Luke turned up the sheepskin collar on his jacket and tucked his chin in. He needed to talk to Scully Anders.

The barn, a big two-story structure with a gambrel roof and weather vanes, sat at the foot of a small slope, enclosed by a small corral and a fenced five-acre pasture. Scully was inside the barn mending a harness in one of the tack rooms.

Good man, Luke thought. New Hope was lucky to have him. Until Luke came back, he'd practically run the place, overseeing the help, keeping track of the cattle. It was he who bought the bulls, did the branding, ran the roundups. And it was Scully who told Molly when and how many boys he needed to help.

Luke had seen three of the older boys riding with Scully and the other men almost every day since he'd been back.

Growing up, he'd done the same, but it was more like training then, a part of their schooling. There had always been a cowboy around, someone to teach a gangly kid how to rope and shoot and break a horse. When they left there, every one of them could get a job on any ranch in the territory. But from what Luke had seen, most of the boys were cleaning barns and shoveling manure, mending fences. Nothing wrong with that, except it wasn't training. That was yardman's work. Molly wanted better for her boys.

He swung down and led Bugle inside the barn. In the dusky light, the pungent odor of manure and hay and animals clung, sweet-sour, in his nostrils. Head high, the big gray stood patiently while Luke unfastened the cinch, lifted off the heavy saddle, and threw it across a partition between two stalls. When he pulled the blanket off, a slight steam rose from the horse's back.

"Mighty fine animal you got there," Scully said, watching Luke rub the sweat and mud off the deep chest with a gunnysack. "What do you call him?"

"Bugle. He was part of my remuda at Stuart's. Grant let me

buy him when I left. I wasn't about to leave him up there." Luke grinned self-consciously, embarrassed to admit how much he liked his horse. Affectionately, he smoothed his hand down Bugle's flank. The horse's muscles rippled in response.

"He's a big one – stallion, too – so how come you ain't wearing spurs?" Scully asked.

"I don't with him. He's a sweet horse. Sometimes I think this critter reads my mind. Move over there." Luke thumped the heavy shoulder out of the way.

Bugle swung his head around and glanced inquiringly at Luke, then did as he was told and hoofed sideways.

"Get him around a mare in season, and I bet you'll wish you had spurs. Sure is a big one. If he was mine, I'd geld him, 'specially one that size."

"I will if I have to, but I'd like a colt out of him first. I've been riding horses all my life, and he's the smartest one I've ever had – the only one I'd ever trust. Twice one winter up at Stuart's, we got caught in a blizzard and had to lie in the snow together. Bugle lay on his side, his back to the wind. I crawled between his legs against his belly, and threw a blanket over us. We kept each other warm until the storm passed."

Scully's eyebrows raised. "I never had one I'd do that with – never. Weren't you afraid he'd roll on you?"

Luke shook his head. "I was more afraid of freezing to death."

With long, brisk strokes, Luke began rubbing down the stallion's powerful front legs, and Bugle came as close to purring as a horse ever could. "Where's all the help gone to around here?" he asked.

"Ain't but six cowhands here anymore," Scully said. "Others

kind of drifted off this past year. Most of them stayed long as they could, but the board's cutting back on the money."

"Who's on the board this year?"

"Same ones as always: businessmen in Repton, the bank president, a preacher, and other stockmen who use this range, including Axel. They all donate to keep this place running."

Under a battered brown cowboy hat, Scully's face was wind-burned and roughened, his cheeks showing a stubble of beard beginning to gray. Forty-odd years of squinting into the sun had etched permanent crow's-feet around his eyes. He held a black bridle rein, straightening it, smoothing it with the heel of his hand.

"I won't leave, though. Food's good and Molly needs me. New Hope's as good as the next place, I reckon."

"I've been riding fences. Some of them are down." Luke watched Scully's face closely for a reaction. "One of them was cut. You know anything about that?"

Scully's eyes widened. "I don't like that at all," he said.

Luke continued to brush the horse. "After breakfast tomorrow, I'm going out to restring those lines. Can you give me a hand?"

"Sure, but there ain't much bob wire left. I used most of it up in the fall."

"Don't need it. Got enough fixing to do with what's already down. I want N-Bar-H cows off the range and back on New Hope property, where we can get a decent count of how many we got. Tell the others I'll need them to work on cutting ours out next week."

When he finished wiping Bugle down, he led him into a stall and threw in extra straw on the floor. "That burns me up," he grunted, kicking the straw around. "Who you suppose cut our fence, anyway?"

"Hard to say. Three different stockmen besides Axel use the range now." Scully raised his voice over the sound of Luke's boots scuffing straw. "To tell you the truth, I wish you'd stick around."

Luke nodded. "I am. For a while, at least. Molly asked me to stay."

Scully laid the bridle aside and walked to the stall. He stood in the doorway, his face serious. "I'm glad to hear it." Then, lowering his voice, he said, "Yesterday when I went up there, someone took a shot at me."

Luke's head snapped up in surprise. "Shot at you? Any idea why?"

"Trying to run me off, I guess."

"Think they mistook you for me?"

Scully looked over sharply but didn't answer.

Luke knew from his expression that the same thought had occurred to him, as well. "Don't tell Molly till we find out what's going on. She's got enough on her mind right now."

"Luke, I don't mean to pry—and it makes no difference to me one way or the other—but some folks around here . . . well, they're a little leery about you. They say you're still part of Stuart's group and you came down here hunting someone."

Luke's leg stopped mid-swing. Hands on his hips, he stared at Scully. "They think wrong. I work for New Hope now, no one else," he said flatly. Inside, the cold feeling in his chest thawed a little more. That was someone else's job now.

"Like I said—don't matter to me either way."

Luke slammed the door to Bugle's stall and latched it. Anger gave way to uneasiness. A little despondent, he shook his head. No matter what he said or what he did, people made up their own minds about things. It was the same in Lewistown. People ask you to do things, and then they're afraid of you when you do. Stiffly, he walked out of the barn and into the yard.

A loose shutter rapped against the side of the house in the wind. The storm must be moving in fast. A curtain of snow swirled across the corral, obliterating everything for a moment.

From the barn door, Scully watched the dark figure of his new boss fade, then reappear from the white whirlpool and track for the house. He heaved a sigh of relief. Whatever was wrong, that man would fix it.

A smile tugged at his lips. As a little boy, Luke had a mind of his own, always fighting, stuttering and fighting. Until he was twelve, he stuttered every time he got upset. Scully used to watch him barrel across the yard on those skinny legs of his and dive into a fistfight on the side of the loser just to even up the odds a bit.

On more than one occasion, Molly had caught him out in the barn sneaking a smoke when he should've been in school. She'd marched him back to the classroom, stuttering and jumping, his ear pinched in her hand. But the next day, he'd be back out there again like it never happened. And so would she.

He outgrew the stuttering, but evidently nothing else.

Scully watched him cross the yard. New Hope needed someone hardheaded and tough enough to draw a little blood, if need be. A vigilante would fit every one of those. But was he or wasn't he?

Scully turned and went back inside the barn, hoping he was.

⁂

Crossing the yard to the house, Luke ducked his head against the snow needling his face. In the three days he'd been back, he'd seen too many things he didn't like. And now someone had taken a shot at Scully. His jaw tightened.

From inside the house came the shrill voice of one of the little girls.

Several times that afternoon, another girl, a bigger girl, had invaded his thoughts. A creamy cameo face and ginger hair swam through his imagination. Impatiently, he forced it away again. He wouldn't waste his time with her. She wasn't his type.

Sticking around New Hope had absolutely nothing to do with her, he told himself. Emily McCarthy was spoiled and stubborn and mouthy. Besides, she didn't like him—and he didn't like her, either.

He fumed to himself, remembering breakfast Christmas morning and yesterday morning and again this morning. Emily McCarthy had taken to acting like she was his big sister, cool and superior. Snooty. And she refused to look at him, absolutely would not meet his eyes. He couldn't fight with her because she ignored him. A line of muscle pulsed in his jaw. He was a grown man, a ranch foreman; she was hardly more than a child. Despite the cold, the back of his neck warmed under his fur collar. Well, old Luke Sullivan gave as good as he got.

Right then and there he decided to treat Miss Emily Mc-Carthy with a brotherly indifference anytime he had to be around her—which was entirely too often to suit him.

Two at time, Luke took the steps to the back porch and crossed to the kitchen door. Stomping his feet, he batted his hat against his thigh to knock off the snow and then went on inside. The big kitchen was steamy and warm and bustling with the women getting supper on the table.

He stuck his head in the door and grinned. "Timed it just right, I see."

"Better hurry," Ida, the cook, said as she took up potatoes from a pot on the stove. A hired girl stood by the side table, ladling out bowls of gravy. He caught a glimpse of Molly's broad figure disappearing through the doorway with a plate of biscuits in each hand.

But no one else was in the kitchen.

Luke hung up his coat and hat on the hook board running down the length of the little room outside the kitchen. A shelf holding a bucket of water and a gray graniteware basin ran along the other side. On the wall behind it hung a small mirror and a towel on a peg. He filled the basin and washed up quickly for supper. Then, two-handed, he combed his hair in the mirror, stooping so he could see better.

Ida called, "Supper's ready."

"On my way."

"Bring the pickles."

He ambled through the kitchen, grabbing up the pickle dish from the side table as he passed, and headed down the hall for the dining room to find Emily McCarthy so he could ignore her.

CHAPTER
6

Luke leaned back in his chair and frowned across the table at Molly. The two of them were sitting at the end of one of the tables after dinner, going over the accounts. Spread open between them was Molly's big black ledger. Papers and receipts were scattered across the table.

"Doesn't make sense," he said, tapping a finger on the page in front of him. "With the railroad into Billings, you should've sold a thousand head more than you did."

"That's what I thought, but we didn't," she answered. "The market wasn't there. Happens all the time. Scully drives a herd to Billings, talks to the yardmaster, and finds out the order was already filled. So we either sell at a lower price or else we bring them back home. Scully did that once when the price went down to fifteen dollars a head."

"Scully was right. Fifteen dollars was giving them away.

You'd have lost money. If we had more help, we could forget Chicago and sell to the mining camps. They never have enough beef."

Molly nodded. "I sold some to Bozeman camp a couple of times, but it's a six-day drive up there and took every man on the place. Nothing got done here when they were gone."

And it still wouldn't, Luke thought. He liked trail-bossing, had gone back and forth to Oregon with Stuart's herds many times, but those days were over as long as he was at New Hope. He couldn't manage the rest of the herd at New Hope by himself.

"Once we get New Hope back in the black, we can hire more cowhands and go for the camps," he said.

Molly wet her finger and flipped back through the ledger pages to the household accounts. "Emily says we should be making our own clothes and bed linen, instead of buying them or paying Ellie Butler in Repton to make them. Emily says we could save five hundred dollars a year if I bought another sewing machine and we did most things here. What do you think?"

"Sewing machines cost money is what I think."

"Fifteen dollars, but the machine would pay for itself in a month with what we'd save."

Luke raised an eyebrow. "Emily McCarthy's a teacher. What does she know about expenses and cutting costs?"

"I'm surprised what all she knows about running an institution." When Luke looked skeptical, Molly smiled. "I grabbed one of the boys running in the hall yesterday, and his shirtsleeve just ripped off in my hand. Straightaway, Emily asked me who made the starch. I told her the hired girl Anna did. She didn't say a word, but a few minutes later, she came back and told me Anna puts too much borax and turpentine in the starch, says it weakens cloth something fierce."

It was getting to be Emily this and Emily that—and getting to be downright aggravating. "She's getting to be a regular little Miss Fix-It," he said to Molly.

With a deep sigh, Molly closed the book. "She's a godsend, Luke. She's taken so much work off me."

He swallowed a twinge of guilt. Molly needed help. If Emily could ease Molly's schedule, he should be grateful.

Molly's head snapped up. "Now, will you listen to that?" She cocked her head and chuckled. Piano chords shattered the afternoon quiet of the big house in a rousing introduction. "Emily does brighten up this place."

"I didn't know she could play like that," Luke said, his eyebrows knotted into a scowl. Sideways, he glanced at Molly.

"There's a lot you don't know about that girl." Her lips pressed tight together, eyes crinkling at the corners, and he could tell she was laughing at him on the inside. "Why don't you try being a little nicer to her?" she said.

He gave a soft little snort through his nose, climbed to his feet, and started for his room. He dragged his feet as he passed the library. Inside, chairs scraped and children squealed. Luke stopped out in the hall and looked inside. Twelve children were yelling and marching, playing musical chairs. With her back to the door, Emily sat at the upright, swaying from side to side with the tempo, pounding out an old steamboat song.

Her hair spilled down her back, the weight of it tossing as

she swept the back of her fingernails up and down the keys in a wacky, syncopated, bobtailed rhythm.

A corner of his mouth kicked up.

Pretty hair. Pretty back. Pretty little everything.

Five-year-old Mary Agnes Kelly pushed against the back of Two Leggings, the young Crow boy in front of her. Shuffling down the row of chairs, she spied Luke in his work clothes and heavy boots smiling in the doorway.

"C'mon in, Mr. Luke," she squealed.

The music stopped. Emily spun around on the stool.

Mary Agnes threw herself into the same chair with Two Leggings, both of them falling to the floor. She looked up, whooping with laughter.

The doorway was empty.

On the staircase at the end of the hall, Luke was taking the steps up three at a time.

The next morning, a child's hoarse wail made Emily stop sweeping the front porch and look up. Frowning, forehead wrinkled like a washboard, Luke strode around the corner of the house, leading a sobbing little boy in knee pants.

"Can you believe it? I hardly know this kid, and he ran all the way out to the second barn to get me," Luke said.

Emily walked down the steps and kneeled beside the boy. "What's wrong, Teddy?"

Though he was only four, he was big for his age and had an odd croaky voice. Now his nose was running, and his eyes were brimming with tears.

"Wait a minute, kid." Luke pulled out a huge handkerchief and gently wiped the boy's nose. "Now tell her."

Teddy sniffed. "My torse's sick and I'm worleed." His voice caught.

Luke looked down at Emily. "Translate, please."

"His tortoise is sick and he's worried," she said.

Luke ruffled the boy's hair, his big hand completely covering the small head. "One of the dogs played with his tortoise, tossed it in the air a couple times. Dog thought it was a walking bone, I guess, and bit it a little. I tried to tell him it wasn't fatal, but he doesn't believe me. He pitched a fit at the barn a while ago, wanted me to bring it to you for some medical advice."

Part of the reason for Teddy's tears, Emily suspected, was the little scene that morning in the dining room and not letting him bring his pet in for breakfast.

"You know the rules, honey. No animals in the house, and that includes reptiles."

"Not a tile; he's a torse, and he's my friend."

Emily hid a smile and held her hand out. "Let me see your sick friend."

Teddy hid his face against Luke's leg.

Luke rolled his eyes, dug deep into a side pocket of his overalls, and extracted a muddy, green and yellow tortoise, shut up as tight as a clam.

Emily frowned and held it up to the light. "You sure it's in there?"

"Was when we left the barn," Luke said.

She sat down on the steps to examine the turtle. It bore several shallow tooth marks and an insignificant gouge in the shell. It wouldn't win any beauty contests, she decided, but it wouldn't die, either.

She held it to her ear. "Hmmmm." She nodded seriously, listening to dead air. "Come listen to how strong her heart is. She's a tough little turtle."

"He's a he, and he's a torse."

"Got it. A torse. And he's going to be just fine. Listen." She held the tortoise to the boy's ear and tapped her fingernail lightly on its shell for a sound effect. "There, you hear it?"

"I do, I do!" Teddy held the tortoise up to Luke. "You listen, Mr. Luke. You said she thinks she knows everything in the world, and she does."

A red flush stained Luke's cheeks. Avoiding Emily's eyes, he held the tortoise to his ear.

"Do *you* hear it, Mr. Luke?" Emily asked in her schoolteacher's *you just got an F* voice.

"Yeah, I hear it," he growled.

Emily checked the tooth marks again. "I don't think he needs stitches. We'll just put some medicine on his back and his tummy and he'll be fine. And until he's all better, Mr. Luke is going to build you a nice little house for Torse with a safe little fence around it."

Luke's eyebrows flew up. "I don't know about that."

Teddy's small face looked as if the sun had burst out behind it. "Oh, Mr. Luke, Mr. Luke, I love you! You're my best friend." He threw himself at Luke and wound his arms around his leg.

Emily struggled to keep a straight face. "That's what best friends are for, Teddy."

Emily went into the house. When she returned, she held up a small red bottle of Mercurochrome.

A minute later, all smiles, and holding on to Luke's hand, Teddy hugged the tortoise to his chest and crossed the yard. Its shells were still shut up like a fist, only now it sported a red splash in the middle of its back.

Teddy looked up at Luke. "Torse wants a house with a window and a door and a fence with a lock and—"

"Yeah, yeah." He looked back over his shoulder at Emily and called, "I'll get you for this!"

Each morning about five o'clock, and still so dark they couldn't see the ears on their horses, Luke and four New Hope cowboys rode out of the complex for the open range.

As a courtesy, he'd gone to see the Paxtons, the Ormons, and old Cecil Bolton, the other stockmen who used the range, telling them he was going into their herds and cutting out his brand.

"I reckon you know you don't have to tell me. You got a right to cut anytime you've a mind to," Carl Paxton said, then grinned and slapped him on the back. "But I appreciate it all the same. Come on in and have some supper with us."

"I better not, Mr. Paxton. You're the last one I had to see today," Luke said. "We're starting early tomorrow."

"Mr. Axel gets a mite touchy about cutting. What'd he say?"

"I didn't talk to him." The answer was crisp.

"I see," Carl Paxton said, in a tone that clearly implied

he did not. He chuckled. "You're polite, but you ain't that polite."

Luke didn't say anything. Instead, he put his hat back on, waved good-bye, and rode off.

Each day they worked another section, cutting the other range herds for the N-Bar-H brand. They usually found a few of their own, for cows weren't fussy. When cattle found a herd – any herd – they strolled over and melted right into it.

Luke was determined to cut out every one of theirs and bring it home. For days, from dawn until dusk, they drove cattle both up range and down range. If necessary, he thought grimly, he'd move his whole herd to another section, for until he got them all collected and together, he couldn't begin to get an accurate head count.

Twice he ran into Axel's crew. Four of them one day. They sat off to one side, rifles over their arms, watching stonily as he and Scully and Henry Bertel worked the herd, circling, plunging into the bawling mass of backs, checking for N-Bar-H brands, dragging out steers.

One by one, they lassoed and pulled out their own, driving them into a makeshift holding pen they'd thrown up on the prairie. Then, back they went again for more, switching horses from the remuda they'd brought along – two or three for each man. At the end of the day, they hazed their own cows down range.

Luke was puzzled. He knew the business, had been around cattle all his life and understood the psychology of range herds. Up at Stuart's they used to say he could think like a cow. He'd never known them to wander like this. He was discouraged and knew they hadn't gotten them all.

Emily untied her apron and hung it on a hook in the kitchen. For days the kitchen had been filled with clouds of sweet-smelling steam from a washboiler full of sap simmering on the back of the stove.

Ida, making bread at a table by the window, looked up. "You're going up there again, are you?" she said, picking up her sifter and snowing a cloud of flour across the dough.

Emily nodded. "Molly says the first sap makes the best syrup. We never made maple syrup in Chicago. Once someone brought a gallon from back east. That's the only time I ever tasted it."

Ida pulled dough off her fingers. "That grove's been up there long as I remember. The Indians taught us how to do it. Cheyenne and Crow have been making syrup and sugar for hundreds of years."

"Molly told me how to do it. Says the sap started early this year because of the warm spells we had."

Ida kneaded the bread with the heels of her hands, then gave a few more smacks to the flour sifter. "Want me to get one of the boys to go along with you?"

Emily shook her head. "Not today. They're studying for a history test, and they're too anxious to get out of class as it is."

Ida straightened. Eyes dancing, she planted a hand on her hip. She stood there, hipshot and grinning wickedly. "I bet Mr. Luke wouldn't mind helping you."

Emily stiffened and threw Ida a sharp look. "I can do it myself. I don't need any help from him." She shrugged on her coat and mittens and hurried out onto the porch. She tossed the scalded tin pails and a big metal bucket into a wheelbarrow at the bottom of the steps. Picking up the heavy handles, she headed out across a field spotted with large patches of snow for the grove of black maples on the other side of the hill.

Outside, the temperature was twenty degrees, but in the smithy it was stifling. Luke's shirt was wet, his upper lip beaded with sweat. Wearing a grimy leather apron, Scully Anders worked the bellows hanging above the forge, jetting air down over white-hot coals. A horseshoe glowed a dull cherry red in the fire.

Bugle stood patiently, his back hoof caught between Luke's thighs. With painstaking care, his master scraped and pared the horse's hooves.

Luke clapped another horseshoe, still warm, against the hoof, measuring. He handed it back to Scully. "Not quite. Bend the ends in a tad more."

Scully shook his head and thrust the shoe in the fire again, muttering, "Never seen a man so fussy 'bout a horse."

Luke heard him and grinned.

A gust of wind creaked the door open. Luke lowered Bugle's leg and went to close it. Standing in the doorway, he watched a small figure trundling a big wooden wheelbarrow beyond the corral.

"Now, where's she going, I wonder?" he said to Scully,

raising his voice over the ringing racket of the older man's hammering on steel.

"Who?"

"Her." Luke pointed to Emily, watching as she shut the garden gate behind her, then grabbed the handles of the wheelbarrow and pushed on across the open field.

Scully stopped his pounding and raised his head. "Looks like she's got sap buckets with her," he said. "Going up to the sugar bush, I guess. They been boiling syrup in the kitchen the last couple days, or ain't you noticed?"

Luke shook his head, not taking his eyes off the girl plodding along in boots and a long brown cape, the ends of a bright blue scarf fluttering behind her. Uneasy, he studied the sky. All morning, a steady northwest breeze had been blowing down from Canada. More snow on the way.

"She always thinks she can do more than she can," he grumbled. "That bucket's too heavy for her."

"Right now that bucket's empty, so shut the door. You're cooling my fire," Scully called. "She'll be all right."

"Snow's on the way. And she's got no business going up there alone."

"Go with her then, but shut the door!"

Luke swung the plank door closed, dropped the wooden bar in place, and went back to shoeing Bugle. Determined to put Emily McCarthy out of his mind, he rested the horse's front hoof on his thigh and began prying out the old nails.

Emily had seen Luke standing in the doorway of the smithy, watching her. Squaring her shoulders, she pushed along faster. As soon as she got to the orchard, she checked the buckets hanging on spouts driven into the trunks. Humming under her breath, she unhooked the pails and drained the watery liquid into the big bucket in the wheelbarrow. It was prime syrup weather, she thought. With the mild, sunny days and freezing nights, they ought to get fifteen gallons of sap from each tree this year. It took about forty gallons of sap – almost three trees' worth – to boil down one gallon of syrup. It was a lot of work, but it was worth it. Drizzled on hot biscuits on a cold morning, nothing could match it.

Emily shivered. The wind had kicked up. She pulled her mittens off and tugged the scarf tighter around her neck. That was when she saw it, a bear cub – a small grizzly, only a few months old. No doubt curious at all her banging and clattering, the cub wobbled on a beeline through the woods in her direction.

And shambling right behind, head swinging, shoulders rolling, was its mother.

Emily dropped the pail. Hiking her skirts, she ran for the entrance to the grove, zigzagging through the trees as fast as she could go. Feet flying, she raced for the edge of the woods and the open field beyond. Behind her, she heard the cub nosing the pail on the ground.

The heavy cape bunched between her legs, slowing her. Her heart pounding her ribs, she kept on running, trying to snatch the cape free. Off-balance, she tripped and fell flat over a root half hidden by snow. The mother bear raised her head and let out a bellow of rage, then made a short lunge in Emily's direction.

With a stricken look, Emily jumped to her feet and stumbled into a run for her life. The bear crashed through the underbrush toward her, huffing, making sucking and blowing noises as it pulled air in and out its nose, as if trying to identify her scent. Emily's heels thudded the ground.

Faster. Run faster!

Blood rushed in her ears. A scream wedged in her throat, because no matter how fast she ran, she'd never outrun the bear.

Ahead of her, a broad maple spread thick, low branches just over her head. She doubted she could jump high enough to reach it. She put on a burst of speed, threw her arms up, and leaped.

Help me, Jesus.

And there it was – the branch, thick and solid under her hand. Straining, she hooked her knee over it, hauled herself up as fast as she could. If it was a grizzly – and she thought it was, prayed it was – she'd read they seldom climbed, even as cubs. They were too big and bulky, and their claws were straight, not curved.

Legs shoving, she reached overhead and pulled herself higher up the tree. She hugged the ridged trunk, cold and rock hard, against her chest, the bark scratchy against her arms. Her scarf caught on a twig, her skirt snagged. She ripped them loose, her eyes riveted on a deep crotch in the tree just above her. Swinging a leg over, she wedged herself down into it and froze, holding her breath.

Through the limbs just below, she saw the bear stop at

the base of the tree, snuffling the ground, a massive animal with shaggy brown fur tipped and frosted looking. The head appeared to grow right out of its shoulders, with a mouth that sliced back to its ears, opening and closing as if chewing air. Slowly, the bear raised its head and peered into the branches, its eyes glittering up at her.

With a roar the grizzly reared on its hind legs, stretching to its full length, pawing, slashing, snarling. A limb splintered. And another. In a frenzy the bear tore at the tree. Emily wound her arms around the trunk to keep from falling and screamed.

A few minutes before, Luke had thrown down his tools and wheeled around, grabbed his coat and his rifle and slammed out of the smithy, leaving a half-shod horse and a surprised Scully Anders staring after him. Muttering under his breath, Luke strode up the hill toward the grove of maples.

Emily McCarthy irritated him. She didn't listen to a thing he said. Every time he was with her, something picked at him.

She didn't like him, and he didn't like her, either.

The air was crisp and clear. He stopped to buckle his jacket against the light snow starting to fall. His nostrils flared. Chin lifted, he sniffed deeply several times. He was downwind of something, a rank odor he'd smelled before, a little like skunk but not as strong. The hairs on the back of his neck raked up.

Bear.

Quickly, he checked the gun and slapped the breech closed. Rifle swinging in his hand, he started for the sugar bush.

When he turned into the woods, he heard it – rhythmic grunts, tree limbs splitting, branches cracking off like firewood. He broke into a hard run and was already pounding toward her when he heard her scream.

"I'm coming, Emily!"

At his shout, the grizzly dropped to all fours and swung around. Luke stopped, brought the gun to his shoulder, and aimed. He fired once. The shot struck the tree only inches from the bear's huge head, stinging the animal with flying bark. With a surprised snort, she leaped aside. Her frightened cub streaked off in the opposite direction, hooting through its nose.

Rocking from side to side on her front paws, stiff legged, the grizzly stared at Luke. If she broke into a full-blown charge, he had two seconds maybe. This time, Luke aimed the rifle at the flat, light-colored area between her eyes. He'd better not miss. The cub, alone and lost, bawled piteously for its mother. Several seconds passed as he and the bear stared at each other. Turning, she charged – but not at Luke. The last he saw of her was a big furry behind running through the trees.

Luke puffed his cheeks and blew out a long, relieved breath. "You can come down now," he shouted to Emily, and lowered the gun. He walked to the tree and looked up through the branches.

Emily stood in the fork of two limbs, hugging the trunk.

"She's gone. Come on down, Emmy," he said gently. With a start, he realized he'd never called her that before.

She gave a little palsied nod and fished her foot in the air for a branch below.

"Take it easy," he soothed. "The bear won't come back. We've got lots of time. Don't hurry."

Slowly, chest heaving, she worked her way down, a branch at a time, until she was on a limb just over his head. Her eyes were as big as pie pans, the red hair tangled and wild looking. Even from this distance he could see her hands trembling.

"Jump," he said. "I'll catch you." He turned to lay the rifle down.

Emily didn't wait. She hurled herself into the air, her cape spreading behind her like wings. From the corner of his eye, Luke caught the flutter of airborne brown cloth. He dropped the gun in surprise. Like a giant bird from space, she landed full on his back and knocked him to the ground.

Stunned, the breath knocked out of him, Luke rolled her off his back and sat up. "What . . . what'd you do that for?" he gasped, and sucked in a ragged mouthful of air.

Lying on the ground in a heap beside him, Emily wrapped both arms around her head and burst into tears. Without thinking, he pulled her onto his lap and rocked her, holding her close.

Emily buried her face against his jacket, shaking uncontrollably. "I'm sorry, I'm sorry. I was scared. I'm so glad you're here," she mumbled into his chest.

Luke stroked the back of her head, trying to sort out his feelings, his throat so tight with emotion he was afraid to speak. Relieved she was all right, he buried his face in her hair.

Briefly, he closed his eyes. She felt good in his arms, and he hadn't expected that. A minute later, he stood and pulled her to her feet.

"Ow!" Her knee buckled.

"What's wrong now?"

"My foot hurts."

Luke sat her down and worked off the boot. Under the black stocking, her ankle was puffed, swelling out over her shoe almost as he watched.

"Here," he said, scooping her up. "You hold the gun." Carrying her high in his arms, he started walking.

"It's too far to carry me. I can make it if we go slow."

"No, it could be broken."

"I don't think it is."

"And I don't know for sure, so stop yapping at me." He shifted her in his arms and hugged her securely against him.

With a little sigh of resignation, Emily snuggled into him. She felt protected and safe, really safe, for the first time since . . . well, maybe for the first time ever. Beneath his jacket, the man was a brick wall, his arms and chest hard. She curved her fingers around his neck. He felt just right, she thought. His skin was warm, and his hair smelled smoky. She buried her face in his sheepskin collar, trying to figure herself out.

"When you shot, you missed that bear on purpose, didn't you?" she said quietly.

He paused, then nodded.

"Why didn't you kill her?"

"Because she woke up too early this spring and she's half starved. And because she has a cub."

"Is that why she came after me?"

"One reason."

"One?"

"Grizzlies are just pure mean."

"Then, you should've killed her."

"I would have if I had to."

She gave a small huff of annoyance. "If she'd gone after *you*, you mean."

He chuckled, and for the first time she saw him smile—a mouthful of straight white teeth. Though his manner was casual and amused, there was a wariness around his eyes. He let no one get close to him and kept most people at arm's length. Ida told her that he'd been a vigilante. Good grief, no wonder he didn't smile often.

A minute later he dumped her into the wheelbarrow alongside a bucket of sap, saying, "I can't carry you, a rifle, and five gallons of sap." He grabbed the wooden handles and shoved the wheelbarrow into a rattling run out of the orchard and across the field, bumping her down the hill.

The sap bucket slid from between her legs and thudded against the front of the wheelbarrow. Sap slopped over the rim. Emily gripped the sides with sticky hands. The wheel jarred into a rock, and she bit her tongue. "What's the big hurry?" she yelled.

"Got to finish shoeing my horse."

"Your horse!"

She snapped her jaws shut. By the time they reached the house, her lips were icy white at the corners. Any tender feelings or silly romantic notions she may have been nurturing for one Luke Sullivan had been jounced right out of her.

CHAPTER
7

The bell rang, signaling the end of art class for the day. Emily collected the slates and stood them up on the eraser rail below the blackboard, admiring them. Wiping her hands on a damp cloth, she called to the children, reminding them to clean their hands before they left. It was a mixed-grade class. Anyone under twelve years old was welcome. The children dropped their colored chalk in the tin chalk box and filed out.

"Tim, wait a minute, please."

Tim Gardner, small and freckle-faced, hesitated, then plopped back onto his bench. He looked up at her as Emily slid onto the bench and sat beside him.

He blinked at her. "Did I do something wrong?" he asked.

"No, indeed. I like to watch you draw. You're good at it, and I thought I'd watch to see how you do it." She laughed.

And patted his hand. "My drawings are so bad. Even my sun looks dumb with all those spikes coming out of it."

She picked up two slates and a handful of colored chalk left on another desk. She handed one to him. She huffed out a breath and then pretended to study her slate.

"What you want me to draw?" Tim asked.

"Anything. I'm going to draw a . . ." Her eyes held on the table by the window with a stack of slates. Tables were in kitchens and kitchens usually had families. It was the family she was after. "I'm going to start with something easy—a table."

He watched her make a few boxlike lines and then began to draw lines on his own slate.

"Tables are easy," he said. He leaned over and smudged out an extra line in her picture, and grinned. "Four legs, not five."

For several minutes they drew together, Tim quiet with concentration. Emily, watching him, drew pieces of furniture she saw in the classroom.

Tim continued to work on one picture. A big room with a curtained window and an open door.

"Yours is better than mine." She tapped her finger under a table he'd drawn. Remembering breakfast in the dining room that morning, Emily had peopled her picture with little stick figures sitting and holding forks.

Tim's table was empty. Except for one stick figure. The chairs he'd put in his picture were empty.

"Who's that?" She pointed to the lone stick figure.

"Me."

"Where'd everybody else go?" she asked.

He glanced at the window and pointed to the sky. "Up there. In heaven."

Emily's heart squeezed tight. It was exactly as she had feared. Tim was withdrawn because he'd lost his parents. He was a hurt little boy.

Orphanages were full of troubled children. At Aldersgate, one of the big universities sent a doctor in from time to time to teach the instructors about painting and art and how it could help ease a child's sadness.

With a pang she realized now how much she missed the extra instruction she had been given.

The slate had given Tim a way to disclose and unburden what was always in his mind. She swallowed and smiled brightly at him.

"I've got an idea! Let's make this picture New Hope's dining room and put lots of chairs with lots of people in them."

Laughing, she sketched a chair at the far end of the table. Then another. And another.

Tim stared at the slate, the solemn little face curving into a smile. With the tip of his tongue in the corner of his mouth, he swiftly drew in more chairs, crowding them into the picture.

"And that's me, next to Mr. Luke," he said, laughing and pointing to another stick figure with big ears in a chair.

"Mr. Luke doesn't have big elephant ears like that."

Tim squealed with laughter. "Next to mine they are!"

"You're right." Emily leaned over and hugged him.

It was a start.

"Sit down, Clete." Bart Axel squeaked back in his swivel chair and waved his cigar to his ranch foreman.

His account books were spread out, a ledger opened to a page scrawled in his big, loose handwriting. "I don't care what Sheriff Tucker says. Sullivan robbed that stage and took the money, and I know it."

Clete Wade shifted and said nothing. Bart swung the chair around again, his back to Clete. Clete shrugged and sat down. Small, steady sucking sounds came from the other side of the chair as Bart puffed his cigar. A plume of smoke wafted toward the ceiling, and a voice snarled from the chair. "Sullivan's been out on the range poking his nose in everyone's herds, rounding up strays. Didn't say nothing to me about it first, neither."

"Regulations say he don't have to, boss. Hunting his own cows—he's allowed to check all herds for his own brand."

"He told everyone else. So how come he didn't tell me?" Slowly, the chair wheeled around. "Suppose you take a few of our boys up there and teach him some manners."

"You want us to rough him up good?"

"If that's all you got the guts to do." Standing, Bart splayed his hands on the desk and leaned his weight forward. His eyes bored into Clete. "I pay you plenty. Any more questions about what I want?"

Clete shook his head.

❧

As the weather warmed and the snow melted, Luke and the men continued looking for N-Bar-H brands. Each day he spotted circling buzzards and followed them into isolated gullies and streambeds. Nearly always he found a few more dead cows and calves frozen in one of the storms. Winter kill, two or three percent, and to be expected. The percentages were right in line.

So winter kill wasn't the answer.

On the range that morning, Luke pointed to three black specks wheeling high in the sky. "I'll check them out," he told Scully and the men, then galloped off before the birds went to ground.

The grassland springing to life underfoot was broken by several small streams and big muddy patches. Gray-green sagebrush pushed upslope to the timberline of white-trunked lacy aspens. The thin, pale green foliage of the trees, full of light and wind, tossed against the sky. The vultures he had his eyes on planed out of sight behind a hillside. He followed them and almost missed it – a narrow ravine, not much more than a footpath between two cliffs.

Luke worked Bugle down a small, pebbled incline and took him at a walk into the canyon, following a trail that curved around boulders. As they picked their way farther in, the canyon widened into bushy meadow walled in by the hills alongside.

He poked through the underbrush and looked for strays. Though the buzzards were nowhere to be seen, he did find one cow belonging to Paxton – dead for months from the looks of it – but none of New Hope's. He reined Bugle around and started back out for the range again.

On the hillside, a mustang slipped between the trees, its unshod hoofbeats muffled by the carpet of pine needles.

Silently, its rider slid to the ground. Moccasined feet crept behind a tree trunk. For three miles, Little Turtle had stalked Light Eyes and his gray horse. Hidden behind a tree or lying in the brush, sometimes so close to the white man he could smell him, he'd watched every move Luke made.

Two crows took flight, squawking and flapping off through the canyon. Little Turtle dropped to the ground and froze. Four men with guns walked their horses single-file into the ravine. Curious as to who else was following the white man, he crept into the brush and watched.

The sounds of a horse approaching carried clearly through the ravine. One of the men raised a hand, warning the others quiet, and all four rode quickly behind a spill of big boulders jutting from the slope.

Head tipped back, Little Turtle cupped his mouth, and the yelping howl of a coyote floated across the gorge, rising and falling.

"Easy, boy, easy." Luke gripped his knees tighter into the horse's sides. Agitated, Bugle sawed his head up and down and tongued the bit. Luke remembered a mile back how Bugle had also acted up when they'd passed two big rattlers sunning themselves on a rock. It was May and the snakes were active now, mating.

Trusting the horse's instincts, Luke reined him in and patted his neck, letting him look around and satisfy himself. Luke scanned the grassy scrub ahead. Nothing.

Then from behind him came a chilling sound, unmistakable: the oiled, sliding clicks of bolt-action rifles. Slowly, Luke twisted around in the saddle.

Four X-Bar-L hands approached him on horseback.

≈≥≈

"Get off, Sullivan."

Luke turned and saw Clete Wade and Wesley Huggins staring at him. The other two of their party, Bud Schmidt and Stu Bronson, rode from behind the rock pile and blocked the way out. All of them worked for Axel.

Clete Wade dismounted. Standing between Luke and the other way out of the canyon, he unbuckled his gun belt and tossed it aside. He made a dusting motion with his hands, brushing them together. "Get off the horse, I said."

"Why? I'm hunting strays, same as you." Luke's senses sharpened, and though he looked straight at Wade, he was aware that the other three men had brought their rifles up and had them resting across their saddles.

Clete gave a nasty laugh. "We ain't hunting strays. We're hunting you, Sullivan, and you're trespassing."

"I'm not and you know it."

"Four of us here say you are."

"Stand aside, Wade. You're looking for trouble, and I got work to do."

"It can wait. Mr. Axel thinks you need to learn some manners." Clete smirked over his shoulder to the men behind him.

Luke lounged in the saddle, his shoulders relaxed. With a tight smile he said, "I'm going out and you're in my way. I'd rather not ride a man down, but you suit yourself about that."

Clete's eyes mocked him. "What suits me right now is teaching you a lesson. You're a little too high and mighty, if you ask me. You learn that up at Stuart's with the rest of your hanging friends?" He braced his legs. "Now get *off* that horse."

A slow burn started under Luke's collar. In a way, he was surprised trouble hadn't come before this. He looked down at Clete, feet planted apart. He'd never run from a fight in his life, and he wasn't about to start. He also suspected riding out of here meant a bullet in the back. He tightened his hands on the reins.

Bugle's head snapped up. Neck arched, the horse flared his nostrils wide, eyes fixed on the man in front of him as if waiting Luke's signal to charge.

"He's bluffing, Clete." Stu Bronson, big and wide-shouldered in a green plaid jacket, shifted in the saddle and spat.

"Don't count on it, Stu," Luke said.

Luke had run into Bronson in Repton a few years before. Bronson was quick to provoke a fight, which he usually won because of his size. Bud Schmidt, beside him, was plank thin and almost as tall as Luke.

"Get off before I pull you off." Clete grabbed for the bridle. Bugle jerked his head and dug his back hooves in. His powerful front shoulders gathered.

Luke hurled himself from the saddle and onto the man beside him. Gouging, grunting, he and Clete went down together in a blur of arms and legs and boots. Bugle galloped off into the trees.

Clete piled on top of Luke. Straddling him, he drove a fist down into his jaw. "That's from Bart Axel, and this is from me." The blow that followed rolled Luke's head.

The warm, salty taste of blood in his mouth pumped rage through Luke's veins. Shaking the ringing from his ears, Luke wrested an arm free and drove a left up into the underside of Clete's jaw, snapping his head back. Clete gagged and rolled aside.

Luke heaved himself out from under and stood up, fists clenching, unclenching. None too gently, he nudged Clete's arm with his boot. "Get up, Clete. I got some questions I want answered."

Arms shot around him from behind. An elbow forked his neck like a vise, cutting off his wind. Stu Bronson's hot breath grunted in his ear. Luke swept his arms upward, rammed an elbow back, and broke the hold. Bronson staggered a few steps, then lunged. Luke spun and swung at the man coming at him. Stu ducked. The punch glanced off his shoulder. The two men sprang apart, facing each other. Wesley and Bud moved next to Bronson, one on either side.

Luke's mind raced. Four of them, no way. This fight he would lose. As a group, the three men stepped forward. Luke brought his fists up.

Clete scrambled to his feet behind him. Luke's immediate problem was Stu and Bud and Wes coming at him. Clete picked up a rifle. Gripping the barrel, he threw his arms back and swung. The heavy stock caught Luke squarely across the small of his back, arched him upright. Pain fired into his thighs. Numbed, his jaw fell open and he dropped his hands.

Wesley and Bud leaped in and pinned Luke's arms behind him. Bronson spat again and smoothed on a pair of black gloves.

A leather fist slammed Luke's stomach.

The gloved fist came at him again. And again. And again.

His legs buckled. With a deep groan, Luke sagged to his knees.

Bud Schmidt stepped behind him. Grabbing a handful of Luke's hair, he yanked his head back. Bronson and Clete tossed their hats aside and stepped closer.

Swearing. Grunting. The crack of knuckles meeting bone.

Luke winced, feeling the mushy give of cheekbone to a jarring right.

"A bullet's faster," Schmidt said.

Clete laughed. "All in good time, Mr. Schmidt."

They mean to kill me!

And it wouldn't be quick. For the first time in years, Luke found himself praying. From deep inside, between the punches and the pain, the words welled up.

I'm sorry . . . sorry.

His face jerked with another blow. Stifling a cry, Luke fell forward onto his elbows.

Help me, Lord . . . please help me.

Light-headed, he stared at four pairs of legs planted around him like pilings. Blood from his nose dripped onto the backs of his hands and ran between his fingers.

A sob caught in his throat.

You never hear me.

Clete laughed and swung his leg back. The sky tipped crazily. Luke pitched facedown. A curtain of darkness drew across his mind.

"Die, Sullivan." Clete grabbed his revolver and shoved the barrel against Luke's skull.

A wild, warbling shriek cut out of nowhere – a piercing, full-throated scream that jerked Clete upright. As he spun around, he heard the dreaded *thu-u-u-p* of an arrow suck past his face.

And another.

Thu-u-u-p.

Stiff cedar shafts struck the dirt at his feet, sinking themselves deep into the earth. Scarcely breathing, Clete stared down at them. Nearly thirty inches long with razor-bladed broadheads, the arrows had the killing power and penetration equal to the heaviest rifle bullet.

Mouths open, Bud and Stu gawked at something up behind Clete. Four braves in buckskins stood on the lip of the canyon above, bows braced. Two others had dropped to one knee, and every one of them was nocking another arrow. Bows at full draw, this time they aimed at the men.

"Why ain't they using guns?" Schmidt whispered.

"Don't know." Stu swallowed. "And I never knowed an Injun to warn first, neither."

"Will you look at the size of them arrows." Wesley pointed to the shafts, rigid as spears in the ground. "They're buffalo arrows!"

"Crows are supposed to be friendly to whites," Clete muttered. "What do they want?"

"Sullivan alive, I reckon." Wesley planted one foot behind the other, slowly backing toward his horse, away from Luke.

"Hold on," Clete said. "We ain't finished here. Boss wants Sullivan dead."

Eyes riveted on the Crow warriors, Wes said, "Why don't you just tell 'em that?" He whirled around, broke for his horse, toed the stirrup, and had his mare running before he got into the saddle. Bud Schmidt was three steps behind him. Bronson took one look and broke into a run.

"You ain't leaving me here." Clete leaped into the saddle on his horse and galloped out of the canyon after the others.

The sound of hooves running on rock faded.

Blue jays scolded back and forth in a pine tree. Head up, black tail swishing, Bugle walked slowly out of the woods and went over to Luke, spread-eagled on the ground. Head lowered, he swiveled his ears and nosed Luke's shoulder up. The shoulder fell back. With a soft, rolling snort, Bugle nosed the shoulder again. Again, the shoulder slumped to the ground.

Raising his nose to the sky, Bugle let out a long, shrill whinny.

Then, head lowered, he pulled and tore at the grass between a pair of legs that never moved.

The jays flew off.

"So go look again. We don't go back without him." Scully frowned at the four New Hope hands he'd worked with all day. "Something's wrong. Luke should've been back hours ago."

The New Hope men headed down range in the direction

Luke had gone and then split up. Half an hour later, two far-off *booms!* from a shotgun sounded. Someone had found him.

Scully and two others galloped toward the shots.

"Where'd you find him?" Scully's feet hit the ground almost before the words were out.

Jeb Simson, a grizzled old cowhand, led Bugle, whose reins were tied to Jeb's saddle. Luke was spilled, belly down across the horse's back. "I didn't find him. The horse found me. Walked up out of the dark and came right to me. He was on his way back to New Hope, looked like."

Scully stooped beside Luke, winced, and looked up at Jeb. "He alive?"

"Barely. Never saw no man beat like that. Face looks like raw meat. Whoever did it tied him on the horse."

Scully looked at Luke, who was lashed securely to his horse. His wrists and ankles were looped together, with the rope made snug underneath Bugle's stomach. Scully shined a lantern under the horse and studied the knots, puzzled by how they were tied.

"No white man tied that rope," he said quietly.

Leading Bugle, the men from the N-Bar-H started back to New Hope. From time to time, Scully glanced back at Luke and shook his head.

"Tom," he called to a young worker, "ride on ahead and tell Miss Molly to send for Doc Maxwell. Tell her what's happened. Tell her it's bad."

CHAPTER
8

He looked dead.

Unconscious, Luke lay stretched out on the bed in his room, his face gray and covered with bruises. Emily felt timid, afraid to touch him for fear she'd hurt him.

"Let's get him out of these dirty clothes," Molly said.

Emily shook off a momentary rush of embarrassment and climbed onto the bed and rolled him toward her, holding the heavy shoulders off the bed while Molly used a pair of shears to slit his shirt and Levi's off. They undressed him, stripping him down to his drawers. They washed him with warm water and soap, flushing the cuts with peroxide, then applying carbolic salve to them.

They rolled him onto his side. His bare chest, dusted with soft dark hair, rose and fell in broken gasps, struggling to breathe. Emily filled a basin with ice from the fruit cellar and kept chilled cloths on his face and his back.

"Did Indians do this?" Her voice cracked.

"No," Molly said, patting away a seep of blood from the corner of his mouth. "Crows don't hit people with fists. They think it's barbaric."

"Then who did this to him?" Emily traced her fingers along an ugly purple bruise on his back, where he'd been struck from behind.

"I suspect we both know the answer to that," Molly said grimly.

They glanced up at a commotion downstairs in the hall. Clutching a small black satchel, Doc Maxwell bounded up the stairs and hurried into the bedroom. Emily shrank back against the fireplace and said nothing, afraid they'd send her from the room. Confused, she watched the doctor examine Luke. Inside, her emotions stormed, leaving her angry and close to tears. She didn't know why, but at that moment she needed to stay close to Luke.

After the doctor left, Emily persuaded Molly to get some rest. They'd take turns sitting with him. Beyond that, there was nothing more either of them could do except to watch him.

Doc Maxwell had given Luke an injection of morphine to dull the pain so he'd sleep. She'd been surprised when Doc pulled a glass syringe from his satchel. In Chicago, good medicine was the norm. Evidently, the rest of the country was catching up.

Emily turned the lamp down to a pale glimmer. As she tucked the blanket in around Luke's chest, her gaze slid across the wide shoulders and muscled arms. He was in the prime of manhood, strong, healthy. But hurt. Still, most women would call him handsome. A small sigh slipped from her. He didn't look like the same man. Asleep, his stern face was relaxed and smooth. Gone was the rugged, strong-willed man who irritated her.

Another spasm of pain shook him. Barely able to move his lips, he groaned, "Please, God, just let me die."

Emily grabbed his hand, as if to keep him there. "Don't do it, Lord. He doesn't mean it. Please don't listen to him."

Smoothing a cool cloth across his cheekbones and swollen nose, she bent and kissed his forehead and poor bruised eyes. She pulled a chair up close to the bed and opened the Bible she'd brought with her to the Twenty-third Psalm, the one she always turned to when things went wrong.

"'The Lord is my shepherd . . .'" she read aloud.

And Luke's shepherd, too, evidently. His calling on the Lord for anything – even to die – surprised her. Despite his claims to doubting, he still believed. When he was desperate, he reached out to God.

He'd been six years old when they moved to the place outside town. He never knew why they moved, only knew something had happened that wasn't Pa's fault, and the comfortable big farmhouse wasn't theirs anymore.

He helped Pa chop long pieces of sod out of the ground. Ma and Mary Beth and he and Pa carried the heavy strips, limber and sagging like a rope in the middle. They stacked them up in rows to make the walls of a house. Even little Benny helped.

The house had a dirt floor and a hay ceiling covered with more dirt outside. In the spring, dandelions sprouted all over the roof. He laughed at how fancy it looked, but Pa climbed up and pulled them out anyway. Too bad. It was the only nice thing about the house – the flowers growing out of it. No matter how sunny the day, it was always dark inside and mice stirred about in the walls. His mother pasted magazine pictures everywhere and told Pa how pretty it looked. She sewed a flowered curtain for the window. But the house smelled funny – like worms. Mama cried when Luke told her that, and Pa yelled at him.

Sitting around the table one warm June evening after supper, Pa read Scripture to them. He finished with the Twenty-third Psalm, as he always did.

"'. . . and I will dwell in the house of the Lord for ever.'" Pa closed the Bible and looked up. "Bedtime, boys."

Luke's mother told him to take three-year-old Benny to the outhouse for one last trip before bedtime.

"Aw, why do I always have to take him?" Luke grumbled.

"Because he's little and he's your brother," his mother said.

"'Cause he's a scaredy-cat, that's what. Nobody had to take me."

Mary Beth giggled. "This year, you mean."

"Luke Sullivan." His father looked up, stern faced.

"I'm going, I'm going." Luke stomped out back, dragging Benny by the hand. At the outhouse at the end of the yard, he pulled him inside. As he helped Benny get his pants down, he heard a horse whinny nearby.

But they didn't have a horse anymore.

Luke squinted through a knothole in the wooden door.

"Oh, Benny," he whispered. Outside, a small war party

of Sioux—six braves, their cheeks striped with red and black paint—slipped off their horses. Time and again, Pa had drummed it into them what to do if Indians came. Hide!

Through the knothole he saw the Indians creep to the house and ease the front door open.

"Shhhh." Luke clapped his hand over Benny's mouth and pulled him down to the floor, shaking him to be quiet, both of them trembling in the smelly dark with the spiders, their fingers plugging their ears until the screaming from the house ended and they heard the horses leave.

They'd scalped his mother, his father, and pretty red-haired Mary Beth, seventeen her next birthday. Somehow, he managed to drag his mother and sister outside into the yard by himself, but Pa was too heavy. He covered him up with quilts and blankets and pushed the table in front of him because it scared him to look at Pa, his face half gone. Kneeling, he held Benny and tried to be brave.

Harder than he'd ever prayed in his life, he prayed for God to bring his parents and sister back. But nothing happened. They never moved. God wasn't listening.

In those awful, silent hours of loneliness and terror, he lost his family and he lost his faith.

The two boys were passed from neighbor to neighbor, no one able or willing to take on two more mouths to feed. Nobody wanted them. And for the first time in his life, Luke began to stutter.

The day came when both of them were taken to New Hope. Until that day, Luke had been dry-eyed about what had happened, a quiet, frozen little boy who blinked a lot. Carrying one small black suitcase holding everything they owned, he held Benny's hand tight and walked through the iron gates and up the long walk to the New Hope Foundling and Orphan Asylum.

Molly Ebenezer waited for them on the porch, her eyes moist, watching the pudgy three-year-old Benny hanging on to his big brother's hand, a big brother who was a child himself. She took one look at Luke's small, somber face and held her arms open.

"I'm so glad you're here. Come give me a hug, little man," she said.

He'd let go of Benny's hand and thrown himself at her, buried his face in her big soft stomach, and burst into tears. Molly had leaned down and picked up not Benny, but Luke, and carried him inside.

Lying in a bed at New Hope twenty years later, tears streamed Luke's face again. The rustle of footsteps moved in the room, and someone softly called his name. With an effort, Luke raised his eyebrows and slitted his lids open. Both eyes were nearly swollen shut. Ragged gaps of sunlight flooded past the curtains, nearly blinding him. Everything too white, too bright. He winced and shut his eyes.

"Luke!"

He pushed his eyelids open again and rolled his head toward the voice. Dully, he looked up. Holding his hand, Emily seemed to float right above him, her face blurring in and out of focus. Her lips moved. He wanted to tell her it was all right, but it hurt too much, and he couldn't stop shaking. His tongue traveled across a puffed upper lip that felt like a sausage.

"Wa-water . . . can I have some water?"

He had trouble swallowing. Little by little, she trickled it into his mouth, a few drops at a time, waiting until his Adam's apple stopped working before dribbling in a bit more.

With a deep sigh he closed his eyes and slipped into unconsciousness once more.

The next day when he woke up, he noted he was in his own room. A fire burned in the grate, and the curtains were drawn. A sharp medicinal smell hung over everything. He vaguely remembered hands probing him and hearing a man's deep voice talking to Molly.

Molly and Mary Beth and Emily. They were all mixed up in his head together.

And Mary Beth had kissed him.

No, not Mary Beth. He opened his eyes. Emily was sitting in a chair looking at him.

"You still . . . still here?" Though his tongue didn't want to work right, his head was almost clear.

"I just came in," she said. "Luke, who did this to you?"

"Bart's men. How'd I get here?"

"Someone tied you on Bugle and sent you back. Scully and the men brought you in."

Luke shut his eyes and tried to concentrate. They'd meant to kill him. The boss wanted him dead, Clete had said. What made them change their minds? He had to warn the others.

He struggled to sit up, every muscle in his body screaming in protest. The room started into a slow, lazy spin. The stitches in the cut over his eyebrow stung like fire. Shakily, he raised a hand to his face. Dried blood, like coffee grounds, was caked in the webs of his fingers.

Emily's eyes widened in alarm as he propped himself up on an elbow, close to passing out again. At once, she was over him, fussing at him. Her hands grasped his bare shoulders.

"Lie down. You've got two black eyes. Your cheek is broken and so is your nose. You're bruised all over. Doc Maxwell just left. He's been here for two days – says it's a wonder you're alive. He says you're not to get out of bed for one solid week."

Luke steadied himself with both hands spread by his hips, waiting for the room to stop rocking. He tried to put on a frown, but it pulled the stitches again and made them hurt. "I have to talk to Molly – "

"I'll go get her. You lie down."

"And Scully – "

"I'll get him, too. He's downstairs. Please, please lie down," she begged.

"The men. I need to talk to all of them."

"They're downstairs. They take turns, waiting."

"Wha' for?" His tongue was thick.

He almost couldn't hear her answer because she turned her face away. "They're worried about you," she'd said.

He let out a shaky sigh. All those people – they'd been waiting for him to die. For the first time, he noticed the open Bible on the table beside her chair. She'd also been waiting, but not downstairs. Up here with him, holding his hand. Silently, Luke looked at her, the meaning of what she'd done sinking into him like raindrops on sand.

"Well, I'm not going to die yet," he said.

She gave him a shaky little smile. "I know that now."

Her eyes were red rimmed, as if she'd been crying. Women don't cry for a man unless they care. Maybe she didn't hate him after all. The tiny ray of cheer didn't last long.

Embarrassment took its place.

All those people downstairs – he was supposed to take care of them. Instead, he'd let every one of them down.

"I have to go see them," he said, and pushed himself up on one elbow.

Vivid green eyes blazed. "Do you, now?" She sounded Irish.

Firmly, he nodded.

Emily shrugged and swept an arm toward the door. "Go ahead, get up! You'll just pass out again. And when you do, I'm going to call every female in this house up here to watch us put you back in bed."

Which made no sense. It wasn't like her to give in so easily. He slid one long leg across the cool sheet toward the side of the bed. And froze. Raising the edge of the covers, he peeked underneath and looked at himself. His jaw dropped. He'd been wearing long johns before. Now he had on summer drawers, close-fitting cotton underwear that ended above his knees.

"Where are my clothes?" he asked.

"We had to cut them off."

"You undressed me?" Heat crawled up his neck.

"Doc Maxwell said to keep clothes off you until the sutures heal." She stepped back and frowned down at him. "I don't believe it. If I didn't know better, I'd think you were blushing."

"Get me some clothes," Luke ordered.

"Lie back down. When he comes today, I'll ask him if you can wear a nightshirt."

"I wouldn't be caught dead in one of those things!"

Unwavering green eyes locked his. "It's either a nightshirt or you stay like you are. Doc Maxwell says cuts heal faster if they stay uncovered for a week."

"We'll just see about that. Emily McCarthy, get me my clothes, I said. I'm going downstairs – now."

"Then you go down bare chested and in your cute little drawers."

He wouldn't and she knew it. There were women and little girls down there. She hated him. She definitely still hated him.

She fluffed his pillow and patted it. Small, strong fingers gripped his shoulders and eased him back down.

"A whole week in this bed and I'll go out of my mind," he muttered. *Or maybe I won't.*

He closed his eyes and smiled.

Emily fumed. For one whole week he ran her ragged. Hand and foot, he made her wait on him. He had her read to him and then corrected her pronunciation.

She snapped at him. "I said it exactly right. You speak with a cowboy twang. I don't."

He sent her chasing up and down two flights of stairs to get him something from the kitchen he forgot – and conveniently remembered only after she left the room.

One afternoon he wrinkled his nose and pushed the bowl of slippery tapioca pudding away. "Looks like fish eyes and glue," he said.

Emily snatched the dish away. The beef tea she'd made for him was also untouched. She put the tea on the tray next to the tapioca. It had taken her all of yesterday to fix that tea, soaking the meat overnight, simmering it for hours, and then drying it and grinding it to a powder. Mixed with the soaking water and served in a thin china cup, it was nourishing and good for him. It most certainly was *not* sticky and clotted and nasty tasting, she fumed.

"And that makes me gag!" he said, turning his head away, refusing the scalded toast she'd brought him for breakfast. "Hot, soggy bread and milk—what kind of meal is that for a man?"

"It's good for you. And it's not necessary to shout." She took a deep breath and silently counted to ten.

"That's not shouting. I'll show you real shouting, you keep feeding me this slop." His jaw jutted. "I want ham and eggs."

"You can't have it. That's too heavy. You're sick."

Hot tears welled in her eyes. She sniffed. Everything she tried to do for him was wrong. Blinking hard, she spooned up a bite of the damp white bread swimming in milk, wondering what she could do to make him like it. She looked at the spoon and then at him. Like a huge baby bird, Luke opened his mouth. Quickly, she popped it into his mouth.

"I am not sick," he said, milk dribbling down his chin. "I never get sick. I'm hurt. There's a difference."

"Oh, it's unmanly to get sick, is it?"

"I didn't say that."

"You implied it. Big stubborn cowboy."

The spoon flew in a silver arc while she argued with him, distracting him, all the while scooping food into him. As long as she fed him, it appeared he'd eat anything. She held the cup and the back of his head. With a shudder he closed his eyes and swallowed down the tea.

But nothing else she did was right. If she made him biscuits, he pouted until she went downstairs and baked corn bread. He carped at her when she was there and sulked if she left him alone.

He wasn't sleeping well. Each night, hour after hour, he mumbled and tossed from one side to the other.

"You should be sleeping better by now," she said, worried after he'd had a particularly bad night.

"Witch hazel rubs might make me relax. It might help if you rubbed my back." His lips twitched.

"Might help if you put a shirt on, too."

"I'll think about it . . . after the back rub."

Emily flounced out of the room and slammed the door. The witch hazel was downstairs in the kitchen, which he knew.

When Emily came back with the witch hazel, she brought along a set of gray winter underwear, a long-sleeved shirt, and pants that reached his ankles. Luke smiled to himself as she shook the legs loose, warming them in front of the fire. He had news for her. He wasn't about to put them on. Bossing him around, was she? He'd give her a dose of her own medicine.

Emily laid the freshly laundered underwear across the footboard of the bed and left the room discreetly. She came back a few minutes later to find the underwear still draped right where she'd left it and Luke Sullivan propped up against the pillows, long hairy legs crossed on top of the sheet. He wore his cotton drawers, an insolent smile, and nothing else.

"Have you lost your mind? Cover yourself up," she sputtered, hands on her hips.

"Why should I?"

"You're sitting around in your underwear, that's why."

Folding his arms across his chest, he raised his eyebrows at her. "How you gonna rub my back if I'm wearing a shirt?"

Emily backed out of the room and stamped downstairs again.

"I'm so embarrassed, I could just die!" she ranted to Molly, waving her arms in the air. "He's gross. What is wrong with him?"

Molly sighed. "I don't understand. He's usually so modest and proper. This isn't like him at all. I expect he's getting even with you for taking his clothes away and making him stay in bed. He's doing it for you—staying in bed like that. He wouldn't do it for me. If it'd do any good, I'd go right up there and shake some sense into him, but I raised that boy. Wouldn't work. You'll see. He'll win. One way or another, he always wins."

"Not this time," Emily snarled. Tight-lipped, she trudged upstairs. Outside the door to his room, she huffed in several deep breaths, pumping herself into the proper frame of mind to deal with one infuriating, bossy cowboy. Shoulders back, she threw the door to his room open.

"I'm ready," Luke said, his back to her.

She poured witch hazel into her hand. The first time she

put her hands on his back, Luke jumped as if she'd stuck him with a pin. After that, he lay dead still, his muscles so rigid it was like rubbing rock. He stared at the wall.

He managed to get her up to three of those rubs a day, until her hands had memorized every contour and curve of flesh and bone that made up the muscular torso of one Luke Sullivan. She went to bed at night thinking of them, and when she managed to fall asleep, she dreamed about them. In desperation one afternoon, she snatched up a can of rose-scented talcum on the dresser and shook a blizzard of the perfumed powder all over his skin. The curly dark hair on his chest went instantly gray.

She stroked the satiny, sweet-smelling talcum across his chest and back, smoothing the silky stuff up and down his arms – and Luke sneezed until his eyes watered.

"If this powder doesn't agree with you, I'll stop," she said.

Shaking his head, Luke grabbed his bruised stomach with both hands. "Aaah-choo! No, it's just fine. I feel – AAH-choo! – better already."

"How nice," she murmured, and socked the bottom of the can with her fist.

"AAAH-CHOO!"

Doc Maxwell shut the door to Luke's room and stood still in the hall outside, his bushy brown eyebrows knitted together. Mentally, he ticked off the injuries Luke had sustained and wondered if he'd overlooked something. Outwardly, Sullivan showed no signs of skull injury, but something had certainly scrambled the man's brains. Imagine, in there around Molly and Emily, wearing only his underwear bottoms.

Doc pulled out a kerchief and mopped his face and the back of his neck. He'd never been in a room so hot in all his life, yet Miss McCarthy kept pitching wood into the fireplace as if it were the boiler on the *Robert E. Lee.*

Luke refused to get dressed, she said sweetly, and she was concerned he'd catch cold, especially since he was red-eyed and sneezing. Then Sullivan, shiny and slick with perspiration, allowed – kinda smuglike – that he preferred a warm room. Miss McCarthy got all red in the face at that and threw a piece of wood as big as a wagon tongue into the fireplace.

Feeling positively light-headed from the heat, Doc had to leave. By that time, even his patient was panting like a lizard.

Doc picked up his bag and started downstairs, shaking his head. From his neck to his navel, Sullivan looked like a ghost. Funny. He'd never acted like one of them sissy city fellas who liked perfume and powder, but there he was, floured up like a chicken and smelling like a bride's bouquet. Doc clucked his tongue. Never could tell about some people.

Shame. Big strapping man like that.

CHAPTER
9

"Sure did a job on you, didn't they, boy?" Jupiter Jackson leaned forward and spit into the fireplace again.

Luke nodded, in no mood for company. Though he felt almost normal, he was still a little shaky on his feet. The swelling had gone down and the bruises faded from his face. Greenish yellow traces were all that remained of the black eyes.

He hadn't seen Jupiter in nearly three years. Today the old man had just come by to say hello. The day Doc Maxwell allowed Luke downstairs, visitors started dropping in – men on their way to Repton or passing by, they said, or who flat-out admitted they came to see him because they didn't like what had happened. Luke and Jupiter sat in the dining room, chairs pulled up to the fireplace.

Weathered and wrinkled, Jupiter's face furrowed into a grin. No one knew how old he was. It seemed he'd always been there, as long as anyone could remember. In his seventy- or eighty- or ninety-odd years, Jupiter had hired on at one time or another at nearly every farm and ranch in the area.

From time to time, the old man rocked forward and spat. "Axel told the sheriff it was a personal quarrel, said you got smart with his men out on the range," he said, in his high, reedy voice. Tobacco juice sizzled in the fire.

"That's his story," Luke said. "Mine's a little different. I was hunting cows; they were hunting me."

"Ain't like the old days. Then, you'd a gone over there, shot 'em, and that would've been the end of it. Now there's all this messing round with the law."

Jupiter rocked back again, quiet for several few minutes, chewing and spitting. "You know, seems to me that range of yours has always been trouble. When I worked here back in the thirties, we had problems with trappers. Frenchies, they were. Wolfers. Came in here by the dozens every year, hunting and laying traps any old place, just like they owned it."

Luke tipped back in his chair and stretched his arms wide. He got stiff if he sat too long. "Guess they figured they did, as much as anyone else."

"They knew better," Jupiter snorted. "Everything from White Dog River to Billings were New Hope's. They knew, all right—just didn't figure to get caught. We fixed 'em, though." He cackled, the weathered face crinkling with humor. "Every spring, we busted their traps and let the critters go. After three years, they got the hint and stopped coming on New Hope land."

"What did Molly do?"

Jupiter shook his head. "That was long before Molly.

Preacher name of Sampson here then. Parted his hair in the middle. Molly's twice the man he ever was."

Luke stared at the fire, seeing a map of the area in his mind. Jupiter had his rivers mixed up. "You can't mean all the way to the Yellowstone River. You mean White Dog to Pryor Creek, don't you? The Yellowstone and Billings are ten miles west of the Pryor. Ten miles—you're talking about one big piece of land."

"I can figure. When I say the Yellowstone, I mean the Yellowstone. Close to thirty square miles altogether is what it is. I ought to know," the old man said. "My backside stayed sore for weeks riding those lines. Main reason I quit."

"Jupiter," Luke said patiently, "everything from Pryor Creek to Billings and the Yellowstone is open range."

"You ain't listening, boy. That ain't open range, never was."

"Axel says it is."

"Well, is that a fact?" Jupiter drawled. "Dunno as I believe him if he says it's daylight and the sun's out. Everybody wanted a piece of New Hope."

Deciding to talk to Molly later about the rivers in question, Luke stifled a yawn and got to his feet, his back muscles knotting again. Putting both hands on his hips, he bent his torso backward until his spine gave a satisfactory crack. If the old man would leave, maybe he could talk Emily into a back rub.

Jupiter sniffed, ignoring Luke leaning against the mantel. "Something smells good."

Luke hid a smile. The old man hadn't changed a bit. It was close to suppertime, and Jupiter was known to hang around until someone had to ask him to stay. "I think I'll just mosey out to the barn and see Scully," he said, looking toward the kitchen. "You still look a little peaked, son. Maybe you ought to lie back down awhile."

Jupiter climbed to his feet and shuffled straight for the kitchen.

Within minutes his voice floated back. "Why, that's mighty nice of you, Miz Molly. I sure would like to stay, yes, indeedy, ma'am."

Luke chuckled. Worked every time. He flexed his shoulders and called, "Emily, you busy?"

As he'd done every morning since he'd been allowed up, Luke hooked a boot heel over the fence rail and watched Scully exercising Bugle in the paddock. The big gray pranced and tossed his head, looking over at Luke. Molly had put her foot down, egged on, he was sure, by Emily McCarthy: no riding or roping for another two weeks.

"Ease up, Bugle. Be nice," he called as Scully sawed on the reins to pull the horse around. Bugle flicked his ears at Luke, swung his head around, and blew his lips at Scully, who burst out laughing. Then, obediently, the horse dropped into a canter.

Lined up alongside the corral fence with Luke, five boys from the school watched impatiently. The youngest, a freckle-faced seven-year-old in patched knickers, fidgeted and scuffed his foot against the post.

Luke nudged his hat back and grinned to the others. "Let's go before Timothy here kicks the fence down. He's the fancy artist in this group, but even they need to be able to shoot, right, Tim-bo?"

A big white grin answered him.

Emily floated across his mind. She knew her kids, and this one needed stroking, she'd said. *"They don't have older brothers or fathers for examples – good or bad."* Then she'd folded her arms and added in a prissy little voice, *"Like it or not, Luke Sullivan, you're it. They idolize you and want to be like you when they grow up."*

He wished for the hundredth time she hadn't told him that.

He waved to Scully, then picked up the old Springfield rifle he'd brought from the house and started off. The little group trailed after him down the grassy slope behind the smithy and into an open field beyond.

He'd been taught to handle guns when he was there, had spent a part of every day practicing, with bullets and without. And he probably was alive because of it.

Patiently, Luke showed them how to reload, to lift the trapdoor quickly, and shove in the big lead-tipped shells. He spent the morning pitching bottles and cans into the air. Deliberate shooting would teach them to shoot the wrong way, he told them, because if they needed to use a gun, most likely it would be at a moving target.

"My arms are tired. It's too heavy. I ain't big enough to hold it up," Timothy said. Disappointment spread across his face when the old Springfield's long barrel nosed out of his arms and down to the dirt again. The other boys laughed.

"It's heavy for me, too," Luke said. The laughter trailed off. "But if you need it and you're scared enough, I guarantee you'll find a way. Aim is what counts, Tim, not size, not strength.

What makes a man is what's in here and here." He tapped Tim's forehead, then the boy's chest with the words.

Taking him by the shoulder, Luke led him to a fence a few yards away and rested the barrel on a rail to take some of the weight. He had Tim hold the gun and picked up a can to throw again. "Now shoot."

An hour later, Luke laid the rifle aside and pulled the Colt from his holster. Instantly five pairs of young male eyes gleamed.

All week he'd debated with himself about whether or not to show them how to draw. He decided he had to. No point in knowing how to use a gun at all, he thought, if you couldn't use it in a hurry. He showed them how to load and to punch out the hulls, then drummed it into them to carry it with the hammer on an empty chamber. "Remember, when you load: five chambers can have shells; one stays empty. Check it every time you load. Otherwise, if you stumble or bang into something, you'll shoot yourself in the leg."

Luke pointed. "John, get that board over there and pound it in the ground." He unbuckled his holster and passed it around, letting each boy put it on and take it off several times. "Most men wear a gun high. I wear mine low, almost on my leg, but that's a personal thing. You've got to find what's best for you. A lot depends on how long your arms are." He reclaimed the Colt, loaded it, and buckled it back on his hip.

Spinning around, he fired in rapid succession, his left hand fanning the hammer back, blasting the board to splinters. Five small jaws dropped. An instant's silence, then a chorus of voices.

Wide-eyed, John breathed, "Why, I never even saw you draw."

"Who taught you?"

"How'd you do that?"

Luke smiled. "Practice. Any man can shoot one of these things. Getting it out before the other man does is what makes the difference. I used to practice for hours with an empty gun." He didn't tell them he still did—every morning of his life, up in his room.

On the way back to the house, Timothy sidled closer and looked up at him, the small face filled with open admiration. "You ever been in a gunfight, Mr. Luke?" he asked, his eyes bright. "I mean a real one?"

"He wants to be like you when he grows up," Emily had said.

Luke tweaked the freckled little nose. In this case, truth was definitely not needed. "Nope. Never have, never want to be."

* * *

While one of the children said grace at dinner that night, Luke gazed over at Emily's bowed head. From where he sat, he could see the umber fringe of eyelashes brushing her cheeks and five small freckles across the bridge of her nose. Sunlight streaming through the window behind her caught her hair, shimmering it from dark copper to pale gold. If this feud with Axel turned into a full-blown range war, what would happen to her if he wasn't around?

His concern for her grew all through dinner. She couldn't defend herself. Axel would drag her back to his ranch, whether she wanted to go or not.

As soon as they finished eating, Luke took his plate and followed her into the kitchen. Emily stood at a table by a window, scraping and slipping plates into a dishpan. Her small hands flew competently in and out of the water as dainty as a butterfly. And pretty enough for three women, with some left over, he thought.

Leaning against the oversized black iron stove, Luke folded his arms and looked at her. "Can you shoot a gun?"

Emily slung water off her hands and turned to face him. "I've never held one in my life, and I don't plan to, either. Guns are for men." She dunked a washed plate into a pan of rinse water and stacked it for drying. Without a word she nodded at the pile of wet dishes and tossed a dish towel to him.

He threw it back to her. "Doing dishes is for women. When you learn to shoot, I'll dry dishes. Finish up in here and come outside with me. It's time you learned."

Eyes flashing, she looked up from the cup she was washing. "Is that an order?"

"No, ma'am, just consider it a stern request."

Face pinched, she smacked the cup down so hard the handle broke off. He pressed his lips together and decided to leave before she threw the rest of it at him.

As he strolled through the back door, she called out, "And any man who walks like that wears his pants too tight."

Shoulders shaking with laughter, he pulled the door closed. This butterfly had teeth!

An hour later, in a field behind the house, Emily blurted, "I'm afraid of guns."

"All guns or just my guns?" Luke slid a shell into place and snapped the breech shut.

She blinked at him. "Both, maybe."

"You still afraid of me?" He thrust the rifle at her.

She hesitated. "Not anymore."

He let his breath out slowly. "Good, I'm glad of that. Now stop talking and shoot the thing."

She took the rifle from him and raised it. The wood stock was heavy, and her arms trembled with the weight of it. Grimly, she pulled the hammer back and jerked the trigger. The gun roared, staggering her backward with the impact. The bullet whistled into the sky.

He smirked. "Just great, if your target's on a roof."

Tears sprang into her eyes. "You stop poking fun at me!"

He sighed, feeling guilty again. Everything he tried to do right for her, he did all wrong. Moving behind her, he reached both arms around her and covered her hands with his. He lifted the gun into place, flattened his thumb on hers, and cocked the hammer back. All at once he felt massive. He'd forgotten how small she was. The gun was too heavy for her.

"I'll hold it; you aim it," he said, and adjusted the rifle butt more comfortably into the hollow of her shoulder. He leaned forward, steadying her, his cheek flattened against hers as she aimed at a tree in the distance.

A strand of soft coppery hair blew across his mouth, filling his nostrils with a cloud of scents—sunshine and soap. As he pulled it off his lips, he made the mistake of looking into her eyes, and the kick of attraction nearly took his breath away. Her pupils had gone wide and dark, and for the first time, he saw tiny flecks of gold deep down in the green around them.

Pretty.

When his gaze slid to her lips, he swallowed. Unaccountably, his mouth had gone as dry as flour.

Her lips were just inches away.

"I want to kiss you," he said softly.

"I'd rather you didn't. You'll just laugh at me."

"Why would I laugh at you?"

"Because I grew up with all girls and" – she jerked away – "and I don't know how." Her voice caught.

Something soft and warm curled in his chest. He put his hand on her cheek and turned her face to him. "I'll show you."

Slowly, he lowered his mouth to hers. Not wanting to startle her, he kissed the corners of her mouth, first one side and then the other. He grazed his lips back and forth over hers. Her mouth was soft and warm and yielded under his. When her eyelids fluttered closed, he cradled the back of her head and kissed her full on the mouth. Hesitantly, lightly, she pressed her lips to his. He made a thick, pleased sound in his throat and gathered her into his arms. Even as he told himself not to, he closed his eyes. And then he *really* kissed her.

Not a good idea.

Though he didn't want to, he raised his face. Softly, he cleared his throat, reminding himself it was just a kiss. Nothing more. But his stomach had turned to air.

She looked dazed, her eyes huge, her lower lip caught between her teeth.

"That wasn't so bad, was it?" he said, relieved his voice was steady.

"Is that all there is to it?"

He grinned. "Pretty much, with a few variations."

She drew a small shaky breath and sat back. Her cheeks were splotched with pink, and her hand trembled under his on the rifle. "You're a good teacher," she said quietly.

Though he knew she meant it as a compliment, it made him feel old and experienced and somehow not very nice. Yet a band of pleasure tightened his chest and set his heart racing again. He was the first. She'd never kissed a man before. He grinned to himself, still trying to wrap his brain around that.

He wanted to protect her, to keep her safe. That was all he'd intended with this shooting lesson. Nothing more, he told himself. He hauled his thoughts away from how good she'd felt in his arms. How right she felt.

He straightened his shoulders and forced himself to concentrate. Something odd was stirring around inside his head. Feeling a little short of breath, he forced himself to explain how to sight the gun.

He liked her. A lot.

"Line up the target with that metal tip at the end of the barrel." He covered the small hand under his and supported the rifle for her. His cheek brushed hers again.

He screwed his eyes shut. He wanted to kiss her again.

"Pull the trigger, Emily," he growled.

But the husky change he heard in his own voice wasn't lost on her, either. She became very quiet and did everything he told her to. And wasn't that a switch?

Emily was ready to drop from exhaustion. Luke kept her out there until she could load the gun, get the rifle up into position, and fire. Only then did they start for home.

On the way back, they cut across a muddy field and down a sloping hill through a grove of cottonwoods. "How's your shoulder?" he called to her.

"What shoulder? If I have one, I can't feel it. My whole arm's numb."

He only nodded, and the sharp retort she expected didn't come. He was different this afternoon. Nice. Once, he'd spread the strands of a barbed wire fence apart for her. As she climbed through, her skirt caught on one of the kinks of wire. Twisting around, she bent over to work it loose. From the expression on his face, Luke Sullivan was getting a good long look at knee-length ruffled drawers and two legs in heavy black stockings.

Facts lined up and marched out of her mind. Frosty, cold-hearted, cold-blooded Luke Sullivan was grinning like a schoolboy. This tough-talking gunslinger holding the fence apart confused her like a Chinese puzzle, and now the pieces of the puzzle were snapping into place. A lot of things were beginning to make sense this afternoon.

He liked looking at her legs.

Her face on fire, she yanked her skirt free. Her stomach churned. She was playing a dangerous game, unsure how to handle this situation, how to handle this man.

She sent a look sideways at him. He had a nice square jaw and was certainly attractive for a gunfighter. Well, not really a gunfighter, but almost. And despite who he was and what he did, his chin was downright cute, with a Y-shaped cleft so deep it folded in on itself. Unbidden, the thought slipped to the front of her mind and hung there. She imagined her fingernail tracing the tiny trench, probing it, even kissing it. Heat slid down her neck.

She smoothed her skirt and wheeled around. Quickly, she started walking away from him.

Luke dumped his hat on the back of his head and loped along beside her. "I've been thinking about what you said a while ago," he said coolly. "Out here, you need to be able to protect yourself. I did not teach you to shoot to be mean."

Emily's lips curved faintly. She'd figured that out for herself.

"I don't know anything about guns," she said, lowering her eyes. "My arm hurts because your old rifle is so heavy."

He stopped dead still, the rifle crooked in his arm. Though he didn't answer right away, she could tell he was considering what she'd said.

Hesitantly, as if she were fishing—which she'd never done in her life—she mentally cast a silken feminine line far out into uncharted waters. Hoping she wasn't misreading him, she said, "Maybe tomorrow you should show me how to shoot your Colt instead."

In a flash, the wiliest, craftiest game fish in the river—twenty-six years old and two hundred pounds—shot to the surface and swallowed the bait, the hook, the rod, and swam off with the line.

"Good idea, Emmy. How's tomorrow, right after dinner?"

CHAPTER
10

New Hope had settled down for the night, the children cleaned up, prayers heard, and sent off to bed. Emily, hemming a dress, sat in the parlor with Molly and Luke.

A few feet away, Luke lounged in a wing-back chair, reading a newspaper. In blue Levi's and a soft flannel shirt, boots off, he'd propped his socked feet on a footstool.

Emily bit off a length of thread, happy that she and Luke had stopped squabbling every time they got within spitting distance. Ever since the shooting lessons, he seemed to be observing a kind of truce. She was, too.

Funny what a couple of kisses could do.

Earlier that evening, like every other evening for the past week, they'd gone for a walk after supper. Twice he took her to one of the fields and let her practice shooting his revolver. The last two evenings, however, he'd steered her over to the corral. He insisted she learn to ride, something she rebelled at every time he took her to the barn. She was afraid of horses, and he knew it, so he'd lift her onto Sheba, a gentle old mare, and have her sit there to get used to the feel of the animal under her.

But not Bugle. She wouldn't go near Bugle.

"He growls at me," she said.

Luke fought a smile and lost. "Horses don't growl."

"He does. And it's not funny."

In the parlor, she looked across at Luke. Dark head bowed, he was deeply engrossed in what he was reading. Lightly, she ran her fingers over her lips, remembering the pressure of his lips on hers, how firm his mouth was.

She glanced down, putting up the hem of a dress she'd made for church, this one plain blue with bone buttons down the front and a soft belt. Every time Molly went to Repton, she brought back several yards of fabric for her. Slowly, Emily was putting a wardrobe together.

"Where'd you learn to sew dresses?" Luke glanced over the top of his newspaper at her.

"Chicago. They taught us to sew and cook and keep house – 'domestic science,' they call it." She shook the dress out and smoothed the silky blue folds across her lap. She grinned as she said, "I also became quite good at sewing boy's underwear. Would you like me to –?"

With a quick "No, thanks," Luke ducked behind the paper.

Molly's lips twitched. She glanced up from her darning. Smiling, she shook her finger at Emily. Emily grinned back. She and Molly had forged a friendship.

"There's an article here about railroad rights-of-way,"

Luke said slowly. "Reminds me of what Jupiter Jackson said about New Hope's boundaries." He lowered the paper and looked over at Molly. "He says New Hope is bigger than we think."

"Oh, there's always been talk," she said, "but it was way before I came. The truth's been exaggerated, I expect. Long time ago, a French fur trader named Olivier owned everything from the Wyoming line to Billings. It was a land grant from before Napoleon – that's how far back it goes."

Molly worked the needle through the fabric, shaking her head. "Olivier returned to France. Story I heard said the Cheyenne captured him and some traveling preacher saved him. Olivier left these parts in a hurry. Before he did, he deeded a large tract of land for a children's house of refuge – New Hope, now – to be run by the preacher. The rest he sold to the U.S. government for pennies an acre. The government bought it and turned it into a reservation for the Crows."

Luke's forehead folded into five straight horizontal lines.

"Count them," Molly had once told her. *"You can always tell what he's feeling. The more lines, the more bothered he is."*

"Jupiter says he remembers when New Hope's range ran all the way from the White Dog River to the Yellowstone," he said.

Molly shook her head. "He's an old man, Luke."

"But you said yourself the deed's messed up, that a piece of New Hope really belongs to the Crows."

Emily did a quick forehead line count. One more. Six wrinkles.

Molly nodded. "It does, but the stretch from Pryor Creek

to Billings was never ours. I've always been told New Hope's line ends at Pryor Creek. It's another ten miles from there to Billings. From Pryor Creek to the Yellowstone is all open range. Goodness, that can't be ours."

"Who said?"

"Everybody." She slipped a darning egg into another black stocking belonging to one of the girls. With tiny, deliberate stitches she outlined the hole, her mouth set. Jabbing the needle into the stocking, she set it aside and looked over at Luke. "Half a dozen people over the years, including Bart. Since he was here before me and on New Hope's board, I accepted his word."

"Where's the deed, Molly?"

She stood up. "I'll get it, but some of it's in French." Shoulders stiff, she left the room.

When she returned, Emily joined the other two at a long coffee table against the wall, where Molly had unfolded the deed.

"What's it say about boundaries?" Luke asked.

"There's nearly half a page about them here." Emily traced her finger under the tiny, cramped French writing down the deed's left margin. "This says 'west from *Rivière du Chien Blanc*' – White Dog River – 'to *Rivière de l' Élan*.'"

Slowly, Molly shook her head. "We all know where the White Dog is, but there's no such place named *Élan* around here."

Emily tapped her finger in the margin. "It's not a place. It's another river."

"Had his rivers mixed up, I guess. No such river named that, either." Luke straightened. Hands on his hips, he stared down at the deed. "Might as well be in Chinese for all the sense it makes to me." He turned to Emily. "What's *Élan* mean in French?"

She shrugged. "A big animal with horns . . . like a moose."

His eyes narrowed, then snapped wide open. "Elk, maybe?"

"That's it. That's the one."

"Jupiter was right!" He grabbed Molly around the waist and swung her feet off the floor. "That's not open range. It's ours!"

"Put me down, you crazy man," Molly said, laughing as hard as he.

Eyes bright, Luke set her on her feet, grinning. "Elk River is what the Indians used to call the Yellowstone." He leafed through the pages of the deed, looking for something. "There." He pointed to the date. "They drew this deed up in 1803. Lewis and Clark didn't explore this area till after the U.S. bought it, two years later. That's when he named Billings's muddy big river the 'Yellow Stone.'"

"I can't believe it," Molly said, her voice cracking. "All these years of just scrimping by. If this is true, it'll make folks mighty unhappy around here."

A shadow spread across Luke's face, his eyes serious. "Correction. It'll make one man unhappy. The Paxtons, the Ormons, old Mr. Bolton—they'll be glad for you. They only drive through, but Axel's days of hogging the range closest to Billings and the railhead are over. That's New Hope land. If he wants to graze it, then he rents it. And the next time he drives through, he's trespassing. Either he pays New Hope or he doesn't go through."

"He'll fight it, Luke. You know he will," Molly said quietly.

"Then we'll fight back. In court. The money problems for New Hope just ended." His face was grim and determined.

"I don't want anybody hurt. It might mean more trouble with him and his men," Molly warned.

He squeezed her shoulder. "There won't be any trouble."

Like an unborn baby kicking, Emily's heart jumped. She stared at the deed and bit the words back. Of course Bart would fight it. Worried for Luke, her gaze swung to him. If something happened to him now, she'd regret it forever.

Molly's gaze held Emily's, as if she'd read her mind.

"Let's not say anything to anyone yet," she said. "Luke, how about you showing this deed to the land office in Billings? Maybe take Jupiter along to back us up."

Coming down from his room two days later, still sleepy and trying to wake up, Luke saw the glow of an oil lamp from the dining room. At four o'clock in the morning, the downstairs was usually dark and quiet. Instead, light shined into the hall, the end of the dining room table lit with a pale apricot glow. The rest of the big room fell into the shadows behind it. He heard comfortable, waking-up noises in the back of the house and the pattering of footsteps. He recognized the hinge creak of the stove's fire door. The aroma of woodsmoke and boiling coffee drifted into the hall. Curious, he followed his nose.

Wearing an apron over a long blue gingham dress, her cheeks flushed from the heat of the woodstove, Emily removed a pan of biscuits from the oven. Luke stopped in the doorway, admiring her as he always did when she wasn't looking. Her hair was tied back with a matching blue ribbon and curled prettily from the heat and steam in the kitchen.

"You're up early this morning," he said.

Holding the hot pan with a towel, she banged the heavy oven door shut and turned to him. "And how about some nice scrambled eggs this morning?" A dazzling smile nearly blinded him.

Instantly his guard went up. Several times in his life he'd used dynamite, to clear a trail covered by a mountain of mud and rubble or to break loose a snowpack threatening to avalanche a herd. He wasn't afraid of explosives, but neither was he reckless with them. The potential for mortal danger was only a heartbeat away. The bright smile she gave him was a lit fuse to something.

Fire in the hole! That was what miners yelled when they ran for cover just before the blast let go. And though the words were ringing in his mind, all he said was, "Don't think I want any eggs this morning. I'm running kind of late." He picked up the coffeepot and the milk pitcher and ambled through the door into the dining room, feeling her eyes boring into the back of his neck every step he took.

Emily followed a minute later with the biscuits on a flowered plate—the good china, he noticed—and an assortment of jams and preserves in little dishes with little spoons, all daintily arranged on a white napkin on a pewter tray. Luke cocked an eyebrow, wondering. A little tea party in the middle of the night? She wanted something. He filled their cups, then set the pot down.

"Would you like some fig preserves?" she asked.

His mouth puckered. Few things in this world made him shudder, but fig preserves did. So did beef tea. "It's a little early. Got any grape jelly over there?"

"Here's some lovely quince."

He wrinkled his nose. "Grape's fine."

She stiffened. Irritably, she pushed the tray toward him and sat back. He moved the fancy dishes around and found some strawberry jam. Almost as good as grape.

Emily stirred a spoon around and around and around in her cup. He set his teeth together and did his best to ignore it, but the small, monotonous whine of metal on china at four o'clock in the morning curled his toes in his boots. She laid the spoon down and looked off into space, her gaze fixed in the air over his head.

Luke waited, relieved she'd stopped scraping the bottom out of that cup but wondering what was on her mind. Whatever she had to say wouldn't come out until she was good and ready. And heaven help him if he didn't want to hear it. Might as well try to hold back the tide.

"Biscuits are real good, Emily," he said, hoping to prod her into conversation.

Silence.

Reaching across, he helped himself to another biscuit, slit it, and spread a thick glob of fig preserves on it. There—maybe that would make her happy. He did the same with a second and handed it to her, using the opportunity to study her face. When she turned her head, the lamplight pooled in deep shadows under her eyes.

"You look tired," he said.

"I didn't sleep much. I've been thinking."

He pushed his cup away and folded his arms on the table. "All right, let's have it. What have you been thinking?"

"I want to talk to you."

"I guessed that much."

The words tumbled out in a breathless rush. "I think it would be a good idea if you'd take me along with you and Jupiter to Billings," she said.

He blinked. "Why?"

"Because I've never really been there and because I can read French, and maybe at the courthouse they can't."

"And maybe they can."

Her eyes met his. "But what if they can't? Then what will you do? You'll have to come back here and get me and go back again. That means you'll make a trip for nothing."

Wouldn't hurt to let her ride along, and what she said about the French made sense. No one around here spoke it. In fact, he'd never met anyone who spoke French before. And he had to take a wagon anyway because Jupiter was too old to ride a horse that far. Her skin looked creamy and soft in the lamplight. His gaze lingered on her lips. She really wouldn't be much trouble. He cleared his throat. "You're talking twenty miles in a wagon and camping out one night."

Emily nodded. "I know."

He picked up his cup and sipped slowly. But there were other things, he knew, that had never occurred to her. Luke glanced over at her. "I'll have to talk to Molly about it. You know how people gossip. It might not look right. Some folks might get the wrong idea if you were to go to Billings alone with two men."

"Oh, for heaven's sake! One of them is ninety years old."

"And one of them isn't."

He meant to shock her with that, but strangely she didn't look at all surprised. It was almost as if she expected him to say that.

Emily let out a long, exaggerated sigh. "You're absolutely right, of course. But then, you are about most things."

He shot her a sharp look.

"I never thought of that," she went on, plucking a crumb of biscuit off the table, rolling it between her fingers. Wide-eyed, she looked at him. "What do you think I should do?"

He drained his coffee and set the cup down, secretly pleased. For the second time she was being sensible and listening to him, just as she did with the guns. She was a stubborn one, all right, but he'd learned how to handle her.

"I'll talk to Molly, but don't get your hopes up. She's a stickler for what's respectable and proper."

Demurely, Emily lowered her eyes. "Well, I'll just have to wait for her answer. I'll do whatever you two decide."

All the way to the barn, and later riding out to the range, their conversation niggled at him. Again and again he played it over in his head, aware of a small warning buzz in the back of his brain. It wasn't like Emily McCarthy to give in to him that easily. She'd sounded too confident, too sure of herself—even a little rehearsed, when you came right down to it.

Like an insect whining in his ear, the thought wouldn't go away: somehow, someway, she was putting something over on him. But for the life of him, he couldn't see it.

Not unless she and Molly had already got their heads together.

Nah, never happen. There wasn't a devious bone in Molly's body. But Emily . . . His eyes crinkled. Chuckling, he went over this morning's breakfast in his mind again. Whatever she was up to, it wouldn't work with him. He was on to her.

CHAPTER 11

Riding home from the range that day, Luke glanced over at the rider on a claybank horse alongside that looked as if it had rolled in red mud. A genial scarecrow of a man with straw-colored hair, Henry Bertel was nearly as tall as Luke and one of New Hope's best range men.

"How many you figure are missing?" Henry asked.

Luke didn't answer for a moment, then frowned and shook his head. "Hard to say. Couple hundred, at least."

Henry gestured his outstretched arm toward a group of heifers grazing nearby, away from the others. "Today I looked for two I know were here before Christmas—a bull with a busted horn and a cow that was snake-bit last summer. They're both gone."

Luke and half a dozen New Hope hands had counted and

recounted cattle since dawn, all reaching the same conclusion: The herd was down. Way down.

"Where in blazes did they go?" Henry muttered.

"Nowhere. I think someone's stealing them," Luke said. The words drawled out softly, belying the angry set of his mouth.

Henry made a disgusted sound. "Hope you're wrong." Looking at the group of heifers in the distance, he gathered the reins. "Be right back; want to check those out one more time." He slapped the reins and set the claybank into a slow canter across the field.

Scully's face had drawn into a deep scowl as he listened. "What you gonna do, Luke?"

"Talk to Sheriff Tucker."

Scully slid a veiled glance at Luke. "Guess I figured you might do something more direct."

Luke shook his head. "Not anymore. Besides, that's something you never do alone. You need witnesses."

"I'd help you, if you needed me."

Luke looked over, touched by the offer. "I appreciate it, but the main reason I came back to New Hope was because they got law here. This is the sheriff's problem now."

But only a few months before, he thought, he would've handled missing cattle his own way. He and three or four men with rifles would have hidden out on the range and watched the herd. Sooner or later they'd have caught the thieves, and that would have been the end of it.

He'd grown up with range law, accepted it, understood it, almost believed in the harsh justice of it. A cow was property. Steal it, you steal a man's livelihood.

And thieves were hung.

But this was New Hope. They had real law here. Cattle rustlers or not, folks wouldn't take kindly to finding local citizens strung up and left hanging out here as examples.

But it worked.

In Lewistown, when Stuart and other ranchers started losing cattle by the hundreds to rustlers, they did something about it. Stuart formed the vigilance committee. Luke, his head foreman, had oversight setting it up and of the men on it. Unlike some, Luke always had mixed feelings about the committee.

Though he hadn't been inside a church in years, some of his upbringing at New Hope had rubbed off. Molly had seen to it that every one of her kids went to Sunday school and church every week.

"Thou shalt not kill."

It got through.

And years later he'd wrestled with it. But after two different preachers told him the Sixth Commandment wasn't meant to protect criminals, he felt a lot easier about running the committee for Stuart. But those days were over. This time he intended to handle it differently, legally, right down to the letter of the law.

At least he would try. First.

The following Saturday morning, Luke and Henry Bertel rode into Repton to see Sheriff Tucker. It seemed everybody had business in town that day. As he waved to Jupiter Jackson coming out of the dry-goods store, Luke saw Bart Axel entering the big two-story Empire Bank & Trust Company next door.

Down the street, a couple of X-Bar-L hands pushed into one of the saloons.

Saturday was market day, the streets choked with buggies and wagons of all descriptions and riders. Noisy freighters with their big teams and heavy wagons waited to be unloaded of goods shipped in from Chicago, Ohio, and back east. Horses were tied to hitching rails, awning poles, anything that would hold them. Women with packages and kids in tow held their skirts out of the mud and picked their way to the other side of the street. When two young boys darted after a dog that ran right between the legs of Henry's claybank horse, the two men swung off their horses and led the animals the last half block or so to a hitching rail in front of Lucky Eddie's Saloon.

"Pleasure before business." Henry grinned and rubbed his hands together. All the way in from New Hope, he'd talked of little else but the girls at Lucky Eddie's.

Looping the reins around the rail in front of Eddie's, Luke straightened his hat and turned to cross the street. "You go ahead. I've got to see the sheriff."

Henry clapped him on the shoulder, his cheeks creased in a wide smile. "Not so fast. You're coming inside with me. You ain't been to town once since you got back."

"All right, all right," Luke said, with an embarrassed grin. He didn't want to admit he wasn't looking forward to seeing Tucker again anyhow.

They crossed the sidewalk and stepped into Eddie's. As soon as their eyes adjusted from the bright daylight of the street to the smoky dimness inside, they walked midway down the bar to an empty section. The bar was a huge mahogany counter, mirrored behind, and running the length of the room.

Luke hooked a boot heel over the railing, his right hand moving automatically to the gun on his hip, thumbing the small leather loop off the hammer, lifting the handle quickly, checking the gun was free, a habit he'd developed years before.

"What'll you have?" Eddie the bartender swiped a rag over the bar top in front of them.

"Just something cold and wet for me. Got any of that new ginger drink they're so crazy about in Chicago?" Luke asked.

The bartender nodded. "Ginger ale, they call it. We got it. Anything Chicago's got, we got."

"While you're at it, he needs a lady to drink it with," Henry said, nudging Luke with his elbow. "Right, boss?"

"Confound it, just order, Henry," he snapped.

"Gimme a whiskey, Eddie." Henry turned to Luke, his long face reddening. "You know what? You been mighty testy the last couple of weeks."

Luke winced. Henry was a hard worker and a friend besides. Irritating as he was, he wanted to help. And deep down, Luke knew he was right. He hadn't been himself lately: short-tempered, worried, and working every one of them too hard, including himself.

"Don't mean to be," he said. "Ignore me. I got a lot on my mind."

"I gathered that, and her name's Emily, ain't it?"

"Did you order?" Luke looked at him, stone-faced.

"You know I did, and you're just changing the subject."

Eddie winked at Luke and tipped his head toward two bored-looking girls sitting at the end of the bar. "Take your pick."

Both women were looking the two of them up and down. One was tall, with a mass of dark hair wound in tight spit curls she scratched carefully with her little fingernail, as if it were a wig. The other girl—plump and pretty—wore a shiny green satin dress cut revealingly low.

Her carrot-colored hair was piled loosely on top of her head in a bouffant style. She smiled at Luke in obvious invitation. He looked away. He hadn't come in here for that.

Henry looked at the girls and then at Luke. "Want to go talk to them?"

"Not today. Soon as I finish my drink, I'm going over to see the sheriff."

Henry beckoned to the girls.

A minute later, a throaty voice purred in Luke's ear.

"Hi, pretty cowboy, my name's Buffy." She settled herself on the stool next to him as if she'd been invited and rearranged her skirt. A thinly plucked eyebrow rose. "My goodness, but you're a big one, ain't you?"

Inwardly, Luke squirmed, feeling like a piece of meat on a block. She was younger than she looked, he decided, and unless he missed his guess, she had a lot of miles on her. Luke's gaze traveled to her hair again—dyed. He wished it were any color but red. With a feeling of distaste, he looked away.

"What's your name?" she asked.

"Sullivan." Hoping she'd go away, he said nothing more to encourage her. Instead, he turned his glass around and around, pretending an interest in making wet rings on the bar in front of him.

Henry, however, had lost no time. An arm wrapped around

the dark-haired girl's waist, he was nuzzling her neck and whispering to her.

"Where you from?" Buffy asked Luke.

"Up north."

Her eyes narrowed. "The strong, silent type, huh?"

Luke grinned and tried to be polite. "No, ma'am. Not at all." He rested his arms on the bar, deciding to finish his drink and then leave.

Around her neck she wore a thin velvet ribbon with a white silk daisy nearly the size of his fist. She touched the flower and looked at his glass. "Eddie, bring me a ginger ale, too," she called.

When it came, she reached to take the drink and brushed Luke's arm as she did. Smiling, she raised her glass in a small toast to him. Her other hand went to the flower again, stroking its petals, drawing his attention – deliberately – to the low cut of her dress. He looked away with a vague feeling of repugnance.

She slid off her stool and lounged against the bar. He was aware of her eyes traveling the length of him, a heated gaze he recognized. Time to leave. He set his glass down, still half full, and started to get up.

Buffy slipped her hand over his. "Don't leave. Let's go upstairs, and I'll fix you a real drink, not this syrupy stuff." Then, with a sly smile, she added, "How's that sound?"

Instead of being flattered, he was annoyed and a little insulted. He was just old-fashioned enough that he liked to do the asking.

He tried to stave off a building frustration at being with the wrong woman. He was no prude and no stranger to bawdy houses, either. But the whole situation had unnerved him completely. Here he was in the biggest saloon and bawdy house in town, with a pretty woman waiting to take his money – and he just wasn't interested. Feeling like the biggest fool in Montana, Luke looked down at Buffy. "Sorry for the misunderstanding. I came to town on business today. I'm only stopping in for a few minutes with my friend."

"Leave him alone, honey," Henry cackled. "The man's pining for someone else. He's got another redhead on his mind today – Little Miss Perfect. Right, Luke?"

"Maybe. And maybe not."

"No maybes about it." Henry tightened his hold around the dark-haired girl's waist. "I got you on my mind. Let's dance, honey." He headed her out to the dance floor.

"Did I do something wrong?" Buffy asked.

"No, I did. Coming in here was a mistake."

"Because of . . . her?"

"Little Miss Perfect?" Luke chuckled and nodded.

"Sounds like you care about her."

"She's just a friend."

Buffy smiled at that and traced a fingernail back and forth along Luke's sleeve. "Most fellers like my hair."

"I'm sure they do. You're a very pretty lady. Now, why don't you run along and find another customer?" he said in a low voice, easing his arm away. Glass in hand, he walked to the other end of the bar, away from her.

Drawing a long breath, he turned around and rested both elbows on the bar behind him. The saloon had filled up. A haze of smoke hung near the ceiling. Through the rising level of men's voices, he heard the sharp crack of billiard balls, the piano banging in the corner.

Emily played the piano better, a lot better. Luke chuckled, trying to imagine her ladylike little figure perched on the red-fringed piano stool, instead of that dandy in the straw hat and striped shirt.

"And you'd be leaning against this bar every night, ready to pound the first joker that so much as talked to her."

Maybe Henry was right.

He glanced down the bar at Buffy, another girl on his mind. He didn't know what to do about Emily anymore.

Henry was laughing and shuffling around the dance floor with the dark-haired girl, his arm seesawing the air.

Luke turned back to the bar. For reasons he never could fathom, women found him boyish and sweet, mistaking his clamped control for shyness, drawn by the slow-talking, easy-going manner he used with the ladies. Other girls wanted to mother him, bake for him, knit things for him.

All except Emily.

Hunched over, he absently turned an ashtray around. An angry exchange of voices on the dance floor interrupted his thoughts.

Luke looked up to see Bud Schmidt shove Henry away from his dancing partner. Henry swore and stumbled backward a few steps.

"Get away, Bud," the girl piped. "I'm dancing with him."

Bud laughed and swung her against him, moving in time to the music, rising up on the balls of his feet in the peculiar pigeon-toed gait of his. "Not no more," he said.

"Says who?" Indignant, she pushed him away.

Arms flailing, Henry waded in and grabbed Bud's arm. Schmidt was fast. A quick punch to Henry's midsection doubled him over and sprawled him facedown on the floor.

Luke pushed away from the bar. "Come on, Henry, time to go," Luke said, intending to drag him out of there while Henry could still walk. Something cold and hard pressed into the back of his neck.

"Stay out of it, Sullivan," Stu Bronson's voice growled in his ear.

Luke heard the click of a hammer drawing to full cock. Before the sound had fully registered in his brain, his reflexes spun him around, ducking, shoulder dropping, right hand going for his gun. Stu fired first. The blast rocked the room. Glass shattered. The wood bar alongside Luke splintered. A second explosion followed as Luke's Colt cleared leather, spitting flame as it came up. Stu clutched the front of his shirt and looked down at the bright red stain spreading under his hand. An expression of shock spread across his features as he slid to the floor.

At the sound of gunfire, Bud shoved the girl away. Bronson lay on the floor by the bar, his head resting at an odd angle on the brass footrail. Luke stood over him, his gun smoking. Bud whirled, facing Luke across a cleared dance floor. A wild, crazy light leaped in his eyes.

"Don't do it, Schmidt," Luke yelled. "Don't draw!"

Bud Schmidt wasn't listening. He clawed for his gun and drew on a man with a .45 pointed right at him. Luke let him get his gun out, an instant, no more. Risky, but he gave him that much. Bud swung his pistol up and aimed. Luke fanned the hammer back and blew Bud Schmidt off his feet.

At the first shots, half the men in the room had dived to

the floor. Now the other half sat rigid, still as statues. In the glow of the overhead lamps in the back, a billiard player froze motionless over the green felt, a lit cigar clamped between his teeth. His elbow and his cue stick pointed at the ceiling.

The room held its breath.

A muscle convulsed along Luke's jaw. So fast! But then it always was—fast and dirty and ugly.

Steel blue wisps of gunpowder curled in the air and coated his teeth. Stomach knotting, he thrust the Colt into its holster and stepped over Stu's body.

I didn't want to do this.

"Eddie, I'm sorry," he said to the bartender. Alert and wary, looking for other Axel hands, he headed for the door and fresh air and sanity.

***

"Hold it, mister. Hold it right there!" Hatless, coatless, and out of breath, Sheriff Sam Tucker crouched in the doorway, a heavy old Smith & Wesson cavalry pistol covering the room in general and Luke Sullivan in particular.

"What happened here?" he demanded.

The bartender broke in. "Not his fault, Sam. The other man drew first. Was self-defense. Sullivan had no choice unless he wanted to get shot in the back. And that light-haired fellow there"—he pointed to Bud, spread-eagled on his back, staring up at the ceiling—"well, he never was too bright. Sullivan warned him not to pull. I guess you could say that one kinda killed hisself." There was a chorus of assent. All around the room, men nodded.

"Don't suppose it'll do any good, but get Doc Maxwell over here anyhow. And you"—the sheriff leveled his pistol at Luke's chest—"I want you in my office. Now." He jerked his head toward the street.

On the way outside, Tucker slipped the Colt from Luke's holster and shoved the barrel hard into the small of his back. "Just take it nice and easy, Sullivan, and don't try nothing smart, or so help me I'll shoot you with your own gun." The door closed.

The billiard player straightened and removed the cigar stub from his teeth. "I'm lookin' right at him, and I swear I missed it," he said. "Anybody see Sullivan draw?"

Five cardplayers shook their heads. "Nobody saw him draw," one said.

"He's either very lucky or very good." The billiard player plugged the cigar back in his mouth and leaned over the table to line up his shot. "Like me," he said, and cracked the ball neatly into a corner pocket.

Across the street, Tucker fixed Luke with a hard look. "By any chance either of those men you killed involved in the beating you took a while back?"

"Both of them were, but—"

"Kinda thought that might be the case," he said tightly. He stacked the papers Luke had just signed. Without bothering to blot them, he tossed them into a cluttered basket on the corner of his desk. He got up and went to a potbellied stove in the corner and poured himself a cup of coffee from an enameled pot. He returned to the desk and sank heavily into his chair again.

Outside the office an excited knot of people congregated on the sidewalk. The town was all upset. There hadn't been a shooting in Repton in five years—longer, if you considered one on a Saturday afternoon in broad daylight.

Voices rose. A shielded face peered in through the window.

"Mr. Sullivan, why don't you go back where you came from? Until you showed up, this was a nice, quiet little town. Most excitin' thing here last year was two dog bites and one outhouse fire. Since you been back, I got a stage robbery, a kidnapping, a beating, and now a double killing."

Tipping back in his chair, Tucker cocked his boots on the edge of the desk and blew into his coffee. With a long-suffering look he waved a hand at the overflowing file basket and sighed. "Mr. Sullivan, you got any idea how much paper work there is when a federal bank loses money—like a thousand dollars? At least I had sense enough not to report the kidnapping. If that's what it was," he added. Tucker pulled out a red bandanna and honked his nose. The swivel chair protested as he raised a hip and stuffed the kerchief back into his pocket.

"'Course you weren't involved in neither one of those. Right?" He looked at Luke.

Luke stared back, silent.

"To my way of thinking, this feud between you and Axel is a personal thing because of Miz McCarthy."

"Shouldn't be," Luke answered.

"This ain't Sunday school, Mr. Sullivan. Don't give me no *shouldn't*s. Is it or isn't it?"

"Sheriff, I did not start this."

"Somebody did. Let me give you some advice. Lots of people round here don't much like Bart Axel because of how he runs his herd, but far as I know, he's legal. Someone tried to beat your head in once. And today, two of them tried to shoot you. Sooner or later, they just might succeed. But that's your worry. Now you take that .45 of yours there and get yourself out of here before I change my mind and lock you up for your own protection."

Luke shoved the Colt into his holster and started for the door.

"Mr. Sullivan."

Putting his hat on, Luke turned.

"What was your business in town today?"

"I came in to see you," Luke said. "I had a couple of things to talk about. New Hope's herd is down. Someone's stealing our cattle."

Unblinking, Tucker stared at Luke. The chair squeaked. Slowly, Tucker uncoiled his long legs and swung around. "So it's rustling now, is it? Why not? Not much else left, is there, Mr. Sullivan?" He rubbed his eyes as if they burned with weariness. "Tell Molly I'll be out next week sometime. What else is on your mind?"

Luke's temper crept up another notch. He fought it down, not answering until the first hot flash of anger faded. This man wouldn't help him. He was back to doing it alone again. "Forget it. I'll handle it myself."

"Not in Repton, you don't. This isn't Lewistown. You catch anyone, you bring 'em in to me. You hear?"

Luke went out and slammed the door after him. Silently, the crowd outside the sheriff's office parted to let him through.

A woman wrapped an arm around her toddler and pulled the child close to her side, her eyes on Luke's face.

"Aw, lady . . ."

Luke headed down the street for his horse, feeling lower than dirt.

CHAPTER
12

"Two of my ranch hands were murdered doing my business in town. And it was murder, Sheriff, cold-blooded murder," Bart Axel said. "I want to know what you intend to do about it."

Tucker looked up from his desk and raised his eyebrows. "Nothing yet. I got no reason to arrest Luke Sullivan. It ain't murder, not unless he shot your men with their guns still in their holsters. Mr. Sullivan didn't do that. A dozen witnesses say your man shot first."

"It was a spite killing, and you know it." Axel's face darkened.

"A saloon full of men say otherwise. If it was a spite killing, Mr. Axel, appears to me the spite was on Stu Bronson's part."

"Of course Sullivan would deny it. And you believed him?"

"Nope. Don't believe nobody involved in a killing. But half

the men in Eddie's saw Bronson shoot first; other half heard Sullivan warn Schmidt not to draw. Near as I can make out, it was self-defense."

Axel hooked his thumbs in his vest pockets and rocked back and forth. Staring at the sheriff, he said, "I want him arrested, convicted, and hung, and not necessarily in that order. This time you better bend a little, Sam. I mean it."

The threat in the gray-haired rancher's voice came through clearly to Tucker. Deep inside, a slow burn started. So long as he was sheriff, any man had a right to keep himself alive. His jaw set. "Then I reckon you'll just have to wait till Mr. Sullivan does something to deserve that."

"You disappoint me, Sam." Bart turned on his heel and left.

Tucker watched him leave, his mind filled with sour thoughts. Luke Sullivan was turning out to be one real pain in the tail.

Riding through the outskirts of Repton on the way back from the sheriff's office, Bart Axel fumed. Repton was a pretty little town, but he was too mad to notice the huge old cottonwood trees lining both sides of the road or the houses with their gardens, still brown but plowed and hopeful. "I got a notion to go to Billings about this," he said to Clete.

"Won't do no good, the way those lawmen stick together. Billings ain't got jurisdiction down here anyway." Clete looked over at his boss. "Speaking of Billings, Jupiter Jackson was in town today."

"That old man still kicking? He ought to be dead by now."

Clete nodded. "He was in the dry-goods store, buying a new hat. I heard him tell Ezra Bobbins he's going to Billings with Sullivan."

Bart's jaw dropped. "What for?"

"Something about their deed. Old Jupiter strutted around like a peacock, trying on hats and saying as how Sullivan was taking him to the land office about New Hope's deed. Seems Sullivan thinks that west section of land into Billings never was open range. Says New Hope goes all the way to the Yellowstone."

Bart's knuckles whitened as he gripped the reins. He felt the blood drain from his face. Trouble. The worst kind.

Years ago he'd studied the maps of the territory, tracing his finger along the valleys and rivers and plotting where he thought the tracks would go when the railroad came through. He began acquiring land in a checkerboard pattern any way he could, a ploy which gave him control over the land between that he didn't own. Sometimes he bought land outright; sometimes he applied for homesteads in other men's names.

Sometimes he misjudged, and the Northern Pacific laid miles north or west of where he'd hoped. He consoled himself with the knowledge his property lay twenty miles on a straight shot to the tracks at Billings—an easy two-day cattle drive. When meat orders came in from the big Chicago markets or the army, Bart drove his steers into Billings and had them in cattle cars and on their way east before smaller ranchers could round theirs up.

What Molly didn't realize was the open range he drove

through was, technically, New Hope land. He knew it, and so did the Crows, but nobody listened to them.

Evidently that was about to change.

Molly wouldn't be trouble, but so long as Sullivan bossed New Hope's herd, there'd be no more driving through, not without a fight. And that meant an extra day added to every X-Bar-L drive to swing north around New Hope, a day Bart didn't have to get his steers to the railroad ahead of the others.

"You talk to Jupiter?" Axel asked.

Clete shook his head. "I was in the back room getting shirts. He left before I came out."

"Did he say when they're going to Billings?" Bart kept his tone casual.

"A week from Tuesday."

When he got back to the X-Bar-L, Bart went directly to his office, to a large black Vulcan safe rolled against the wall. He spun the dial, opened the safe, then unlocked the separate steel inner door. Another key unlocked a drawer on the left. From a small notebook inside, he took out a loose slip of paper with a name and a general delivery address written on it.

Bart studied it for a minute, then folded the paper and tucked it into his shirt pocket.

Jupiter talked too much.

CHAPTER
13

Shortly after midnight, dogs barking and a horse's frantic whinny snapped Emily bolt upright in bed. Light flickered against the wall, and an eerie orange glow brightened the windowpane. She leaped out of bed and ran to the window.

The north side of the big two-story barn on the hillside was ablaze. Flames shot through the roof. Black smoke churned into the night sky.

"Luke! Molly! The barn's on fire!" she screamed.

She threw on a robe, pulled on her shoes. Hands shaking, still shouting to Luke, she lit a lamp, grabbed it up, and charged out of her room and across the hall. She beat her fists on Luke's bedroom door, yelling for him to get up. An instant later she ran downstairs, pounding on the walls and the other bedroom doors, yelling at everyone to get up. Get up! She lit another lamp and left it on the table for the others, then raced through the dining room, out the back door, down the steps.

"Oh no . . ." she gasped, and broke into a run across the yard. The horses were in there!

Behind her, doors slammed. High soprano voices of frightened children cried out in the summer night. Male shouts rose as Scully and Henry and all the hands poured out of the bunkhouse. Half-dressed men grabbed up buckets and shovels and raced after Emily across the field to the burning barn.

Shirtless, in work pants and cowboy boots, Luke burst out the back door. "Emily, wait!" he bellowed, and leaped off the porch.

He caught up with her as she wrestled with the heavy barn doors. Luke pushed her aside and shoved them wide open.

Immediately, a hot, acrid haze gusted out. Coughing, shielding his face with an arm, he disappeared into the smoke.

One section of wall at the far end was already burning. Locked in a stall away from the mares, Bugle neighed and stamped his feet. Luke threw the stall door open.

"Out, boy!"

Bugle stared at him, wild-eyed. Terror-stricken, he backed away, crowding his rump against the wall. Lips raised, he pointed his head at the ceiling and let out a long, shrill neigh.

Overhead, a bale of hay *whumped* and hissed into flame. Bugle bucked and drove his hind legs straight out behind him. Two iron hooves crashed through the boards.

"Luke! Luke! Where are you?"

"With Bugle. Stay out!"

Emily ducked her head and followed the sound of his voice, running through smoke that opened and closed around her.

An oily black cloud blew down from above. She leaned against the wall of the passageway, coughing.

"Where's Scully?" Luke choked.

"Trying to put out the fire."

"There's no way. The barn's gone. Tell him to get in here fast or we're going to lose the horses."

"There isn't time! I'll help you. Now, get moving, Sullivan! I'll get the stalls on the left; you get the ones on the right." Robe billowing, she ran down the center passageway. At the first stall on the left, she yanked the door open. The old mare inside was smart and stood with her head lowered close to the floor, breathing where the air was clear.

"Come out, Sheba!" Emily shouted.

Sheba didn't budge. "I said, come out!" Emily whipped off her robe and stepped inside against the wall. She flapped the robe, popping it like a huge white towel, and shouted, "Run, you silly thing. Shoo! Shoo!"

Sheba shot from the stall.

Luke yelped in alarm and threw himself against the passageway as Sheba tore by.

One by one, Emily worked her way back up the line of stalls, jumping inside, popping the robe, and shrieking like a crazy ghost. She got all the horses out on her side. Though it took him longer, Luke managed to grab the halters and run them out on his side. All except Bugle.

Hot air seared her lungs. Overhead, burning rafters snapped and crackled as the fire leaped across the loft.

Grim faced, he went back in for Bugle.

Pressing his back against the wall, Luke slid in alongside his horse. A piece of plank dangled in one hand.

Bugle, slathered with sweat, chewed air and foamed long strings of saliva.

In all the time he'd had the horse, he'd never hit him. Not once.

"Run!" Two-handed, Luke raised the board and belted a stinging wallop against the horse's rear end.

Bugle let out a blaring whinny and reared like a wild stallion, pawing his front legs in the air. Luke dropped the board and dived out of the way as the hooves came down, expecting him to rear again. Instead, Bugle wheeled and shot out the stall with Luke right behind him. A spotted mare and two cow ponies in the passageway saw Bugle. All three bolted for the barn door.

Luke threw Emily against the wall as they stampeded after Bugle. Necks stretching, tails streaming, they charged through the barn and out into the corral. They kept right on running—through the corral gates, up and over a fence, and across the field on the other side.

A beam burned through the loft and plummeted to the floor, exploding into a fountain of red-hot sparks. Fiery clumps of hay sifted down. With a creaking sound of nails pulling, the floor above them began to sag. Luke snatched Emily up and leaped for the open door, running through the smoke and out into the corral with her.

"Oh, thank God! There they are. They got out!" Shouts went up from the men in the yard.

Chest heaving, sucking in deep, sweet breaths of air, Luke set her down by the corral fence.

A red glow lit the sky. In the strange, wavering light from the burning barn, a human chain of figures thrust buckets from hand to hand. Children in nightclothes grabbed the empty pails and raced back and forth between the outstretched arms of the line of men and the wild-eyed teenager in his nightshirt, working the pump handle as fast as he could.

"You all right?" Luke's face was streaked with soot, his eyebrows singed and powdery.

Emily nodded. Hands trembling, she reached up and batted out wisps of smoke curling in his hair. A sinking feeling dug at the pit of her stomach as he sagged back against the fence holding her in his arms.

She'd almost lost him. Her arms clenched his waist.

From across the corral came a ripping sound and a chorus of shouts. A burst of sparks sailed upward. The men in the barnyard threw their buckets down and ran. In a blaze of flame and brightness, the barn caved in.

They should have died in there. But they hadn't.

Her arms tightened around him. *Thank you, God.*

He pulled her closer. "You know you're only in your nightgown, don't you?"

She looked down at her front and shrugged. She'd dropped the robe in the barn. "No time for modesty. We saved the horses! I can't believe we got them out."

"Thanks to you and your robe. If you'd come at me flapping that thing, I would've run, too." His chest shook with silent laughter. "You little peanut, you yelled at me in there. I love it!" He looked down at her. "I also love your nightgown."

And his mouth came down hard on hers.

He didn't sleep well that night, overwhelmed by the whimsies of life and death, who lived and who didn't, and how close they'd both come to dying. Without a moment's hesitation, he'd gone after her, risked his own life to save hers.

She was *that* important to him.

Arms folded under his head, he stared up into the darkness and tried to make sense of what he'd done and why. He couldn't. His mind swam with confusion, thoughts ramming into each other. When did this happen? With no warning she'd become a major part of his life that he wanted to keep.

He rolled over and punched up the pillow. He wasn't ready for this.

After breakfast the next morning, Emily was at the clothesline, hanging out a basket of wash when Luke walked over. As she pinned a pair of boy's corduroy trousers to dry, he grabbed the clothesline with both hands and looked down at her.

"I'm going into town to talk to the sheriff about the barn. That fire was no accident. We found coal-oil cans. No question, the fire was set." He forced a smile, knew it came out all wrong, and covered her hand with his. Gently, he squeezed it. "Ride along with me?"

On the ride in, they chatted like brother and sister about New Hope — an awkward, self-conscious conversation about the fire, about the weather, about everything except what was really on his mind.

Them.

When they got to Repton, Luke dropped her off to shop, and he crossed the street to the sheriff's office.

A few minutes later, Tucker let out a long sigh. "So it's arson now, is it? I reckon I better come out today before something else happens. Good-bye, Mr. Sullivan." He tossed the paper Luke had just signed into his overflowing file basket, and that was the end of the visit.

Luke stalked out and slammed the door so hard he thought the glass would break. He wasn't quite sure what he'd expected, but Tucker's high-handed attitude wasn't it. Luke had turned his back on the raw justice of range law, swearing he'd never go back to it, but sometimes — like now — he wondered if Tucker's law was any better.

Luke stepped off the boardwalk and crossed the street.

Repton's main street was wide, dusty, and nearly three blocks long. Four other small streets ran into it from the north. The town had grown. The two-story Strand Hotel on the corner had a streetlamp out front, lit by the owner himself every afternoon at four o'clock. The Northern Pacific Railroad now crossed the whole territory, and the Burlington Quincy's new spur line operated daily from Repton to Billings. Every spring saw another business, another store, another saloon open its doors.

A school and two new churches, one a white frame Methodist on the outskirts of town. In the heart of the downtown, and just finished, stood an imposing brick Lutheran with a bell tower that pealed every Sunday. Both churches drew overflow congregations. A thousand people lived in Repton, and the town was taking on city airs now.

Two more cafés had opened up, one with a hand-lettered

sign in the window that read *Pie Every Day*. Luke grinned. Maybe he'd take Emily there when they finished in town.

He walked past Atkin's Feed Store, then the new Grange Hall that hadn't been there last time he was home, and past Bobbins General Store, which had always been there as far back as he could remember. Inside the store, in a clutter of bolts of fabric, racks of clothes, a counter of ladies' hats, chairs, and cookware hanging from the ceiling, Ezra waited on Emily. He raised his arm and waved as Luke passed by.

Three doors down, Luke turned into the Beartooth, the oldest café and billiard hall in town. After the glare of the noon sun, it took a minute for his eyes to adjust to the dim interior. The sweet, sharp scent of frying meat mingled with the stale smell of sweat and men. A wide counter had a footrail so highly polished he could've shaved in it. Behind it a mirror reflected the pool tables crowding the room.

Will Baxter, the Beartooth's owner, leaned over and grabbed Luke by the shoulder. "You rascal, you! Ain't seen you since you got back. How are ya, boy? What'll you have?"

Luke grinned. "Nothing, thanks. I can't stay. Just came in to say howdy." He propped his foot on the railing and thumbed the loop off the Colt's hammer. Leaning on the bar, he looked around. At this time of day, the place was nearly empty. Along the far wall, four men sat at a table, laughing and playing cards. The billiard tables stood empty, the balls racked in the center. Halfway down the counter, a lanky cowboy in a black hat slouched over a cup of coffee, a cigarette smoking in his fist.

Will Baxter wiped his hands on his apron and leaned closer to Luke. In a low voice he said, "I heard what happened to you with Axel's men. Must say, you look healthy enough now, but I don't mind telling you we were all mighty worried for a while. We've known you since you was a little shaver."

"Someone new?" Luke inclined his head toward the stranger to his right at the end of the counter.

Will shrugged. "Never saw him before. Rode in on that leopard Appy little bit ago." He inclined his chin to a handsome black Appaloosa with a white-spotted rump outside, then picked up a towel and began drying glasses. He carefully set them down on a shelf in front of the mirror, lining them up like cavalry. "What're you in town for today? You come by yourself?" he asked pleasantly.

"No. Miss McCarthy needed a few things and rode along. I came in today to see Sheriff Tucker."

"About your barn, I guess."

"Good news travels fast, I see," Luke said dryly.

"The whole town's heard. A bunch of us'll be out to New Hope next weekend to start raising you a new barn." Baxter shook his head. "Sure hate to see this start up again. Too much like the old days. You know who did it, I guess?"

"Not really. That's the sheriff's job."

Baxter leaned closer. "If one of Axel's men did it, you're wasting your time with the sheriff. Sam Tucker's a good man, but he can't do nothing about Axel. Sometimes I think . . . well, you know what I think about Axel."

Out of the corner of his eye, Luke caught a flicker of movement. The cowboy at the end of the counter raised his head. From under his hat, small, deep-set eyes stared fixedly at Baxter.

"But I don't," the stranger said. "S'pose you tell me what you think 'bout Mr. Axel." In one fast movement, he swung his elbow onto the counter and leveled a gun barrel at Will Baxter's stomach.

Leaning forward, arms folded, Luke looked down the counter. "No call for that. Put the gun away, mister. This conversation doesn't concern you."

"You're wrong. It does. Directly. I just hired on at the X-Bar-L and that's my new boss he's talking about." His eyes glittered at Luke. "And this doesn't concern you, neither. So keep your nose out of it."

The four cardplayers interchanged glances, laid down their cards, and stood up. Single-file they followed each other out the front door.

Luke straightened, the back of his left hand easing a bowl of peanuts aside. "I said to put the gun away." His voice was a monotone.

"Big talk for a man who ain't drawn yet."

"If I draw, I use it. And I'd rather not."

The man's eyes flicked to Luke's right hand resting on the counter, fingers widespread, relaxed. Ready.

When Luke first slid onto a stool at the counter, the quick pat down he'd given his Colt had got him a hard stare from this man. The stranger was aware of Luke's automatic gun check. Luke checked other men himself—looked for it, in fact. It was a dead giveaway to a fast draw. Luke tensed inside, his senses alerted.

Takes one to know one.

Who was he?

He spoke better than some cowboys, but he wasn't a rancher. His eyes were wrong.

"You shoot Mr. Baxter, it's murder," Luke said, quietly. "I shoot you, it's not. And I will."

Axel's new man shrugged. "It ain't your fight," he said, then flipped a dollar onto the counter. "I got no quarrel with you." He slipped his six-gun into its holster and pushed away from the counter. Spurs jingling, he moved toward the door. Holding it open, he looked over his shoulder at Luke. "Name's Haldane. Kid Haldane. What's yours, mister?"

"Sullivan. Luke Sullivan."

"I'll remember that."

"Good idea."

With a curt nod, Kid Haldane turned and pushed his way outside.

Will Baxter wiped a sleeve across his forehead and leaned weakly on the counter. "Much obliged. I owe you." His voice wavered.

Luke leaned over and squeezed his shoulder. "No, you don't. You'd do it for me." He put his hat on and walked out.

He went up the wooden sidewalk, his boots rapping the planks. The gunfight jitters that always hit him afterward closed like a hand around his throat. He walked faster, wanting to find Emily and then get out of town.

Down the street in Bobbins Store, the bell above the door jangled as Luke stepped inside. "You about ready to go?"

She looked at his face and snapped her purse closed. "I'm ready."

Silently he collected her packages and carried them out to

the buggy. As he stowed them behind the seat, he noticed the spotted Appaloosa belonging to Haldane still tied to the rail in front of Will Baxter's place, its owner nowhere in sight.

Luke looked across the street at the café where he'd planned to take Emily for lunch and shook his head. Food was the last thing he wanted. He was too churned up inside to eat.

She laid her hand on his forearm and looked up at him. "You're upset."

He glanced at the black and white horse again and then back to Emily. "I look it, huh?"

"I guess you don't want to stop for lunch, then." Her mouth pulled down at the corners.

He gave her a lopsided smile and pretended everything was fine. They didn't get to town often, and she was disappointed. "I didn't say that. You want to get something to eat?"

"I kind of hoped we would."

Luke looked down at her. In the sunlight, her hair shone like a new copper penny.

"Then that's what we do," he said, keeping his voice casual. He could manage to get down a cup of coffee.

He took her arm and tucked her close to his left side, keeping his gun hand free. Eyes checking every face in the crowd on the sidewalk, he walked her across the street and into the little café.

About halfway home, he turned the buggy off the road onto a sandy trail.

"Where're we going?" she asked.

"Someplace private so we can talk." He looked over at her. "We've got a lot of fighting to make up for."

They crossed a covered bridge, its board sides plastered with notices and bright circus posters. The buggy rolled over a small rise, then turned off into the protection of a line of trees and stopped. For several minutes, Luke looked straight ahead, not speaking.

Emily shifted around in her seat. "What happened in town?"

"Looks like Bart went and hired himself a gun. Name's Kid Haldane. He butted into a conversation Will Baxter and I were having, and he pulled a gun on Will for no reason. I threatened to pull mine to keep him from shooting Will."

She swallowed. Her face went dead white.

He stared into the trees, not wanting to say the rest. "Will Baxter's got three little kids. He's a family man, a churchman. If Haldane had shot Will, I would have killed him, Em."

"And Haldane might've killed you."

"Not likely."

"You're that good?"

He nodded.

She looked dazed. He stared into the cool, green depths of her eyes. Worry for him, mixed with disapproval of what he'd done, moved in the back of them.

He took her hand in both of his. "I know how you feel about me and guns, and I know it upsets you, but I didn't shoot. I didn't want to shoot. Instead, I talked him out of it."

As he said it, an odd feeling of satisfaction welled up. Exhilaration. That piece of him he thought he'd never lose—the part that could so easily destroy another – didn't surface. He hadn't wanted to kill Haldane.

She looked at him as if she'd never seen him before. "And Will's alive because of what you *said*."

He let out a long sigh. "And because I had a gun to back it up."

She smiled, as if the sun had come out behind her face. "A gun you didn't use. I'm so proud of you."

Eyes closed, she began praying for him, thanking the Lord and asking Him to show them both the right way.

Luke looked down at her hand in his, surprised and moved. He squirmed, a little embarrassed. Being prayed over in a buggy with a pretty girl holding his hand was a new experience. He closed his eyes to block her out and listened to her words asking forgiveness and comfort for him.

No one had ever prayed for him before.

Then something odd happened.

For the first time in years he knew God was listening. To Emily, yes, but waiting for him, Luke Sullivan, to open his mouth and say something.

He wanted to pray. Oh, how he wanted to pray. But he didn't know how to begin. He screwed his eyes shut and tried to form the words in his mind.

He felt . . . different . . . surrounded by a faith so fierce he nearly went down on his knees.

God was waiting.

Lord, help me. I don't know what to say . . .

His plea went winging upward, hanging on to her prayer like the tail on a kite.

A soft feeling of peace wrapped around him.

Emily spread her hand and wound her fingers through his. He squeezed her hand tight. The next time she paused for breath, he added a strong "Amen" out loud, hoping God understood that sometimes a man gets other things on his mind.

He untied the ribbon under her chin holding her hat in place and slipped it off her head. He pulled her to him and looked at her for a long moment. "You know I love you, don't you?" His voice was quiet.

A small smile lit her face. "I do now."

Soft, warm arms wrapped around his neck. As soon as she touched her lips to his, he gathered her close and kissed her long and hard.

Haldane stayed hidden in the trees, watching the couple in the buggy. When he'd seen enough, he headed the Appaloosa for the X-Bar-L.

"What do you mean you've already met him?" Axel demanded of the tall, light-haired cowboy standing in front of his desk.

"In town, at the pool hall," Haldane answered, omitting a few details of his meeting with Luke Sullivan. "We chatted a little, you might say. By the way, I don't like him."

Axel leaned back in the chair, his face hard. "That makes two of us. He's an ex-vigilante from Lewistown and more trouble than a nest of snakes."

Haldane's eyebrows lifted a fraction. "Lewistown?"

"Stuart's group."

"He's bad news."

"Sullivan quit them. You'll never see them."

Haldane was quiet for a moment, then looked up. He nodded. "You're paying me a lot of money, Mr. Axel. Who – and how you want this handled?"

"There's an old man who knows too much." Bart leaned forward and studied the wiry blond man across the desk. "Unless I can head it off, I'm going to have a range war on my hands, one I'll lose. I've got a boundary dispute with an orphanage coming up."

"An orphanage? You serious?"

"Place is called New Hope, about five miles from here. Sullivan runs their herd now."

Haldane gave a quiet whistle of surprise. Hitching a pant leg up, he sat on the corner of the desk.

Axel swiveled his chair around and stared through his office window at the hot July afternoon and his barn beyond.

"Sullivan's taking New Hope's deed and Jupiter Jackson, an old guy with a long memory, into the land office in Billings next Tuesday," Axel said. "I don't want either the old man or the deed to get there."

"How about Sullivan?"

Axel swore and slammed his fist on the desk, his face dark with anger. "He's been trouble for twenty years. Everything comes back to him. There's a woman I want at New Hope. He's even in my way there."

"She a pretty young redhead, by any chance?"

Axel shot him a hard look. "Why do you ask that?"

"Because he had a girl with him in town. I followed them into the woods. From what I saw, he's a lot more than *in your way*. Any man kiss a girl like that better be planning on marrying her. And from the way your lady friend had her arms wrapped around his neck, I'd say she's sweet on him."

Axel stretched across to the brass humidor and unwrapped a dark Havana. He wetted the cigar between his lips and lit it. "I waited months for things to calm down at New Hope with my girl. And now, looks like Sullivan's gonna get her, too," he said.

Haldane slid off the desk and looked down at Axel. "Not if he ain't around, he won't."

"But he is."

"That can be changed."

Axel puffed the cigar, his cheeks sucking in and out until the tip glowed red hot. "How much?"

"You can afford it."

CHAPTER 14

Right after breakfast Tuesday morning, Luke pulled up in front of the house driving a green ranch wagon with a bowed canvas top. Emily grabbed a satchel off the porch and ran down the walk. Cheeks flushed, she hopped on the wheel hub and handed up the brown traveling bag. He threw it in the wagon, stretched for her hand, then pulled her up next to him.

"Did you put my things in the back?" She bounced around on the seat and peered inside the wagon at the jumble of blankets and cooking gear and food supplies and extra clothes. He'd never seen her so excited, except for the night he met her. His mouth curved into a broad grin.

"I could drive a herd from here to Texas with less stuff than you have back there," he said.

"Drive, Mr. Sullivan, just drive." She flicked her hand with a flourish.

"Hold on, there. Not so fast. Where's the deed?"

"In there." She pointed to the brown satchel in back.

He worked on a pair of buckskin gloves, gathered the lines in his hands, and slapped the reins. "Giddap!"

The wagon lurched. The horses moved out on command, taking them down the lane. At the end, harnesses jingling, they swung a wide, walking turn through the gate and onto the road to Repton and Jupiter Jackson's house.

As soon as they were out of sight of New Hope, Emily propped her feet up on the footboard. She ran a thumb around her hat brim and sniffed, looking at him with mock seriousness. Thrusting out her hand to him, she said, "Name's Clyde, mister. What's yours?"

Amusement spread across his face as he took the small hand and shook it. He chuckled and eyed her clothes. "You look ridiculous. You know that, don't you?"

Instead of a dress, she wore a blue denim jacket and boys' Levi's, a plaid flannel shirt, and thick-soled work shoes laced to her ankles. Her hair was pinned on top of her head and stuffed under a wide-brimmed black cavalry hat that was too big for her.

"Molly and I thought it was a good idea. No one will ever guess it's me. If we meet anyone, they'll think I'm one of the boys from school."

"From a distance, you just might pass for a boy. But not up close." His gaze slipped to the telltale fullness of her shirtfront. Bunching all four reins in one hand, he stripped off the bandanna around his neck. "Here," he said gruffly, "put this on.

And button up your jacket. For your information, boys don't have bustlines."

"I didn't think you noticed such things," she mumbled, her cheeks on fire.

He fixed his eyes on the big swaying rear ends of the horses straight ahead and smiled. "I noticed."

❧

Jupiter Jackson lived with his granddaughter and her husband in a cabin deep in a pine woods outside Repton. The old man was ready and waiting in the yard, alerted by the dogs barking long before the wagon came into view. His granddaughter fussed over him, helping him up, while Luke loaded his gear into the back.

"Morning, Emily," Jupiter whispered out of the side of his mouth as he settled his back against the seat.

Her jaw dropped. "How'd you know it was me?"

Jupiter arranged his new hat on his head and spat over the side. His eyes twinkled at her. "I may be old, girl, but I ain't blind."

And she wasn't dumb. A few miles down the road, she climbed into the back of the wagon and rearranged a few things inside her shirt.

Luke held the horses down to a monotonous, slogging walk that ate the miles slowly but relentlessly, a pace the horses could keep up for hours without tiring.

Emily listened to the rise and fall of hooves and the crunch of wagon wheels. A few months ago, these sounds would've been foreign to her. Now they were part of her life, and she found them oddly comforting. She could hardly remember what the *clang* of a streetcar sounded like.

The voices of the two men droned beside her, discussing the weather. Jupiter's voice was frail and thin; Luke's, a deep rumble.

Jupiter scanned the sky overhead. "Probably gonna rain in a bit. Moon had a ring around it last night."

"Maybe, but I've been fooled by that before," Luke said, smiling past her at the older man.

"One of the few advantages of getting old, my boy, is experience – being able to read the signs of what's coming at you."

"I'm in no hurry for that." Luke threw his head back and laughed, a hearty sound that warmed her and made her smile.

He doesn't do that often enough, she thought, watching the creases fold in around his mouth.

Luke had taken his jacket off and unbuttoned the collar of the rough blue cotton shirt he wore. Relaxed, hat tipped up on the back of his head, he held the reins loosely in his big hands and let the horses plod along by themselves.

How could she ever understand a man whose lips told her one thing and his eyes another?

Sometimes she thought there were three of him. The one she liked least was the public one, the ex-vigilante, arrogant. Pulling a gun on him was suicide, they said. She'd seen that Sullivan only once, the night he took her off the stagecoach, and that one was squint-eyed and scary.

Then there was the quiet, serious Sullivan who smiled

easily and was comfortable with books and figures. That one had talent and brains.

And lastly, there was the private Sullivan, slow talking and gentle. She didn't know that one well yet and suspected he was like that only with her. Whenever he kissed her, he was a different man. His guard dropped then, the toughness gone, replaced by a teasing playfulness.

The road to Billings stretched for miles across a pheasant-colored countryside. The vast emptiness of the prairie cast a spell, a landscape that swallowed people up. Plains, waist-high with grass, rolled from one horizon to the other, broken here and there with high flat-topped hills.

Much of this land before her belonged to New Hope, the deed said. Between the dirt road and a steep slope off in the distance, a herd of longhorns grazed.

"Are those ours?" she asked Luke and pointed to the herd.

"Should be, but they're not. They're Axel's." He bit the words off.

"How many does he have?"

"Close to ten thousand head. Most of the other stockmen on this range run under five thousand. New Hope's the smallest. When I was a boy, we used to run about five thousand, but nothing like that now. The herd is way down." He swept his arm in a wide arc in front of him. "With all this land, we could run double that and not crowd anyone else out."

"Sounds like you want to change things."

"I'm going to, but it takes time. And money."

Emily turned back to studying the landscape, overwhelmed by the enormousness of the rangeland in question. Uneasy, she chewed at her bottom lip. No wonder Molly expected trouble. They weren't talking acres of land; they were talking miles of land.

They ate lunch from their laps—cold chicken and biscuits and a jar of pears, and buttermilk for Jupiter and her. Luke hated the stuff, so he drank water. Occasionally, he handed her the lines, jumped down, and walked beside the wagon for exercise. Only once did they stop to rest, letting the horses drink from a rocky little stream before resuming the slow trek toward Billings.

In late afternoon, Luke spied what he'd been looking for: a sheltered place to make camp for the night. A mile distant, a flat hilltop with a few pines butted against an outcropping of rock. Whistling, calling to the horses, he turned the team off the road and headed them across the plain for the cliff and the trees.

"Whoa," Luke called, and stopped the team in the shade.

As soon as he had the animals unhitched and picketed, he looked for a spring and brought back buckets of water for the horses. Then he was off again, this time to gather wood and kindling for a fire.

Inside the wagon, Emily bustled around for the makings of supper, digging out the cornmeal and a slab of bacon, clattering through a stack of cooking pots for a knife to slice the meat. She didn't hear Jupiter the first time he called, but when he beat his fist on the side of the wagon and shouted, "Listen to me," she stuck her head out.

"Go tell Luke someone's coming." Jupiter jerked his thumb in the direction of the road. Kicking up a cloud of dust behind him, a lone rider on a spotted horse was cantering directly for them.

"Maybe he's just—"

Jupiter's eyes snapped. "And maybe he ain't. Git, I said!"

Alarmed at the urgency in his voice, Emily grabbed her hat and scrambled across the pile of cookware in the wagon, dropped over the back, and darted into the woods, running through the trees. Luke was nowhere to be seen. She turned left and scrambled through a tangle of underbrush leading up to the top of the cliff, yelling, "Luke! Luuuu-ke!"

Only the raucous call of jays overhead answered her. Panting, she leaned against a tree at the top to catch her breath. She cupped her palms and yelled again.

"Luuuu—"

A hand shot around from behind the tree and clamped hard over her mouth. Instinctively she clawed at the hand over her face and struggled to break loose.

"Shhhhh! I saw him, too," Luke said softly.

Her knees sagged with relief. He eased his hold on her and came around the tree. Clutching her throat, Emily stared at him and gulped. "I almost had a heart attack."

"Sorry, but I had to shut you up," he said, his face tight with tension. "Who's coming?"

"I don't know. Jupiter sent me after you."

From a distance, the horseman's hat hid the upper part of his face. Although it was warm, he wore gloves—fringed leather gauntlets—and a black jacket buttoned tight at the throat. He rode the black and white horse up close, stopping a few feet from Jupiter.

"Evening, gramps."

Jupiter narrowed his eyes. "My name is Jackson," he said. "Jupiter Jackson. I didn't catch yours."

The horse shuffled sideways as the rider drew off a glove. "Who was the boy who ran in the woods as I came up?"

"You didn't see no boy. I'm alone."

"You're lying, old man. Call him back."

Jupiter stiffened, staring up at the rider. "You better state your business, mister."

"I said, call him back." The words dropped like stones. He slipped a Winchester rifle from the saddle boot and pointed it at Jupiter's chest. Smoothly, he pumped the metal lever out and back, the click of the shell as it chambered sounding unnaturally loud. His finger curled around the trigger.

Jupiter blinked rapidly, staring up at the hard-eyed man on the horse. "Now, mister, get on out of here and—"

Boom!

The blast hurled Jupiter backward to the ground, his arms outflung. Feebly, he jerked his legs in a futile attempt to sit up.

Boom!

Emily spun around at the shots. Luke grabbed her, jerked her to the ground, then crawled to the edge of the cliff and looked over. Through the back of the wagon, he saw the stranger tearing open boxes, dumping out bags of flour and cornmeal. On his stomach, Luke inched backward to Emily.

"I'm going down. He just shot Jupiter." His face was hard, his lips a thin white line.

She grabbed his arm, panic exploding in her mind. "Don't go, please don't go." From his expression, he intended to even the score.

He shook her hand off. "If I tell you to cover me, do you know what I mean?" His eyes bored into hers.

She nodded. "You want me to shoot anybody shooting at you, but I don't want you to go."

"I have to. If he doesn't find what he came for, he'll come after us."

Luke thumbed a handful of bullets out of his gun belt and slipped them into her shirt pocket, then pulled one of the Colts from its holster and handed it to her. He pointed to a shelf of rock jutting over the edge. "Lie flat on that and wait till I get down there. When I start running toward the wagon, you start shooting at the back of it and keep shooting. Understand?"

She bit her lips to stop them from trembling.

"Don't worry. You won't hit him. You're too far away, but I'm hoping he won't realize that. Just keep him pinned down until I get close enough to get him."

She took a deep breath, held it a moment, then let it out. Gun in hand, she started crawling out on the piece of rimrock.

"Emily?" When she turned, he said, "Remember to cock the hammer back each time."

She gave a little spastic nod and continued working her way out onto the jutting piece of rock.

"Emily?"

She looked back over her shoulder again.

"Please don't shoot *me*."

❧

On her stomach, Emily elbowed herself forward and peered over the edge. Luke had pulled their wagon well off the road into a wide meadow with a tiny brook and a steep-sided butte. A small plateau topped the butte and overlooked the clearing a hundred feet below. Yellow sandstone boulders from an old rockfall lay at the base of the cliff, and a grove of young cottonwoods grew in the clearing beyond.

She scanned the clearing. Those trees in the clearing weren't big enough to hide her, let alone someone the size of Luke. With no cover he'd be out in the open, an easy target for someone with a rifle. Then, in a flash of understanding, she knew why he'd stationed her up there – to protect her. She squinted at the big Colt pistol clutched in her right hand. It was all she had to help him.

She took in every detail of the clearing, the rock pile, the wagon, the horses, memorizing where things were. If Luke got into trouble, he'd need her help.

She sucked in a deep breath. Who was she kidding? He already *was* in trouble. She shoved herself backward to the steep little path she'd come up on, a narrow strip of dirt, no wider than a rabbit run. Shoulders hunched, she started down, sliding some of the way on her backside. At the bottom she crawled through the underbrush up to the rock pile at the foot of the cliff. Slowly, she eased the bushes apart and peeked out.

The wagon was twenty or thirty feet away, its long green side almost right in front of her. She wiped her sweaty palms down her thighs and mentally positioned Luke and herself. If the gunman was at twelve o'clock, she and Luke were at eight and four.

Her mouth went dry. She was closer to the gunman than Luke was. She took a deep breath and stared at the gun in her hand. The gunman inside the wagon was tossing cutlery and metal plates around.

She stretched out on her stomach under a thick, droopy bush and waited. The instant Luke broke into the open, she'd begin firing to hold the gunman off. She stiffened.

Luke eased himself out from behind a boulder.

There he goes!

She thumbed the hammer back as Luke bolted across the clearing. Zigzagging, he headed for the wagon.

The spotted horse saw him and whinnied. A rifle barrel poked through the curtains in the back of the wagon and pointed at Luke.

Emily aimed at the curtain and squeezed the trigger.

BANG!

The Colt jumped in her hand. Her mouth fell open when the side of the wagon splintered. She *did* it! The rifle barrel jerked back inside.

Luke fired three more shots into the wagon. Emily joined

in, holding the gun steady and whispering to herself, "Cock the hammer – fire. Cock the hammer – fire."

The gunman leaped out the front of the wagon and squatted behind the wheel. Luke got off a shot that nicked the edge of the wheel.

Emily shot again. This time, the gunman snapped his rifle around and fired back in her direction.

SPANG!

The slug struck a big rock alongside her and sent chips flying. Startled, she gave an angry huff and crawled away. Her fear faded, replaced with determination. Up on her knees, she held the Colt in a two-handed grip and fired twice more. One bullet went through the wagon and out the front; the other ripped through the canvas top and ricocheted, clanging the iron pots inside.

Luke fired almost at once from the other direction, the shots so close together it sounded like a small battle. The gunman hunched toward his horse. He yelled something unintelligible, threw himself into the saddle, and kicked the horse into a leaping gallop for the road.

Emily scrambled to her feet and tore out of the bushes after him. Reloading on the run, she and Luke chased the rider, firing until they heard the frantic, fruitless clicks of their empty guns.

Luke swept up his hat, which had fallen off in the run. Looking at her, he brushed the dust off. "Why didn't you stay up there where I told you? You could've gotten yourself killed," he said, his lips barely moving with the words.

Her chin shot up. "And so could you. There was no way you could dodge across that clearing and not get shot. You needed help down here, not up there."

He dropped an arm around her shoulder and hugged her. "You're right. Didn't mean to snap at you, but you scared me to death. Coming in close like that and both of us shooting is what drove him off. You probably saved our lives."

That night Emily held the lantern while Luke dug Jupiter's grave. Driving the shovel in savagely, his dark shadow swept over her as he attacked the ground, wrenching out the earth, propelled by sorrow and grief and anger. When he finished, he leaned on the shovel for a moment, rib cage heaving. His face, when he climbed out of the grave, frightened her.

"I loved this old man," he said, wrapping Jupiter tenderly in a blanket. Together they lowered him into the hole and covered him over with dirt. Luke placed three heavy stones to mark the grave, then stood silently, hat in his hands, his head bowed.

Shoulders sagging, he turned to her. "That's the best we can do for now. We'll talk to Sheriff Tucker and bring him back here. Jupiter's family will want a proper burial."

"You were praying back there, weren't you?" she said quietly.

A mixture of surprise and embarrassment flitted across his

face. "I didn't realize it. I guess I was." Not looking at her, he led her away from the gravesite.

"No one knew we were going to Billings, so it must have been a robber, someone looking for travelers on their way to Billings," she said.

Luke took her hand. Winding his fingers through hers, he shook his head. "I'm afraid he was hunting us. The horse belongs to Axel's new hired gun, Haldane. He wanted something, and the only thing we've got that Axel would want is the deed. I'm afraid Haldane found it."

"No, he didn't. I put it in a safe place." From under her shirt she withdrew a large piece of heavy tan paper and held it out to him.

Puzzled, he frowned at the deed in his hand. "Why did you put it there?"

"To flatten my front after your remark in the wagon about bustlines."

The corners of his mouth dug in. "Guess I'll have to watch everything I say to you. In a way, it was kind of a compliment."

She met his gaze directly. "I didn't think so."

"Then you know nothing about men."

In case Haldane returned after dark, they dragged their bedrolls up the cliff and spread them out under an overhanging tree away from the edge.

"Why don't you get some sleep? I'm going to watch for a

while." He sat and leaned against the trunk, the Colt within easy reach.

In minutes he heard her squirming. She rolled over and sighed, evidently trying to find a soft spot. He barely noticed how hard the ground was. In ten years of trail-bossing and chasing cows, he'd probably slept on the ground more than in a bed. Came natural now. But not to this soft-skinned little teacher.

Holding the Colt, he sat motionless, listening. A low overcast moved in and hid the stars. Night stretched. Shadows deepened. The silence was profound.

His throat ached with the hurt of losing Jupiter. Raw anger welled up again. Mentally, he ticked off ways to get even with Axel, then shook his head hard, as if to clear it. In Lewistown, perhaps, but not here. He lived at New Hope now, and so did Emily, which meant there could be only one way: the law.

An owl ghosted in, feathered wings sweeping soundlessly. It landed in the branches overhead and went into its nightly routine. The ominous snarls and whistles sent Emily crawling for Luke, fast. Her knee rammed his leg in the dark, and she sprawled across him. He hauled her up and sat her beside him.

She shuddered. "What *is* that?"

"An owl." He smiled in the dark.

"I thought it was a wildcat." Her confident little teacher's voice cracked.

"It's all right, City Girl," he said, and covered her hand with his.

He heard her swallow. "I'm not upset anymore. I don't know how to thank you. You saved my life today."

"And you saved mine, so we're even."

"I think I'm all right now."

"Well, I'm not." Luke pried her twisted hands apart and wound his fingers through hers. She gripped his hand in response.

Guilt tightened his chest. So much had happened to her today. She'd seen things, done things that no woman ought to. She needed someone now, needed the closeness and comfort of another human being. He puffed his cheeks and let out a quiet breath. And so did she.

He'd never held her like this, and never at night. She made a satisfied little sound and inched closer to him. He composed his face and concentrated on keeping his emotions in check.

She knew what he was, what he had been. She was a lady. Under other circumstances, she wouldn't have let him get within a mile of her. But the attraction between them got around that. He held her tighter.

Miles away, the horizon flickered with silent bursts of lightning.

"Looks like Jupiter was right about the rain," she said.

"True, except *that* one is someone else's storm. The last thing we need tonight is to get soaked."

The owl shrieked again. This time, Emily yawned. "I feel better just knowing you're here. I'm so tired, I'm falling asleep sitting up."

He relaxed his hold on her as she moved toward her bedroll. He debated with himself about kissing her good night.

No. Definitely not.

Kissing her wasn't a good idea. He was still churned up inside, and the way he felt tonight, it wouldn't end with just a kiss.

He pushed to his feet. "Go to sleep. I'm going to check things out up there."

CHAPTER
15

The clock on the Billings depot said nine fifteen the next morning when Emily and Luke rattled across the railroad tracks into town. Except for a sweeper pushing a broom and a cowboy asleep on a luggage wagon, the train station was deserted.

Nicknamed *Magic City*, Billings had sprung out of the prairie almost overnight when the Northern Pacific came through on its way west.

The city was only two years old, but you'd never know it, Emily thought. Workmen were everywhere. Hammers pounded and saws whined, building more hotels, shops, and saloons. There were fortunes to be made here, and cowboys, gold prospectors, cattlemen, and settlers flooded in by train, steamboat, and wagon.

It was rough and noisy, with a saloon every thirty feet, a place where cowboys unwound and relaxed – or wound up and hoo-rawed—after a long cattle drive to the railroad. The streets of Billings, unlike those in Helena, the territorial capital, ran straight as an arrow. In Helena, the streets twisted back on themselves, snakelike curves laid out deliberately to cut down on the gunfights.

Billings struggled for respectability, realizing its prosperity was tied directly to the success of the big ranches. To ensure this, the town and the Northern Pacific jointly appointed a yardmaster to oversee the honest shipment of cattle.

Emily wrinkled her nose as they passed the stockyards. A line of cattle cars stood empty on a nearby siding, doors open. Only a few steers milled in the muddy lot.

"A few hours ago," Luke said, "that stockyard was a cloud of stinking dust, bawling cattle, cussing yard hands, and hooves running up the ramps to the cars."

She shook her head. "Sounds awful, and you just love it."

Laughing, he reached over and patted her hand. "It's my business."

Luke drove the wagon to Stuncard's Livery, where the horses would be unhitched and fed and watered. After he'd seen to the animals, he led her across the street, smiling down at her on his arm. A little thrum of pleasure skipped through her. He'd been doing that a lot this morning.

She looked nice, and she knew it. Instead of the boy denims she'd worn yesterday, today she'd changed into a rosy pink dress she'd made last week especially for this trip to the land office. Her hair was held back with ribbon that matched the dress.

A guest came out of the Headquarters Hotel and tipped his hat at her. Luke gave him a curt nod and hurried her on by. Every time she stopped to look in a store window, he kept looking over his shoulder for Haldane.

When a screen door slammed, Luke shoved Emily against the wall of the building alongside. He spun around into a half crouch in front of her, his gun out and up and in his hand. Across the street, two ladies in big hats dropped their packages and ran squealing into a store. Emily hustled him into a café behind them to get him off the street and calm him down.

He slouched into a chair in a corner at the back of the café, red-faced. She went to the counter and ordered coffee for both of them.

"What's the matter with you? You're scaring everyone to death, including me," she said, putting the cups on the table.

"Just jumpy, I guess. I wish we hadn't come. I'm afraid something else is going to happen." His eyes softened in a slow smile for her.

Her cheeks warmed, and she looked down at her coffee cup. He wanted to kiss her. "Don't look at me like that in public," she whispered.

"How am I supposed to look at you?" he asked quietly.

"I don't know."

"Neither do I."

She looked over the cup at him. His mask of cool indifference didn't fool her a bit. He wasn't as tough as he pretended to be. He was as unsure of himself as she was in this relationship, seemed torn between wanting to stay and wanting to run away. He picked up his coffee cup and slid his free hand over hers on the table. She smiled. For now, at least, he'd decided to stay.

"The other day in the buggy, you said you loved me. Did you mean it?" Inside her chest, her heart waited for the answer.

With a long, deep sigh, he turned her hand over and worked his fingers through hers. "I meant it, but I didn't mean to say it," he said. "Not yet, anyway," he added softly.

His face had gone soft, his lips somehow fuller. "We're going to do this right, you and me. And we both need more time. You especially." He paused. The café owner was wiping off a nearby table.

When the owner moved to the front of the store again, Emily turned to Luke. "More time for what?"

"To get used to living out here, for one thing."

She gave a small huff. "To get used to *you*, you mean."

"That too. Give yourself six months, maybe a year. You're a little city girl. You know nothing about western men."

She smiled. "I think you're the one who needs time – to get used to *me*."

He chuckled and sipped his coffee. "I'm already used to you."

"Yes, but you don't like me *that* way."

He gave her a look she didn't understand and let his breath out slowly. "I like you very much that way." He pulled back and touched his thumb to her chin. "I thought you knew that, also, from the other day in the buggy."

When she'd prayed for him.

Understanding washed over her. Luke didn't say it – couldn't say it yet – but he was just beginning to get things straight with God, and he didn't want to mess it up.

Out in the street again, Luke stopped a workman carrying boards on his shoulder and asked where the land office
was. The man pointed to a nondescript log building squeezed
between the blacksmith and the saddlery. From the sawmill
across the street came the shrieking whine of a ripsaw and the
resinous smell of cut pine.

Luke and Emily spent two hours at a long mahogany counter with the land office's big registration book opened out flat,
painstakingly comparing the boundaries listed there with New
Hope's original deed signed by Monsieur Olivier.

Ed Watson, the registrar, tapped his finger on the deed.
"As you can see, Mr. Sullivan, the deeds are identical, even to
the note up here in the corner. I don't speak French, so I don't
know what it says, but I reckon it just clarifies something in
the deed." Ed Watson pushed his small, round glasses up onto
his forehead.

"It does," Luke said. "When Olivier wrote this deed, there
was no Yellowstone River. He called it what the Indians called
it—Elk River. That's what this note says."

Ed Watson flipped his glasses back down and peered at
the words again. "I don't read French, sir."

"Neither do I, but Miss McCarthy here does," Luke said.
"Emily, would you translate, please?"

When she finished, Watson whistled softly and shook his
head. "That's a fair-sized chunk of ground you're talking about,
Mr. Sullivan. I'll have to talk to Helena about this. I don't see
a problem, mind you—this deed is good as gold, but it'll take
time to straighten out, verify the French, and get the proper
name of the river put on it. It's been eighty-some years since
this deed was filed."

Watson pointed to the chimney-shaped piece of land belonging to both New Hope and the Crows. "But this section here"—he shook his head—"now, that may be a problem. Montana Territory has nothing to do with that. It's a federal matter, you see. Or was. You have to talk to Washington about that."

Luke stiffened. "Washington? How long will that take?"

Ed Watson snorted in disgust. "May be easier just to deed it to the Crows yourselves."

"Can we do that? Legally, I mean?"

"I'll have to check. But it's complicated. Once upon a time, the piece of land you're talking about was French government land, then Olivier's private land, then sold to the U.S. government, who ceded it to the Crows. Now, technically the Crows are a foreign nation, too, so it looks like you got three countries involved here. And our government made a mistake, you say, and gave a piece of New Hope land to the Crows?"

"No," Luke interrupted. "The other way around—they gave Crow land to New Hope."

"See what I mean?" Watson said. "And now you want to give something that belonged to the United States of America back to the Crow Nation—who already owns it—so it's really not yours to give." He shrugged his shoulders and turned his palms up. "May take another eighty years to straighten this one out."

Off to one side, Emily was busily copying the French from their deed to two separate pieces of paper. She slid them across to the clerk. "Send one of these along to Helena. They'll need to verify my translation, anyway." Quietly, she added, "And file this with the one you have here. That way, at least you'll have one full copy in case . . . in case something happens to our deed on the way home, I mean."

⁂

"Well, that was one wasted morning," Luke grumbled, and shut the door behind him.

Emily took his arm and let him lead her toward the hotel down the street for lunch.

"Look over there! Hey, Luke!" a voice called from across the street.

Luke snapped around, his face breaking into a huge grin. "Hey, boss!"

Three men in dusty work pants and Stetsons jumped into the street and headed across to Luke. Arms outstretched, they met Luke in the middle of the street, shaking hands, thumping backs, and laughing.

On the sidewalk again, Granville Stuart swept off his hat and bowed to Emily. "And who would this beautiful young lady be?"

Luke introduced her to his old boss and Will Lawson and Burt Miller, two of Stuart's ranch hands from the big D-S ranch in Lewistown.

Nice men, Emily thought. They seemed so normal, impressive even. Not at all like what she'd heard about them.

"What are you doing in Billings?" Stuart asked Luke.

Within minutes, Luke was explaining why they were there and what had happened to Jupiter yesterday. Stuart listened somber-faced and nodded. Emily's gaze jumped between the two men. From what Luke had told her, Stuart was a powerful politician with a sharp legal mind. Luke valued his opinion.

President of the Territorial Council, Stuart was widely known and respected. Emily smiled to herself. Though Stuart was dignified and courteous, this day his face was dirty and he was wearing work clothes, dressed as roughly as his men.

"Excuse my appearance," he said. "We got nine hundred head out this morning. The cattle train that left a while ago was taking our beef to Chicago. I'll follow them up on the train tomorrow and finish some business there."

"You drove them down here yourself, did you?" Luke asked with a grin.

"Me and the rest of the crew. They're all around here some-place." Stuart narrowed his eyes at Luke. "You see, when I lost my high-and-mighty ranch manager, I wound up having to do a lot of his work myself."

And the nature of that "work" disturbed Emily. Luke was so gentle and easygoing with her, she almost couldn't believe what they said he'd done with Stuart. And yet, when he took her to Repton, she'd seen for herself how certain men shrank away from him, their faces guarded. No one had proof of what Stuart's committee had done—still was doing, some said—but just knowing Luke used to work for him was unsettling.

True or not, horse thieves and rustlers had cleared out of Montana Territory.

A glow of pride warmed Emily. "How did you two meet?" she asked.

Stuart's eyes crinkled with laughter. "I won him in a card game."

Emily cleared her throat quietly. "You what?"

"You heard right," Stuart said. "He was a twenty-year-old trail boss at the Double A ranch, about fifty miles west of my place," Stuart told her. "A trail boss that young? Unheard of.

"Six years ago, Angus Aberdeen, owner of the Double A, ran into me in a saloon in Helena, and we played poker together. Angus, as usual, put away a lot of bourbon, and when he does, he talks and he talks. Started bragging about his good eye for cattle, for picking horseflesh, and especially for hiring help. To hear Angus tell it, his Double A had the best crew in all Montana Territory." Stuart chuckled. "Just about glowing with whiskey, he was, boasting about his crew and mentioning his young trail boss. I just wished he'd stop running his mouth and pay attention to the game. I was getting some really good hands that night.

"'Why, he even doubles as my bookkeeper,' Angus says to me.

"That perked my ears up. I asked him if he let him handle his money, and Angus said of course he did. I looked at him like I thought he was crazy.

"And Angus looks me right back and says, 'He ciphers better than I do and can do it in his head besides. He don't gamble a-tall and don't drink, neither. Rides five miles to church every Sunday, regular as a clock.'

"Disgusted, I threw my hand in and said Sullivan sounded like a saint.

"And Angus comes right back, rakes my money in, and says, 'Not quite. A little too quick with his fists. Still in all, I trust him with anything I got—anything 'cept my daughters, that is.'"

Emily stiffened. Turning, she raised her eyebrows at Luke.

Luke covered his mouth and turned away, his shoulders heaving. "I didn't know he even had daughters," Luke said.

This time Stuart's eyebrows went up.

"By then I was getting interested," Stuart continued. "I was just starting the DHS and good people are hard to find up here, but long-winded old Angus was tired of losing and ready to quit. I kept talking to keep him there. I asked him if this boy trail boss of his could shoot.

"And Angus gets all puffed up and says, 'Shoots like a hired gun. Got a draw like chain lightning. Awesome. Downright awesome.'"

Stuart nodded at Emily. "If I wanted to steal Sullivan away from Angus—and by that time, I did—then that was one card game I had to lose, so I threw in winning hands, kept Angus talking and taking my money till I got all the particulars on his trail boss and exactly where I could find him. I had to track him down quietly, you see. Couldn't very well just ride up to the Double A and offer him a job.

"Two months after that game, I had Sullivan and his horse moved up to Lewistown. And now, I understand, he's settled in all nice and comfortable out there at New Hope."

Stuart rubbed his hands together with an evil smile at Luke. "I'm looking forward to seeing Molly again. Haven't seen her in a couple years. By any chance, she play poker?"

Afraid Haldane might be lying in wait for Luke and Emily, Stuart and his crew of cowboys rode along to New Hope with them. "A little show of support never hurts," Stuart said.

"Particularly if he recognizes *you*," Luke said softly.

Stuart nodded. "Decent folk don't know us, but the outlaws do. If Haldane recognizes us, he'll think twice before he pulls something like this again on you. The implication is we'll come get him. And we will."

At the spot where they'd camped the night before, Luke reined the horses off the road and into the clearing to see their campsite and Jupiter's grave. Stuart and twelve D-S cowboys rode in with them.

Luke took them up the cliff, and they sited where they were and where the shooter had been. Fanning out over the clearing, riding and walking, they checked the ground for tracks and found spent rifle brass. The cartridge casings could identify the rifle they came from. Luke slipped the brass casings into his shirt pocket.

"I'll turn these over to the sheriff," he said.

From the wagon, Emily watched the interaction of Luke and the men he used to work with. There was an easy give and take between them all, and yet something stamped him and Stuart with an attitude she'd seen before. Her throat went dry. All lawmen had it.

Two hours later, thirteen men on horseback escorted a green ranch wagon, its canvas sides and bowed top peppered with bullet holes, up the lane and into New Hope's courtyard.

Doors slammed. Squealing children poured out of the house and down the front steps. One of them, four-year-old Teddy, was beating a pot with a spoon. Up the hillside, three boys ran out of the barn and raced down the hill, whooping like Indians.

"Teddy, stop that noise!" Luke bellowed.

Emily jumped over the side of the wagon, skirt flying. On the run she grabbed Teddy, who was heading for the group of men and their horses with his noisy pot.

Stuart, already on the ground, yelled, "Men, hold your horses! These kids are gonna get stepped on."

Restraining Teddy, Emily took his spoon away and shouted over the racket. "They're just excited. They've never seen this much company in their lives." She led Teddy to the wagon and handed him up to Luke.

The D-S men swung down at once and held their horses, while the kids jumped up and down and hollered and hugged everybody.

Granville Stuart, along with two little girls holding his hands, eased himself through the group toward Molly, who was coming down the steps.

Molly threw her arms open. "Grant, what a nice surprise!"

"Molly, sweet thing," he called. "I'd give you a hug, but I got my hands full. I swear, a herd of cattle is easier to handle than all these kids."

Later that afternoon, his face solemn, Luke snapped the reins and drove the buggy away from Jupiter's house. "I'm glad you were along for that," he said to Emily. "I'm no good when a woman starts to cry." He drove at a steady pace down Jupiter's driveway. "I think it helped that we both saw what happened.

There was nothing Jupiter could've done. She needed to know that."

Emily turned away from him in the buggy and waved at the group of men ahead of them on horseback, walking the horses to Repton. Stuart insisted on taking them all to dinner at the Manor House Hotel in Repton. He and his men would stay the night there before returning to Billings tomorrow. His crew would collect the horses, wagons, and other trail equipment they'd left there and head back to Lewistown. Stuart would take the noon train to Chicago.

To Emily's disappointment, Molly begged off because one of the children was sick.

While the Lewistown crew got their horses settled in the Repton livery for the night, Emily strolled the hotel's cobblestone promenade along the White Dog River. Slate green, flecked with foam, the narrow little river tumbled out of a ravine between two mountains and splashed into a wide pool of late summer sunlight.

"Like that?" Luke asked, coming up alongside her.

"It's pretty, a fairy-tale river."

A short man in spectacles, talking with Stuart a few feet away, walked up and joined them. "Excuse me, I couldn't help overhearing," he said. "Small as it is, it's a little workhorse of a river. A mile downstream it powers two mills." He smiled. "If you'll excuse my butting in, I'm John Armstrong, editor of the *Repton Tribune*." He took his hat off. "And you would be the lovely Chicago lady, Miss McCarthy."

Luke stuck his hand out and stepped in before Emily had to respond. "Been a long time. Good to see you again, John."

Armstrong grabbed his hand in a hearty grip. "Luke, I heard

you'd come back. I just heard about Jupiter getting killed. You're going to talk to me about him after a while. Right?"

Luke puffed his cheeks and exhaled hard. "After I talk to the sheriff. How'd you find out?" he asked the editor.

Stuart edged in. "I told him. John recognized me and some of the men. He put two and two together and came up with fourteen."

CHAPTER
16

Fall was roundup.

Just after daybreak, seven riders and a small caravan of mules and wagons loaded with firewood, cooking pots, equipment, and saddles pulled out of the barns at New Hope. A remuda of extra horses, roped together, followed behind, headed across the north pasture for the open range.

Relaxed in the saddle, Luke whistled softly under his breath. The horizon was a misty blur, the pewter sky above stained with the pink streaks of morning. Spreading his arms in a wide stretch, he gave a contented grunt. It was great to be alive on a day like this.

Near a stand of scrubby willows, they began unloading. First thing, Jeb Simson got a hot fire going with the wood they'd brought, put a pot of coffee on to boil, and shoved the branding irons into the pile of burning oak logs to heat. Not until the metal glowed and was ash colored would they be hot enough and fast enough for a quick skin burn.

A column of white smoke billowed and rose. Caught by the early morning breeze, it quickly dissipated and vanished into the sky.

Luke and Henry and Will Brown mounted their horses and trotted toward the herd of brown and black and spotted backs and horns.

"Nice and easy with them. Don't chouse 'em up," Luke called. Working a herd of excited cattle was a nightmare and dangerous. A smart man took nothing for granted with cows. His knees gripped the horse tighter.

Dust swirled. The herd spread out at their approach. Sitting easy in the saddle, the men plunged into the blaring confusion of lowing cattle and clacking horns, letting the horses do the work, shouldering their way into the herd. Bulls bellowed and swept their horns at the men. Luke listened, not with his ears but with his eyes, soaking up all the other signals. One large black bull in particular he watched warily, a thick-muscled giant with a massive chest, a five-foot spread of horn, and an extra doggedness he didn't like at all. Luke let out a quiet hiss of relief. Ponderously dragging its tail on the ground, the big slab-sided steer moved off.

Luke singled out a calf for a head catch and let the reins lie loose. There was a bond, a linkage, between him and the horse. Bugle made a quick dash and worked the youngster's mother to the edge of the herd. She ran, her calf following. When the cow dodged, Bugle gauged instinctively which way she would break, keeping himself between her and the rest of the herd so she couldn't go back. She swerved out right where he wanted her. Bugle sprang forward and cut her off from the calf.

Luke coiled the rope for a quick throw. He stretched up straight in the saddle and whirled the rope over his right shoulder.

"Yaah! Yaah!" he yelled.

The calf raised its head in alarm. Overhand, Luke cast his arm straight forward with a quick leftward twist to his hand. The loop sailed, spreading left, the rope running through his fingers. He played it out. When he had the loop over and ahead of the calf, he stopped it, dropped it. Still spinning, the loop rolled on its side, standing in the air. The calf ran right into it. Luke yanked, taking up the slack, and tightened the noose.

The instant the rope had left Luke's hand, Bugle veered in the opposite direction. He pulled up short, half squatting, digging in, braced for the shock when the animal hit the rope at the other end. The calf hit it, tumbled, grunted, and fell down in a cloud of dust. Sidestepping, always facing the calf, Bugle kept the line taut as Luke dallied the rope around the saddle horn and hauled the animal in.

Together, Luke and Bugle dragged the bawling calf over to the fire. John Cosgrove, a young New Hope hand, worked as a flanker, to help the rider haul a calf in. John grabbed the rope and pulled himself out along the taut line to the straining calf. He seized her tail and twisted her off-balance. The animal dropped onto its shoulder, its hind quarters sticking up. John fell on its neck and pinned her. Luke slid off and jerked the calf's hind legs out from under her, and the calf fell into the dirt.

The branding crew worked fast. John's brother, Tom, moved in quickly on the downed calf and slapped a glowing white-hot iron against the animal's left hip. There was a sizzle of burning flesh. Sides heaving, the calf rolled its eyes and bawled a bewildered cry of pain. The stink of scorched hair and skin rose from a blackened *N-H* still smoking on its flank.

The men jumped back. The calf scrambled to its feet and bucked its way back to its mother.

An hour later, when Luke was working the edge of the herd, a white-spotted bull calf with a torn ear ran by. The blood had dried and crusted.

"Hey, Scully, look at that one."

"Reckon a coyote got him last night?"

"Something sure did."

Bugle sidled closer to cut the calf out of the herd. Luke whirled the lariat and sailed the loop out. As if it knew the rope was coming, the calf cut left. The loop caught one ear and slid off. Bugle swung in sharply after him. Quickly, Luke hauled the rope in, coiled it, getting ready to throw again. The calf broke—not toward the herd and its mother, as the horse expected. Instead, it broke for the open range and darted right in front of him.

Bugle almost ran him down, the big horse's momentum barreling him straight ahead like a runaway locomotive. Luke tried to manhandle him into a pivot, but Bugle couldn't get his legs under him fast enough. Stumbling, he went down on his knees, catapulting Luke out of the saddle and over his head into the dirt. The calf scrambled away, blatting. Belly swinging, its mother lumbered into a swaying run after it.

Luke climbed to his feet and grabbed up his hat. Dusting his pants off, he glared at Bugle. The horse slung its head and blew his lips, as if oblivious to Luke's dirty look.

Back in the saddle, Luke headed into the herd again for another calf, puzzling about the one that got away. *The critter acted like it had been roped before*, he thought.

∾

At noontime Luke slid off fast. Hot and tired, he was stiff up to his shoulders. He poured himself a cup of coffee and drained it, hardly tasting it, trying to wash the grit from his throat and mouth. He felt like he'd been eating dust for hours.

"Whew!" Scully took off his hat and mopped the front of his neck. Carrying his plate of beans and bacon, he crossed to where Luke was and sat down cross-legged facing him. "We must've done fifty this morning."

"Fifty-three, but who's counting," Luke said. Wearily, he leaned back against a tree trunk and closed his eyes. Puffing his cheeks, he let out a long, slow exhale. His shirt was soaked with sweat.

"How long's it been since you done this?" Scully asked, talking around a mouthful of beans.

"Not long enough," his boss said, not opening his eyes.

It had been a long time since he'd had to rope and brand like this himself. On a big spread like Stuart's, it wasn't required. He'd been the boss. But at one time or another in his life, he'd done everything there was to do on a ranch—from line riding to cooking to trail-bossing. He knew cattle like he knew his own name.

But at that moment, tired and sore, Luke wondered if maybe he'd left Stuart's too soon. Over the years he'd saved almost enough to buy a small ranch. It was what he'd always dreamed about—a place of his own, the kind of cows he'd have. And no more wild longhorns. He intended to crossbreed with those white-faced Herefords from Kentucky, a hornless breed. He'd had enough horns to last him a lifetime.

He lay back, cocked his boot up on his knee, and tipped his hat down over his nose.

Build my own house, too, a small place to start.

Funny, whenever he'd imagined it before, the house had always been empty. But now it took no effort at all to slip one cat-eyed redhead and a bunch of babies into that dream. The problem was keeping her out of it.

Easy enough to say when she wasn't around. It was when she wrapped her arms around his neck and kissed him that his mind shut down. Until now, he'd never felt a need for a permanent relationship. Caught in any girl's net, he'd have been miserable. Just the thought of settling down in one place with one woman and raising a family had always turned his insides to jelly. But he'd almost asked Emily to marry him that night on the mountain, and he knew it. And he'd come close again last night when they went for a walk.

A long time ago he'd learned to recognize the marrying look in a girl's eyes. Because he could, he'd always managed to stay two long jumps ahead of the preacher and broke it off before anyone got hurt. Emily didn't have that look. So how come he was waiting for the net to settle around his shoulders? How come he wasn't running this time?

Because she'd brought something into his life, filled a

hollow place inside him that he didn't know was there. And she was on his mind all the time, there when he went to sleep, there when he woke up.

Dear Lord, I hope you know what I'm doing, because I sure don't.

He pushed Emily from his mind and sat up. Luke regarded New Hope's crew, mentally sizing them up. Today was the first chance he'd had to see them work. They did all right, he thought proudly. Old Jeb Simson, his face windburned and tough as rawhide, might limp a little when he walked, the result of a horse falling on him a few years before, but he had cow sense and was wily as they came. Henry Bertel and Will Brown, both his own age, came up from Texas on a cattle drive a few years before and never went back.

The last two were a pair of ropy, towheaded brothers named Cosgrove from over near Billings. Of the two, he liked John better. Young Tom Cosgrove talked too much. The big bony Swede was always singing under his breath or squirming in the saddle. *Can't keep his backside still for ten minutes*, Luke thought. Just a kid really, a year older than Emily.

The six of them had worked like twelve that morning, and every one of them was tired, himself included. Tom Cosgrove and Henry Bertel were stretched in the shade of a tree, napping. The others were sitting around the fire. Jeb, closest to it, had his stiff knee bent awkwardly and was trying to roll a smoke. Luke watched Jeb fumble the drawstring closed on the small tobacco pouch. He dropped it. Tobacco scattered across his legs.

Luke frowned. Not a good sign. Jeb was branding. A man could get hurt when he got that tired.

"Let's call it quits. We've done enough today," Luke said.

The instant relief he saw in their faces told him he'd done the right thing. They were all tired. "Better get your appetites back," Luke said. "The ladies in the kitchen were peeling apples when we rode out this morning. I'll bet we get pie tonight."

"Especially if the boss put in a special request before we left, which he did," Jeb Simson said. "I heard you myself. You know something, Luke? You got those ladies eatin' out of your hand, Miss Molly included. How you do that?"

"Practice, Jeb. Just practice." Luke laughed. "Miss Molly's like a mama to me."

Lying on his back, Tom Cosgrove chuckled, his voice muffled by the hat over his face. "Bet Miss Emily ain't like a mama to you though, is she?"

Luke rocked to his feet, his face heating. "Watch your mouth, kid!" Fists balled, he stood over Tom. "Get up and let's go." His voice was like a blast from the arctic.

Luke rode on ahead, alone. *What's wrong with me?* Tom was only teasing, yet Luke knew he'd come dangerously close to punching the kid out. One of these days the boy might make a good cowhand, if the little snot ever learned to keep his mouth shut.

When Luke was safely out of earshot, Tom turned to Scully. "I didn't mean nothing. What'd I say to make him so mad?"

"Not a thing, boy. Not a thing. The man's in love."

Scully studied the man on the gray horse riding up ahead. For someone as worried as Luke was about missing cattle, he'd seemed mighty cheerful all morning. Scully wondered if all that whistling and happiness had anything to do with the walk he'd seen Luke and Emily take last night. For the first time, Luke had his arm all comfortable around her waist, as if he didn't care who saw.

Scully kept his head down and hid a smile from Tom. "Right now he's like a bull that ain't been branded before. Most likely, he's trying to sort out his own feelings about the little lady."

"You mean he ain't made up his mind yet?"

Scully's weather-beaten face crinkled around the eyes. "Oh, I reckon he's done that all right," he said, chuckling. "He just don't like it none. I got a feeling that young bull's trotting himself over to the fire right now, and he knows it."

A sly grin stole across Tom's face. "Well, he better get a move on, 'cause I just might ask Miss Emily to go for a walk with me after supper tonight."

"Then you ain't got a lick of sense," Scully said softly. He pointed to the man in the black leather jacket sitting stiffly on his horse ahead of them. "That's your boss up there, boy. He's twice your size, can ride anything with hair on it, and handles a gun like no man I've ever seen. What happened back there ain't like him. He don't get mad easy, but right now I'd say you got him riled right down to his saddle. If I was you, I'd back off till you see which way the wind blows."

Tom studied the back of Luke's jacket for a minute, then looked at Scully and shrugged. "I like her, too. She sure is pretty."

Scully snorted. "So's heaven, I hear. Get between him and his lady, I reckon you might find out."

Emily selected a dark green skirt with side pockets from a rack and took it over to Bobbins's main window. She held it up to the light and examined it. It had to do for a day and a half on the train.

Just right.

Molly wanted something to wear on the trip tomorrow that wouldn't wrinkle too much or show the dirt.

Emily walked back to the rack and flipped through the garments hanging there until she found a large-size pale green sweater to go with the skirt.

"Miss McCarthy, you find what you're looking for?" Mr. Bobbins called from the back of the store.

"Yes, thank you."

"I've got the perfect hat to go with that," he said.

She smiled across the rack of sweaters. Repton, Montana, was a thousand miles from nowhere and yet Bobbins knew merchandising and sales appeal. Like the big department stores in Chicago, he displayed his clothes on hangers. The other merchants in town still stacked garments in piles on tables.

The bell on the front door jangled, and Luke came in. He'd used the telephone at the express office.

With Molly's new outfit over her arm, Emily hurried to him. "How's her brother? What'd the doctor say?"

"He's going to be fine. Says he's in some pain, but that's common with broken bones. He agrees with you and Molly. Thinks it's a good idea for her to go stay with him until he's off the crutches."

"And you don't?"

Luke took the skirt and sweater from her and handed them to Bobbins to ring up. "Until Molly gets back, you'll have to run New Hope by yourself. It's a lot on you."

"Not a problem."

Emily forced a confident smile on her face, hiding how she really felt. Twenty-four kids. Could she do it?

She had to. It was a family emergency for Molly.

She'd answered the front door at New Hope yesterday, and the Western Union man from Repton had handed her a telegram from Molly's brother. The Reverend Eli Ebenezer of Dickinson, North Dakota, had been in a stagecoach accident. The coach he was riding in plunged down a ravine and overturned. Eli, who'd been on his way to New Hope to visit Molly, now had a broken arm and a broken leg.

"She has no choice," Emily said quietly to Luke. "He's all the family she has. But I admit I hate to see her go. She's the disciplinarian, not me."

"Let's hire someone to help you," Luke said.

Emily shook her head. "Our budget's not big enough as it is. Money's tight, and the board will deduct anything else from our allowance. It'll only be a month. We'll be all right."

But what if they weren't all right? she wondered the next morning on the porch, watching as Luke drove Molly down the lane for Repton and the stage to Billings, where she'd take the afternoon train to Dickinson. Molly waved good-bye again to Emily and the collected children, and the buggy turned onto the main road.

Emily let out a sigh. That morning her insides felt squeezed and jumpy. She could feel herself trembling inside.

Dear Lord, help me.

Just the thought that she wouldn't be able to run both the school and the orphanage made her stomach hurt. Molly, bless her heart, had been so calm about it.

"You love children, and it shows," she'd said.

"But they were all girls, all second or third graders. I haven't had much experience with older kids," Emily replied, omitting that she had no experience at all with boys, old or young.

And two of the boys at New Hope were taller than her.

***

Thirteen-year-old Pete Brewster herded all the boys together in the hall before their morning history class.

"We got orders," he muttered, and repeated Luke's lecture to him earlier, a combination of threats and bribes to guarantee good behavior for Miz McCarthy.

A wide-eyed fifth grader interrupted. "That's for girls. I ain't gonna take no sewing class."

"You cause any trouble, we both do. You, for causing it — me, for not stopping you," Pete said. "And I guarantee you'll be sorry." None too gently, he shoved the boy into the classroom ahead of him and flopped down beside him on the bench.

Chalk in hand, Emily turned around from the blackboard where she'd sketched a picture of an animal with a row of pointed plates along its back.

"Let's start today's lesson on prehistoric animals by

comparing it with something we already know. Teddy, did you bring your tortoise today?"

Later that morning, when the horses were inside the barn, Emily led the students up to the pastures behind. They tramped over several acres, looking for dinosaur eggs in the grass and under every bush. With a straight face she told them a discovery like that was most unlikely. In class she'd told them about a Chicago scientist who'd recently discovered dinosaur fossils in nearby Dakota Territory. Right then her students clamored to look behind New Hope.

They found only arrowheads, which Two Leggings and Red Cloud assured them, importantly, were not made by the Crow.

An hour later she led them back down the hill to the house. Walking toward them were four men she recognized, members of New Hope's Board of Directors.

"And what are you kids out digging for?" John Armstrong, the newspaper editor, gestured to the spoons and trowels the children carried.

"Dinosaur eggs," croaked Teddy.

Armstrong laughed and said, "That's great. How many did you find?"

Emily filled them in on the morning's fruitless search. "Only arrowheads and a few rocks in that pasture, nothing more."

"No dinosaurs here, I'm afraid," Mr. Bobbins added.

"But they used to be next door in North Dakota and just possibly were in Montana," Emily said, aware of the disappointed faces on the children. "There was an article in the Chicago paper last week about recent discoveries. We're reading up on them."

She turned to the children. "Run along so the grown-ups can talk," she said, and shooed them around to the back of New Hope to go in through the washroom.

"Let's go inside and sit down. I'm sorry we weren't here when you first came. What can I help you with?" she asked.

The editor spoke up first. "We were concerned with your having to run the classes by yourself and wondered if you needed anything, if we could help."

"Besides dinosaur hunting, what classes have they had today, Miss McCarthy?" Bernard Stanton, the local banker cut in, his tone implying she was neglecting their education.

Emily gazed at him a moment and decided she didn't like the man.

"Reading and arithmetic before the egg hunt," she said, and smiled. "After lunch we'll do geography and English, if we can squeeze it in. Today is art class, and sometimes English comes in second to art and music."

Stanton cleared his throat and stepped forward. "The dinosaur hunt was ridiculous, if you don't mind my opinion. English is important, my dear. I insist you shelve the art and music and teach them about the world they live in."

Emily weighed her answer before she spoke. "I agree English is important, but so is art and music. We'll fit it all in."

He pulled a paper from his pocket. "And this request of yours for free tickets to the Repton Music Festival next month is over the line. As long as I've been here, no one ever asked for that before."

"Repton never had a music festival before, Bernard," Mr. Bobbins said quietly.

Mr. Bolton, one of the ranchers who used the same range that New Hope did, smiled to the others and said, "I'm glad we stopped out. Miss McCarthy has everything under control." He paused. "How many tickets do you need?"

Emily swallowed. "We have twenty-four children, if I can bring them all."

"Twenty-four it is. You'll have them. Plan on it."

CHAPTER 17

Scully said it was a bad omen.

High overhead a red-tailed hawk screamed, hunting its breakfast. It wheeled and soared in the updrafts in the early morning sunlight, then dived and sped a foot above the ground. Legs outstretched, it struck. Powerful wingbeats climbed for altitude, a small rabbit clenched in its talons.

Scully reached back and slipped his rifle from the scabbard.

Luke followed the bird with his eyes. It had carried its prey to ground and was now feeding a short distance away.

"Ah, don't shoot him, Scully," he said softly. "It's not an omen, good or bad. It's just nature for both of them."

Every morning he and the New Hope crew were out by seven, cutting calves and branding. Another couple of days and they'd be finished. Everything should ease up a little then. Maybe things would go right after all.

Axel had taken the closing of the rangeland with a strange silence. He hadn't said a word to him, just sent a crew in the next day and turned his cattle back.

Luke wondered if Sam Tucker had something to do with that. On the way back from Billings, Luke had stopped by the sheriff's office. Stuart had come inside with him and introduced himself as a friend and former employer.

Tucker had listened, growing increasingly quiet as Luke recounted Jupiter's murder and described the gunman.

"Lots of men ride spotted horses around here, Mr. Sullivan," Tucker had said. "You could be wrong about it being Haldane."

"I don't think so. He never took his hat off, but I'm sure it was Haldane."

"Well, I'm going out there tomorrow to talk to Mr. Axel about something else. I'll keep it in mind."

Luke reined in and pulled Bugle up. Sitting astride the big gray, he watched the cows, his brain clicking along, making mental tallies of each group, filing it away in some side pocket of his mind to be pulled out and added in with the others later.

At first he thought the herd had just scattered more than usual, that the roundup had made them jittery, and they spread out. But by midmorning, the vague perception that something wasn't quite right had jelled into the solid conviction something was quite wrong.

On the surface, things seemed little different from the day before: the heaving brown backs in front of him, the clouds of dust rising as Henry Bertel and Tom Cosgrove moved deeper into the herd. The weather was the same—clear and sunny and not a sign of rain in the sky—a twin of the day before, and the day before that.

Numbers flashed in his head again. They didn't add up. The herd was smaller. He was sure of it. Fifty or sixty fewer, he guessed, maybe close to a hundred. Exact figures were hard to come by in a herd that size. Twenty head would never be missed. But fifty? Maybe. If you had good eyes.

He rode back to the branding area and slid down. Hand curled around the saddle horn, he waited until Scully and Tom Cosgrove straightened up over a calf. The young heifer scampered back to her mother, mooing at them from the edge of the herd. Luke stepped over to the fire.

Scully looked up. "Something wrong, boss?"

"I'm not sure," Luke said, pushing his hat up with a finger, "but I think more of this herd is missing. I'm going up to the north section and take a look. They might've roamed up there yesterday."

Scully shoved the cooling N-Bar-H iron back into the fire. He stood and dusted his pants. "I'm coming with you, then. I remember the last time you rode up there alone."

Half an hour later, Luke pointed to a large herd spread like a mirage across the horizon in the distance. A breeze rippled over the rangeland, lifting and smoothing the ocean of grass ahead of them like wavelets. "Don't see how they could've roamed that far," he said to Scully.

"They probably ain't ours, then. Axel's, most likely."

"Let's go see." Luke tapped his heels, and Bugle quickened his pace.

In a few minutes they were pushing into the mass of cattle,

checking brands. Most were Axel's X-Bar-L. There were only a few strays belonging to the Paxtons and the Ormons. Then, as they tunneled in deeper, they began to find N-Bar-H steers. And cows. And calves. Luke's jaw took on a granite hardness. Axel wasn't stupid. He didn't need to rustle cattle. So what was this all about?

"What do you make of it?" Scully asked.

"About twice as many as I figured."

"They could've been here all winter, you know."

Luke shook his head. "That's what I thought until I saw him." He pointed to the spotted calf with a torn left ear.

"That critter was miles down range yesterday. Someone drove him here last night!" Scully snapped a look at Luke. "What's going on?"

"Looks like we got a thief out here," Luke said.

A rush of sour thoughts filled his head. One man seemed to pull the strings in his life, jerking him around like a puppet.

Bart Axel.

The noon sun was warm on his back, but inside he felt cold. A slow procession of thoughts moved like ghosts across his mind. His parents . . . Mary Beth. He'd forgotten what they looked like. Sometime when he was around thirteen, he'd cut himself loose from old memories of a family he couldn't remember and decided to make do with what he had. And Molly and New Hope was the family he had.

After that beating, it had been all he could do not to go gunning for Axel. No one knew how many nights he'd lain awake in his room, figuring how he'd do it. But he didn't, because the law said there was no proof that Axel was involved and because Molly and Emily begged him not to. Then the barn . . . and now this.

Beneath the broad-brimmed hat, a glare of sunlight warmed his lower face. His jaw tightened.

Enough was enough.

Bart Axel leaned back in his chair. "Well, did he find his brand?"

"Just like you said he would," Clete said, laughing. "Sullivan was out there checking our herd early this morning. Then he and Scully Anders took off for New Hope like their tails were on fire. You reckon they'll be back?"

Bart stroked his cigar ashes into an empty glass. "I'm counting on it. But before he does, I want you to cut out two hundred of our own today and mix them in with theirs. Then Haldane and the men will drive them to Parker and put them on the train up there for Chicago."

Bart chuckled, a dry sound with no humor. "The yardmaster in Parker isn't fussy about brands, except the ones on his whiskey. Couple bottles of the right stuff, a box of cigars, and he'll load anything I want him to."

"And Sullivan will come after what he thinks are his cattle, because of where we're taking them—to Parker," Clete said.

Bart ran a knuckle down one side of his mustache, then the other. "Don't underestimate him," he said. "He's smart. He won't come too close, and he won't come in right away. He'll hang back and follow for a day or so till he sees what we're up to. Once he's figured it out, then he'll come in and try to take the herd—or what he thinks is his herd. And when he does"—Axel picked up the nickel-plated Schofield from the desk and aimed it at the hat rack across the room—"bang! Nobody can blame us for looking after our own."

Clete nodded. "Sullivan's been asking for it for a long time." He smacked his fist into the palm of his other hand.

"But not you," Axel said quickly. "Sullivan is Haldane's job. We stay out of it. You and me will be miles away when that happens. We split the New Hope cows off and take them south to Wyoming. A man I know down there will take them off our hands."

At sunup the next morning, the horses snorted and stamped in place. Luke and the men led their mounts, already saddled, out through the double doors of the barn. Blanket rolls were tied behind the cantles of the saddle, the saddlebags loaded. Every horse had a rifle scabbard slung on its left. Together, the men swung up and settled themselves, taking off a moment later in a muffled clatter of hooves across the corral and through the gate. They pushed the horses at an easy, rolling canter for the North Quarter, intending to cut out their own before Axel's crew got started. Luke had brought as many men as he dared, hoping that the small army from New Hope would make Wade or Wesley or Axel himself think twice before starting trouble. But he wasn't counting on it.

"Make sure those rifles are loaded," he reminded them again. Though each of them carried a pistol or revolver on his left, butt forward, they wouldn't be close enough to use them.

At least he hoped not. "Look sharp. We're getting close," he warned.

Ahead of them, the plain stretched endlessly for miles—empty. There was no herd. Instead, the pasture was a mud wallow. It looked as if the herd had panicked, tracks criss-crossing everywhere, the grass trampled deep into the dirt, clods of earth dug out by hundreds of running hooves. The men swung off and looked around blankly. Leading Bugle and frowning, Luke walked a wide circle and tried to fit the pieces together. It made no sense.

Scully pulled off his hat and ran a hand through his thinning hair. "Looks like they took 'em out of here in a hurry, but why east? If they wanted to hide them, they should've gone south. There's nothing east of here."

Luke pulled himself into the saddle again. The horse shifted nervously. "Yeah, there is," he said, his voice calm, deliberate. "Parker. They're going to take them out by train. And they just might get away with it, too. Let's go. We got a long ride ahead of us."

They rode for more than an hour after dark, moving in closer—but not too close—to the herd they knew was up ahead. A few miles from the banks of the Bighorn River, they made camp in the open. Luke and Henry and Will Brown unsaddled the horses, picketed them, and turned them loose to graze while the Cosgrove boys helped Scully get a fire going. Supper was coffee, fried fatback, and the cold biscuits they'd brought with them. Lying around the campfire, eating and drinking, the men talked, speculating about the herd and why Axel had taken up rustling.

Legs outstretched, Luke folded his arms under his head, more aware of the sawing throb of crickets in the background than the drone of the men's voices. He gazed into a sky bright with stars and, one by one, sifted the facts through the sieve of his consciousness, examining what he knew, guessing at the unknowns.

Why was Axel stealing his neighbor's cows? He had thousands of his own. Anger welled up inside Luke again. Axel had to know they'd follow him, find him out. Did he really want the beef—or did he want Luke Sullivan?

Will Brown's voice interrupted his thoughts.

"Luke, they ain't more than five miles up ahead. Let's go in and get them tomorrow."

Luke shook his head. "Can't. Not tomorrow or the day after, either. There's nothing between Repton and Parker but prairie—sagebrush and a few scrub bushes for cover. If there's one place we don't want trouble, it's there."

"You looking for it?" It was Henry.

"Don't know for sure, but let's get ready just in case. Treasure Canyon is two days ahead. If we come in from the north end, we ought to be able to turn the herd and start them back this way before Haldane's crew know what's happening."

Luke sat up and stirred the fire higher. A slab of pitch pine popped in a small explosion of sparks. "With any luck, they'll be too busy trying to catch their cows and stay out of the way of the herd to worry about us. But I repeat: There's apt to be some shooting, so if anyone wants to go home, the time to do it is now."

There was no hurry the next morning. Scully treated them all, made flapjacks and boiled two big pots of coffee, while the men lolled around, joking and killing time, waiting until Haldane and his crew got well on up the trail. Leisurely, they broke camp, mounted up, and rode out at an ambling walk, staying out of sight, miles behind the herd. Once, they got close enough to see the dust on the horizon. Another time, they saw where the cattle forded the Bighorn River and turned north. They waded into it themselves and swam the horses across.

On the other side, a few minutes later, Henry Bertel pointed to Luke. "What's he doing?"

He did look peculiar. Leaning far out of the saddle like a trick rider at a fair, Luke kept Bugle moving, zigzagging him back and forth across the cattle tracks. He stopped up ahead, got off, and waved to the others to do the same. Dropping into a high-kneed squat, he thumbed his hat back and pointed to a clear set of tracks.

"This herd's been cut since yesterday," he said.

"Cut again? When? Where'd they go?" Scully asked, his face registering surprise.

"Wish I knew," Luke muttered.

He sent the Cosgrove brothers, Henry Bertel, and Will Brown off to follow Haldane and the herd going to Parker. He and Scully doubled back to where the tracks first crossed the river and turned north, where the Little Bighorn emptied into the Bighorn River. Luke pointed to a V-shaped spit of sand and rubble jutting into the center where the two rivers joined.

"How come it's busted up out there?" Luke said.

"It's where they went across, I guess."

Luke shook his head. "No. Haldane drove them over about a mile back, remember?"

"A couple got loose, maybe?"

"Take more than a couple to chew it up like that." For a full minute, he sat there, staring at the confluence of the two rivers. Again and again, his eyes pulled back to the Little Bighorn River curving to his left. "Let's go down there a ways."

Sully hesitated. "You forget that's Crow territory?"

"No." Luke hadn't forgotten. His stomach was already knotting.

For the Crows, raiding was expressly forbidden by the treaty. Yet twice since he'd been back, Luke had seen signal fires in the mountains. Every chance they got, small war parties of Crows stole off the reservation, riding miles out of their way to avoid a ranch or a farm and being seen by the whites. Then swinging back, they swooped in on an enemy camp of Lakota Sioux or Cheyenne. So far, they'd left the whites strictly alone. But that could change.

Indian life had changed. All too often for the Crows, bad things happened after white men came in. But increasingly, there were signs of hostility. Until recently, the Crow had been the one tribe the white men trusted. But now, still unexplained, was the disappearance of two itinerant trappers last seen taking a shortcut through the reservation on their way south to Wyoming.

"I ain't going in there," Scully said grimly, shaking his head. "I like my ears right where they are."

"We don't bother them, they won't bother us. Wait for me here. I won't be long."

He heeled Bugle into the river, and the horse swam the short distance in the middle for the bank on the other side. Water sheeting from his flanks, Bugle drove his powerful hind legs and scrambled out of the water and up the bank.

Scully watched and debated with himself. Tail swinging with each step, Bugle moved rapidly along beside the river, his rider erect in the saddle.

After a minute, Scully sent his own horse down the embankment and into the water, and caught up with Luke. A mile farther on, they stopped.

"Nothing," Luke said. "Not a sign of them—they didn't come this way. Let's go back where they crossed and look again."

From somewhere in the trees, the mournful howl of a coyote cut across the canyon like a knife, gliding, wavering. A brother answered, unseen but almost at their elbows. Both men spun in their saddles. Their eyes met. From far away, widely separated, others took up the call, not faint or fading but approaching, howling on the run.

"Those ain't coyotes," Scully whispered.

"Let's get out of here."

They wheeled their horses and kicked them into a gallop, racing along the riverbank to get out of the reservation. Leaning around a sweeping bend of the Little Bighorn, both men reared back in their saddles and plunged the horses to a stop.

Bows at full draw, a Crow war party crouched on the path in front of them.

CHAPTER
18

Luke started to sweat. It seemed as if these copper-faced men had been chosen for their vicious appearance, for the nightmare of Indian cruelty they represented. There was nothing they wouldn't do. His breath trapped in his lungs.

His stomach had turned to air, hollow as a shell, and a muscle ticked out of control in his cheek. He shot a look at Scully. Eyes wide, Scully's face sagged with fear. Until that moment, Luke had always thought Scully to be rock solid. Now he wasn't so sure.

A tall, bare-chested Crow in buckskins and a breechclout held up a hand, palm out, and stepped forward. Attached to the heel of each moccasin was a coyote tail that flopped the ground with every step. He stopped a few feet from them and drove his lance into the earth, then nodded abruptly and pointed to the trail in front of him.

Relief flooded across Scully's face. "I've seen him before. Name's Little Turtle. Came to New Hope after Black Otter's boys a time or two. He's kind of a junior chief, so don't go getting ideas about pulling your gun," Scully warned. "Some say he's a captain in the Dog Soldiers, a secret society you don't mess with. The spear in the ground means he's friendly. He wants to talk."

"Go ahead," Luke said.

"Ain't me he's looking at."

Slowly, Luke stood in the stirrup, swung his leg over, and stepped down, stalling for time, studying the Crow waiting for him.

Crows were handsome people, tall and fine-featured, with narrow non-Indian noses. This one wore soft yellow-gray deerskin, his moccasins beaded and trimmed with tufts of fur. Around his neck hung a small leather pouch and an eagle claw. Hair, black as night, was cropped into a stiff brush above his forehead, the remainder bound loosely into two strips hanging to the front over his shoulders.

Over six feet tall, the man stood eye to eye with Luke and was in superb condition. Luke blinked slowly and dragged in a long breath.

For centuries, Sioux fought Blackfoot, Blackfoot fought Arapahoe, Arapahoe fought Cheyenne. The Absaroka – the bird people, the Crows – fought every one of them. With a fierce bravery, they ran a constant warpath, protecting what belonged to them.

And this reservation was theirs.

He and Scully were not only armed and trespassing on Crow land, they were following a herd of cattle bearing the

New Hope brand and driving right through the middle of their reservation. Somehow, Luke had to convince Little Turtle that it was all a mistake. He cleared his throat and shook off the sweat trickling down his jaw.

"My name's Sullivan. I'm from New Hope."

Flat black eyes stared back at him.

"We're looking for cattle. Our own cattle. They were stolen."

Not a flicker of movement.

He doesn't speak English, Luke thought, and chided himself that he didn't know sign language, that he'd refused to learn it. Palm up, Luke lifted a hand in a gesture of openness, and turned to go. "We will leave now."

"No."

Luke wasn't sure if Little Turtle had spoken or if he'd imagined it. The lips appeared not to have moved. The face before him could have been carved from leather.

"We meant no harm," Luke said. In spite of himself, a tight anger coiled in his chest and thudded his heart against his rib cage.

"Come." With a jerk of his head toward the trees, the Crow yanked his lance out of the dirt.

Luke didn't move. Instead, he stared at the Crow brave in front of him. The man's dark eyes locked on his, each man staring the other down.

Pictures flashed in Luke's mind again, misty, detached. His mother, his sister, his father with his face half gone. Bitterness clawed at the back of his throat. Why was he spared then only for this?

No fair, Lord.

He went for his gun.

The Indian blistered out a stream of Crow. Luke took a step backward and collided with bodies, which weren't there a moment before. His holster was empty, the Colt already in an Indian fist. Two braves pinned his arms high behind him, rounding his shoulders, stooping him over. Men on ponies moved in and surrounded them. One Indian with a long, thin strip of rawhide in his hands stepped in and bound his wrists behind him, lashing his thumbs together tightly.

Not taking his eyes off the Indian in front of him, Luke gritted his teeth. "What do I do now, Scully?"

Scully's voice cracked. His own arms were being tied behind him. "I told you not to go for your gun. Crows are supposed to be peaceable to whites. I ain't so sure now."

The Crows took their rifles, pistols, even Scully's pocket-knife. One of them held Bugle's bridle; another grabbed Luke's shoulder and indicated with his head for Luke to mount the horse. Roughly, Luke was boosted into the saddle. Then the Indians boxed them in, crowding their ponies around the white men's horses.

Bugle made an ominous rumbling sound in his neck and hoofed a step sideways in alarm. Not wanting the horse hurt, Luke pressed his knees into Bugle to reassure him.

Up and out of the canyon, they rode into dense woods, shadowed and thick with ferns. Here and there, a shaft of sunlight slanted through the branches. Only the stiff creak of timber overhead and the muffled thud of hoofbeats broke the silence. Hands tied behind him, Luke rode in silence, wondering if they were the first white men to pass through.

Deep into Crow land, the trees thinned. They broke into a

large clearing filled with mud-and-stone lodges, wooden huts, and smoking tipis. The camp dogs ran at them, barking and snarling around the horses, setting up a racket.

Black-haired, dark-eyed people were everywhere, working, talking in small groups around campfires. Outside their houses, cinnamon-skinned women ground meal or scraped animal skins pegged to the ground. Two women in knee-high moccasins were weaving on a loom strung between two poles. A baby hung in a cradleboard on one of the poles.

All activity ceased at their approach, the villagers falling silent, staring at the two white men. Luke's mouth went dry, remembering what he'd heard Indian women did to white male captives. In front of a large lodge, the Crows dismounted. With a Crow brave steadying each of them, Luke and Scully were pulled off their horses.

Little Turtle pointed to the low doorway. Luke and Scully exchanged wary glances, ducked their heads, and went inside.

Chief Black Otter looked from Luke to the brave standing beside him. In Crow, he asked, "Is this Light Eyes?"

"Yes. They came after cows. I told them nothing," Little Turtle said.

"Why you tie him up?"

"He is angry inside."

Black Otter nodded. His sons had told him about the Sioux attack on Luke's family. "He has reason. Untie him," he said. He gestured for Luke to sit on a pile of buffalo skins on the floor. "Rest easy in your mind, Sullivan. You welcome here."

Luke's eyes widened at the use of his name. "Are you Black Otter?"

The chief nodded, a faint twist in the corners of his lips. "My sons know you. They say you teach them to shoot."

Luke let out a long, ragged sigh of relief, and he sank down onto the buffalo skins. Slowly, his heartbeat smoothed to something close to normal. Rubbing his wrists, he said, "White men stole our cattle. We thought they drove them here," he explained.

"They did. They here."

"We looked. There are no tracks."

"You no see tracks. Men come with one called Iron Hair. They drive cows through river—a long way."

"Bart Axel's men?"

"Two are same men who beat you. Little Turtle, his braves, they stop them." Black Otter frowned. "You not know we tie you on horse, send you home?"

"That's right, Luke," Scully broke in. "I knew those were Injun knots!"

Luke looked at Little Turtle, caught a slight softening of expression, then a brief nod of affirmation. A pang of guilt needled Luke. If they hadn't grabbed his gun, he would have shot the man.

He pulled in a deep breath. "I'm sorry," he said to Little Turtle. "I was wrong."

As quickly as he could make Black Otter understand, Luke explained about the two herds of cattle. When he'd finished, the chief stood and left the lodge without speaking. He called for his horse, then beckoned Luke and Scully to come outside with him. He led them back to the Little Bighorn River. A mile downstream from where his braves had found them, he showed them the tracks. For a hundred yards the bank was caved in where cattle had climbed out of the river.

"From the looks of it, he sure didn't want nobody following this herd," Scully said.

And Luke thought he knew why. "Chief, did you get a look at the brand on these cattle?"

"They yours. All New Hope's," Black Otter said.

"Axel took a chance bringing them in here," Luke said to Scully. "He knows this is Crow land. And I bet the man taking the herd to Parker knew we were following them." He slammed his fist into his hand. "I was so sure those were our cattle! Every cattle thief around here dumps in Parker."

Scully was confused. "If the other herd ain't ours, why's he want us to follow them?"

"He's setting us up," Luke said.

"To kill you," Black Otter added.

Luke's mind raced, going over in his head what he had to do and how he had to do it.

"I want to come in here after our herd, Chief," he said, "but Axel's men won't let them go without a fight."

Black Otter nodded, his face serious. "I show you good place."

Luke reached out an arm, touched the chief, surprised that he considered the man an ally. "I don't want to cause your people trouble with the government."

For the first time in his life, Luke Sullivan heard an Indian laugh. Black Otter threw back his head and burst out laughing, deep belly laughs that shook his shoulders. "No trouble, Light Eyes. You take cows. That day, Crows see nothing."

"Luke," Scully broke in, "the minute we stop trailing them, Haldane will guess we're wise. What'll he do then?"

"Come after us," Luke said.

His face impassive, Black Otter stared out over a bend in the Little Bighorn, stroking his upper lip thoughtfully. "No. You come." Winding his hand in the pony's mane, the chief sprang easily onto its back.

It was long after dark when Luke and Scully found where the New Hope crew was camped.

"We were getting worried about you two," Henry Bertel said. Tom and John Cosgrove and Will Brown were sitting in front of the fire. An owl hooted in the trees. Henry stiffened. "Something moving out there. We got company, Luke," he said, reaching for his rifle.

"Easy, Henry. It's all right. They're with us."

Six Crow Indians stepped into the firelight.

"Little Turtle," Luke said, "over here, so we can talk."

The Indians dropped to the ground, eyes moving from white face to white face. They sat silent, expressionless, while Luke told New Hope's crew what Axel had planned.

"They want us to follow them so they can bushwhack us in Treasure Canyon. But we're not going there. With the help of the Crow we're going back to the reservation and get our herd. Little Turtle and his men will take our places and follow the Parker herd instead of us. Haldane won't know we've gone."

Standing, Luke started unbuttoning his shirt. "We need to

switch clothes and horses, so let's get started. We want to be off this range before daylight."

Half a dozen red men moved around the fire, trading clothes back and forth with half a dozen white men. Crow fingers fumbled with buttons and snaps, both races wrinkling their noses at the unfamiliar odors of the garments.

"Ugh! What these people eat make them stink bad," a brave muttered in Crow to Little Turtle.

Little Turtle, the tallest of the Indians, didn't answer. He sat on the ground, wrestling Luke's riding boots over his feet. Standing, he teetered back and forth, a look of near dismay spreading over his face.

Running Wolf, a fierce-looking brave with a shaved head, strutted around in a pair of long johns in a peculiar manner. Reaching behind him, he fisted the buttons off the drop seat in back. A quick yank and a square of ribbed fabric sailed into the fire. Running Wolf bent over and touched his toes, his naked skin visible through the open window of the underwear. "That better," he said.

"Look what he done to my drawers," Will Brown sputtered, fishing the flap of his burning underwear out of the fire with a stick. It was too late. The edges were blackened and a tongue of flame curled around one corner. Disgusted, Will kicked it back in the fire and tugged at the breechclout hanging down his front. "I miss my underwear. It don't feel right with nothin' on under these skins."

Scully sniffed and spit. "Drafty too."

"Gives me the creeps. Skin almost feels alive on you, don't it?" Tom Cosgrove whispered, stretching his arms out and shaking the fringe on the sleeves of the buckskin shirt he had on.

Henry stroked a fringe of silky strands sewn across the cuffs of his shirt and woven into the side seams. "Sure is soft. Wonder what kind of fur this is?"

"Ain't fur. It's hair," Scully said.

Henry's mouth fell open. He snatched his hand away from the hair just as Running Wolf pulled off a necklace of bear claws and rattled them over Henry's head. With a wary look, Henry plucked the string of yellowed toenails away from his chest. "They're real nice, Running Wolf," Henry managed to say. "Real nice."

"Better bring your ropes and your rifles," Luke said. "We've got to switch horses and get out of here."

Red-skinned *cowboys* with braids and breezy, unbuttoned flies boosted six clumsy *Indians* onto Crow ponies for the ride back to the reservation. Wordlessly, the Crows watched the men from New Hope jounce bareback off into the night. When a heartfelt cussword floated back, they slapped their thighs and doubled over with laughter.

All except Little Turtle. The captain of the Dog Soldiers sighed and shook his head. Walking bowlegged, he limped back to the fire and sat down. His feet hurt.

The next morning Bugle's nostrils flared wide and held. Once again, he rolled his eyes to the side. His rider was like a feather. Only the pressure of weight dead center in the middle of his back revealed the saddle held a man. The horse swung his head around. The stirrups flapped loose and empty at his sides, the rider's legs dangling free.

Barely opening his lips, Bugle stretched his neck and nickered to Henry's mare plodding beside him with lowered head. Peevishly, she flattened her ears and nipped at him. With a hop sideways he managed to get his muzzle away from her just in time. She was in a foul mood herself that morning. Someone had braided her tail.

~~~

Out on the range that night, Haldane stretched his long legs toward the fire and sipped his coffee, staring into the flames, going over in his mind the events that had followed an odd conversation with Axel. Funny, he thought, the way Axel had reined him in after the trip to Billings.

Granville Stuart showing up with his Committee and escorting Sullivan and Miss McCarthy home worried Axel as nothing else had.

The plan had been for him to pick Sullivan off on the range—from a distance, nice and clean—and then leave for Kansas.

But then Axel changed his mind, saying no just ten minutes after the sheriff had left. Tucker had made him nervous, all right. In fact, from what Haldane had seen, Bart Axel's hands shook when the sheriff started nosing around Haldane's big Appaloosa like he'd never seen a spotted horse before, talking about murder and attempted murder and what a coincidence it was that two of the three attempts on Sullivan's life—the beating and the gunfight in town—had been by X-Bar-L hands. "And whose horse did you say this is, Mr. Axel?"

Absently, Haldane scratched the mat of straw-colored fuzz

covering his arms and the backs of his hands. Never could tell about people. Haldane yawned and slung the dregs of his coffee into the fire. Spreading his bedroll, he rolled onto his side and was asleep in minutes.

The next morning they were packed and ready to head out when Wesley rode in fast. He'd been out scouting the New Hope party, making sure they were still back there. With Treasure Canyon coming up, losing them was the last thing Haldane wanted.

"Haldane," Wesley called, jumping off his horse. "Something strange going on back there."

"Like what?"

"They were eatin' rabbits for breakfast."

Haldane looked at him in surprise. "So Sullivan likes a little meat with his flapjacks. What's strange about that?"

Wesley shook his head. "Weren't no flapjacks. No coffee, neither. Just berries and rabbits on a stick."

Haldane wrinkled his nose. The stink of rabbits cooking that early could make a man puke. "What'd you get that close for, anyway?"

"Figured I'd maybe pick up something we need to know. Then, just as it's getting light, I see three of 'em go into the woods. They were back in five minutes, I swear, with a whole armful of dead rabbits – and I never heard a shot."

"Look," Haldane said, "I don't care what they eat or *if* they eat." He massaged his midsection. "I got a weak enough stomach as it is, and you ain't making it one bit better."

Wesley bristled. "I'm just doing my job. You don't like it, you send someone else. And another thing – you know how Sullivan babies that big horse of his? Well, those horses were saddled and ready to go with daylight still an hour off. I bet they ain't been unsaddled since yesterday." With that, Wesley stomped off.

Haldane pursed his lips thoughtfully. *Saddled all night? Now that *was* strange.*

CHAPTER
19

"They've spotted us, " Axel said in a low voice, looking straight ahead.

Side by side, the two men rode through the Crow reservation ahead of the New Hope herd. From the moment they'd entered the ravine, both had been alert for Indians.

Uneasy in this barren landscape, Clete's hand slid across and closed around his pistol. On both sides, menacing dark cliffs dropped like slate waterfalls to the canyon floor. Nothing but rock and stone and sagebrush, the eerie silence broken only by the clopping of their horses and the whispering of trapped wind as it funneled through the canyon. Clete's eyes darted. Not an Indian in sight.

"I don't see them," he said.

"Didn't see them the day you jumped Sullivan, either," Axel said, "but they saw you. Most likely, what's up there is a scouting party, wondering why we're here, so forget about pulling your gun. If they meant to kill us, they would have by now."

"How many are there?" Sweat beaded Wade's forehead.

"Half a dozen. Probably more. Knowing Injuns, there's probably three times that many up there. Play this one nice and easy, you hear? Because one way or another, we're going through." Axel rode silently for a minute, his mind working. "Tell you what. Go back and stop the herd, let the cattle graze where they are. Maybe the best thing is to go see Black Otter himself."

"Not me."

"Then you better go on ahead." Bart gave a nasty laugh. "I'm going to call our red friends down, and I don't think they like you."

Clete jerked the reins. He had no desire to powwow with Crows, not then, not ever. Clucking his tongue, he kicked his horse into a trot back in the other direction to hold up the herd.

Axel squared his shoulders and sat tall in the saddle. He cupped his mouth and shouted up at the empty rocks above. "Black Otter, where's Black Otter?"

On the ridge above the canyon, Luke grabbed Tom Cosgrove's shoulder and pushed him down. "Keep that yellow head of yours out of sight. He thinks we're Crows." Frowning, he turned to the young brave at his side. "Curly Bear, it seems Axel wants to see your chief."

The brave nodded, then stepped into the open. Like most of the Crow men, Curly Bear was over six feet tall. In buckskins, silhouetted on top of the cliff, the big Indian was an impressive sight. He raised his arm. "Ho," he called, pointing to a flat area near the end of the canyon.

By the time Axel got to the spot, Curly Bear was already there. Without a word, the Indian turned his pony and galloped over a small rise for the forest beyond, leaving Bart Axel sitting on his horse. Axel had no choice but to follow.

Curly Bear reached over and seized the bridle of Bart's horse, slowing him to a walk through the camp. He stopped, indicating the large lodge on their right. On a tripod behind Black Otter's lodge hung the chief's red and blue war shield, painted with zigzag lines and a running bear. Made of shrunken buffalo hide, it was handsome and smooth and tough enough to stop an arrow or a bullet.

Standing inside, Black Otter gestured an open hand toward the pile of soft buffalo robes across from him. Three other lesser chiefs sat cross-legged around the fire.

Now that he was there, face-to-face with Black Otter, Bart hesitated, unsure quite how to begin. The Crows looked at him silently, expressionless, yet he had the distinct impression they'd been expecting him, been waiting for him.

It had been years since he'd seen Black Otter. For some reason, he remembered him as being a smaller man, a younger man. Certainly not this imposing Absaroka chief with the beautiful manners, towering over him in a buffalo-horn headdress. Axel stared at the lethal pair of horns curving from a close-fitting feathered cap and wondered why this man who had pledged "everlasting friendship" with his white brothers was wearing a war bonnet.

Bronze skin across jutting cheekbones was pulled taut by

a heavy jaw. Pinpoints of light from the fire glowed blood red in the black of his eyes.

Axel cleared his throat, reminding himself to be careful. Black Otter had been a ferocious fighter. The scar on his face was a monument to that. Underestimating this man would be a grievous mistake. This chief was no fool. Though he could neither read nor write English, he was a keen thinker, a pretty fair philosopher, and as vindictive as they came.

Crows never forgot a wrong, and that worried Axel. He remembered a white trader – a blustery, big-nosed giant of a man from Canada – who once tricked a River Crow chief out of three horses, three potbellied ponies. He had the good sense to leave the territory. Before he did, the Canadian compounded his misfortune by leaving the chief's daughter with a half-white baby to raise.

Seven years later they found him – or pieces of him – in Louisiana, minus his scalp. From the hole in his chest, where his heart should have been, stuck the handle of a Crow knife. Axel shuddered. Louisiana. Fifteen hundred miles away.

In Black Otter's lodge, Bart glanced over at the hatchet-faced chief in the headdress facing him. The points of the curved buffalo horns gleamed like ice picks in the firelight.

He tucked his legs under him, imitating the chief. So far, no one had spoken a word to him. Protocol required Black Otter to speak first, but Bart was in a hurry.

"I'm driving a herd through your land," he said.

Black Otter stared back coldly for a moment, then nodded for him to continue.

Pretending to be exasperated, Bart let his hands fall heavily in his lap and shook his head. "Now, mind you, Chief, we did not drive them here. Strangest thing I ever saw. I was taking my cows to Wyoming and something spooked them at the river junction – a snake, most likely." Axel gave him an ingratiating smile. "I'll pay you, of course, to let us through."

After a long pause, Black Otter said, "The cows you driving, they New Hope cows. Why you drive New Hope cows to Wyoming?"

Axel blinked in surprise. "Why . . . ah . . . they're mine. I bought them from New Hope."

The chief stared at him. Slowly, he shook his head.

Axel's mind raced to come up with something better. Then he remembered. The chief couldn't read.

"Yes, they are. I got the paper right here says they're mine." Axel fished inside his jacket for a leather folder and took out a newspaper column – the advertisement he had placed for a bride months before. He shook it out importantly. "There," he said, handing it to the chief, "you can see for yourself."

Black Otter stared at the meaningless black marks on the paper for a full minute, then solemnly handed it back.

It worked. Bart tucked the clipping back inside the folder and made a great show of replacing it in his jacket. "I'd like your approval to drive my herd through. Just this once, I promise."

Black Otter said nothing.

Axel held up two fingers. "I give you two cows to let us pass."

The chief spoke to the other men seated around the fire – short, guttural sounds, deep in his throat. He grunted and shook his head. Holding up both fists, Black Otter snapped his fingers open.

Ten! Bart Axel swore under his breath. He'd hoped to get away with one, perhaps two at the most. The fool Indian had been around whites too long.

"Ten, it is," he growled. With a little bow he started to rise. He had to get back to Clete and the men and get those steers moving.

Black Otter reached over and grasped his arm, pushing Axel back down. "You give me paper say so."

A sheen of perspiration broke out on Axel's forehead. "But no one would doubt Black Otter," he said.

"No paper, you no drive herd. Soldiers say we steal them."

Axel sighed. That did it. He didn't dare put anything in writing about those cows. Or did he? Black Otter wouldn't know. Out came the leather folder again and a stub of a pencil. Axel scribbled on the back of an envelope, then signed his name with a flourish and a jab of the pencil. He handed the envelope to the chief, saying, "This is a legal bill of sale. It says that I, Bart Axel, give you ten cows in return for permission to cross your land."

Black Otter turned the paper over in his hand and nodded. "Good. We will feast."

Axel watched the chief rise, cross the dirt floor, and disappear into the long entryway leading outdoors. Apparently, the Indian had gone outside to get Axel an escort. It had been easier than he'd thought.

Axel looked around the earthen lodge. Over forty feet across, the floor had been dug out a few feet in from the walls, leaving a wide shelf for seats running around the outer edge.

The air was thick and warm, not smoky at all. A constant current of fresh air drawn through the vestibule by the fire carried the haze up and out the smoke hole in the top.

Outside the lodge, Black Otter's hand closed on his son's shoulder as Two Leggings chased by, playing a game with his friends. He led him behind the lodge. Standing next to the tripod holding his shield, he handed the boy the envelope.

"Read this to me," he said in Crow.

Two Leggings ran his finger under each word. He grinned and looked up at his father.

"It no say Iron Hair give me cows?" the chief asked.

His son shook his head.

"What it say?"

Two Leggings read aloud:

> "When the moon comes up, and the sun goes down,
> Sullivan, the cowboy rides to town.
> Bang! Bang! Sullivan, Sullivan!
> Bang! Bang! Bang!

"Is silly song we sing in school to tease Light Eyes," Two Leggings said and shrugged.

"As I thought. Iron Hair lies to me." Black Otter stared at the paper and then back at Two Leggings. "Sullivan your friend. You not ever sing that song again."

The wide forehead of the chief of all the Absarokas dug into deep lines, and an unforgiving bitterness settled around his mouth. The white man had made a fool of him. Three times he clapped his hands and shouted. Every brave within earshot ran to the chief. As Black Otter spoke, the men's dark eyes began to shine. The chief laid a finger across his lips and pointed to his lodge.

In minutes, dozens of braves with bows and arrows and spears and rifles slipped out of the village. Many of them squatted beside their ponies before they mounted, scooped their fingers through the black earth, and dragged broad dark stripes down both cheeks.

Fighting off a wave of nausea, Axel started to rise. "I must leave now," he said. He felt a little green. Waving his hand, he refused another gourd full of pemmican. His mustache was oily and plastered around his mouth, with buffalo grease covering his lips and hands. The dried raw meat and crushed berries were glued together with layers of melted fat and marrow and then poured into animal bladders.

Axel shuddered. Nasty stuff. Only sheer willpower and a herd of cattle marooned in Indian territory had enabled him to swallow it and keep it down. And he wasn't too sure about the latter. He averted his eyes from the heaping gourd. It made his insides churn just to look at it.

For nearly an hour, the men sat there, feasting, celebrating their agreement about the cows, Axel blatantly flattering the chief and pretending great interest in the Crow Nation, praising its "achievements," as he called them, biding his time until he could leave and get the cattle moving south for Wyoming.

Black Otter munched his food with gusto and smiled at Axel. Four pretty girls in soft, fringed dresses and high moccasins padded around silently, waiting on them. For reasons Axel didn't understand, the chief had kept him there in the lodge, talking, as if stalling for time.

Axel climbed unsteadily to his feet, determined to leave. "Let's go get your cows, Chief," he said.

~~~

Luke and Tom Cosgrove stationed themselves high on the ridgeline, while Henry, John Cosgrove, and Will Brown spread out halfway down the cliff behind the rocks.

At a shout, Luke looked up. Nearly fifty braves lined the rim of the canyon, tall, grim-faced men with cheeks and foreheads streaked with circles and bars of mudlike war paint. A wave of red-skinned men washed down the hillside, digging in, blending in with the surrounding foliage.

Turning to the Crow beside him, Luke said, "Curly Bear, keep those men out of sight. Get them to the other side of the canyon and get them up high. Make sure they know those cows will run once the shooting starts."

Curly Bear's eyes gleamed. "Like buffalo?" he asked.

"I guess you know." Luke grinned and squeezed the Indian's shoulder. To Curly Bear, with three eagle feathers stuck rakishly over his ear, two hundred docile cows were nothing. He'd ridden bareback into buffalo herds of thousands.

~~~

Ahead of the herd, Clete Wade rode along, scouting the terrain, speculating why Axel was gone so long. From time to time he shifted around in the saddle and checked the horizon. Not a cloud in the sky, and yet an expectant heaviness hung in the air, as if a storm were coming.

From the time they pulled the herd out of the Little Bighorn the day before, he hadn't liked it.

They were driving the herd due south from where the Little Bighorn and Bighorn Rivers came together. It was a rolling landscape, rough grassland parted by a few low hills and ravines, gouged through by the occasional deep canyon like the one he was riding in now.

He slowed the horse to a walk and rolled himself a smoke. It had taken him two days to swallow his anger at not going with Haldane to Parker. He'd wanted to be there when they took Sullivan out. Clete put a hand on his chin and worked his jaw from side to side, his eyes narrowing at the popping sounds it made. Luke Sullivan would pay for that if it was the last thing Clete did. He looked up, scanned the dark gray walls of the cliffs. There!

One minute, they weren't there, and the next minute they were. *Give any white man the creeps*, he thought. When he spotted a tall figure in buckskin slipping behind a rock, Clete's scalp rippled. And over there, another one. On the rocks above, three more hunched and moved into the trees. It seemed everywhere he looked, copper-skinned men clung like brown spiders to the cliffs on both sides of the canyon.

Images of Sullivan, bleeding and down on his knees, flashed in front of him, and arrows coming from nowhere. Riding a horse made him too easy a target. Clete kicked his feet free of the stirrups and slid off the horse. Running, he dove headfirst into a dry ditch carved out by the rains.

Axel and Chief Black Otter appeared on the ledge of the cliff above. Clete slid the barrel of his Winchester over the side of the ditch and lined up the Crow chief in his sights. He squeezed the trigger. A white scar blew out of the rock at the chief's feet, the slug ricocheting down the canyon.

Quickly, Clete cocked the rifle and fired again, trying to get the range right. This time, the bullet whined over the Indian's head. Better. As Black Otter broke for the shelter of a boulder, Clete's Winchester roared once more. The bullet's impact sent the chief to the ground. He slid on his back halfway down the hillside. His leg useless, Black Otter elbowed his way behind a boulder and shouted in Crow.

His braves shot to their feet with yells of fury. Until that moment, not a bow had been drawn. Axel shouted down at Clete, gesturing wildly, pointing behind him. Clete lifted his head and peered over the edge of the ditch, saw what looked to him like a whole tribe of enraged Crows swarming down the hillside after him. He scrambled out of the ditch and made a frantic dash for his horse.

Luke aimed and fired. A geyser of mud and dirt blew out of the ground between Clete and the horse. Half a dozen archers drew.

Clete snatched the bridle and held the frightened horse still. He had his boot in the stirrup when the first arrow hooked in hard in his upper arm. Face twisted, Clete grabbed for the shaft and tried to pull it out. A red-hot poker drove into his hip, burying itself and a piece of his trousers deep into muscle, and slamming him against the horse. The animal snorted and ran away, holding its head at an odd angle to avoid the trailing reins.

Clete had hardly hit the ground when Little Turtle and three Crow braves shinnied down the cliff and dangled from an overhanging ledge. They dropped, landed on their feet. Knives drawn, they ran to the downed white man.

Clete tried to get his gun up but with no success, as he was knocked flat on his back by a moccasined foot. Cursing, he grabbed the fist clenching his hair, and then his oath turned into a long, hoarse scream.

On the hillside across the ravine, Luke's stomach roiled. He'd heard those screams before. Swallowing, he turned away, and for the first time, Bart Axel got a look at the Indian in buckskins who'd shot at Clete.

"Sullivan!" he yelled.

Face twisting, Axel yanked the Schofield from its holster and fired. The impact of the slug tore into the fleshy part of Luke's arm and knocked him to the ground. Red gushing from his sleeve, he slid in the dirt partway down the embankment.

Axel turned and jumped down the hillside, zigzagging, sliding, half falling in a race for the ravine and Clete's excited little mare. Grabbing the saddle horn, he threw himself onto her back and kicked her into a run.

Luke struggled to a sitting position. Leaning into the steep incline, he braced his feet against a rock, lifted the butt of the rifle to his shoulder, and clenched his teeth into the fringed sleeve on his left arm, pulling it up like a sling. The buckskin was slimy with his blood, and pain stabbed down to his fingernails.

Supporting the barrel with his injured arm, he raced the sights ahead of Axel on the horse and fired. Missed.

Clumsily, he tried to cock the lever to shoot again, but his left hand had gone numb and shook uncontrollably. He couldn't hold the gun up, couldn't feel the weight of the barrel anymore. Feeling sick and shivery, he watched Axel ride away.

He felt it before he heard it—the ground vibrating under his hips. Like a distant avalanche, the rumble of hooves came from around the bend. Hemmed in by the high rock walls, the herd thundered around the curve.

Axel heard it too, and looked back over his shoulder, then flailed his legs into his horse. Lashing the reins back and forth in a stinging arc across its neck, he drove the animal faster, trying to get out of the way of the herd.

The lead bulls barreled alongside him, jostling the little mare and her rider, spooning up clods of dirt. The others followed right behind, overtaking them, surrounding them. Caught in the middle of a crushing mass of steers and clacking horns, Axel fired his revolver into the air and whipped the horse toward the outside of the herd. Encircled by crazed cattle on all sides, Axel galloped along in the suffocating din with no choice but to ride it out.

From the ledge above, Luke saw the horse's shoulder dip as it broke stride. For a moment, she seemed to rise above the heaving backs of the herd around them, thrust upward by the surging momentum. Axel's hat flew off, cartwheeled across a steer's back, and disappeared. Then horse and rider sank together into a cloud of yellow dust and hooves. The last of the herd disappeared down the canyon.

The distant rumbling of the herd grew louder, and with it the bellowing racket of cattle approaching.

Luke slid down the hill to Black Otter, snatching, grabbing at brush with his good arm. Crows at the other end of the canyon had turned the herd. Confused, the cows were stampeding back this way.

Black Otter started to slide. Wide-eyed, he reached his hand up to Luke.

Luke grabbed it and crooked a leg around a small tree, praying it would hold them and keep them both from rolling into the herd below. The ground trembled with the pounding of hooves.

Lord, quick, I need some help down here!

Feet first, three braves dropped over the top led by Curly Bear, digging their heels in, skidding down to the two men. Luke bent over the chief and tugged at his leggings, trying to get to the wound to stop the bleeding. Curly Bear shoved him aside and drew his knife. With a flick of his hand, he slashed the leather open from hip to ankle.

Luke tied a strip of the cut legging into a tourniquet.

The gush of blood slowed. It wasn't nearly good enough, but it was all he could do for now. "Let's get him to New Hope and a doctor," he said.

Wincing, Black Otter said something to the men that Luke didn't understand, then closed his eyes. The four of them, lifting and crawling, got the chief up to the top and boosted him over the edge. Tom Cosgrove, lying on his stomach, hauled Luke up the last few feet.

Luke sagged against a tree trunk, panting and holding his arm. "Go get Doc Maxwell. Tell him to meet us at New Hope. Tell him to hurry."

CHAPTER
20

As night settled in, the Indians began arriving at New Hope. Some walked, while others rode in on horseback, dragging loaded travois through the woods and setting up their tipis in the field beyond the barn. Members of the Dog Soldiers and Fox Warriors, solemn, straight-backed men with braids down to their waists, simply appeared a few hours after the stampede. In small groups of two or three they stood around the yard, talking quietly, waiting for word from inside about Black Otter.

On the back porch, three braves stepped aside, one of them holding the kitchen door as Emily came out with a bucket and headed for the well again.

Every window was ablaze with light. Inside, Doc Maxwell and Emily had turned the library into an infirmary, a makeshift operating room. He and Scully rolled the piano against the wall, while Emily padded the long oak reading table with newspapers and quilts and covered it with sheets. It took three men – Doc and Scully and a Crow medicine man – to move the big Indian onto the table. They worked on him for hours.

The chief's face was sunken, wrinkled with pain. From hip to ankle, his leg was splinted and wrapped in bandages. Maxwell squeezed his shoulder gently. It had been an ordeal for all of them. Twice, his patient had fainted on the table as Doc struggled to stop the hemorrhaging, set the bones, and stitch the gaping wound closed. Maxwell gave him another injection of morphine.

Black Otter's gaze held on the shaman kneeling by the fireplace. At the chief's request, he'd remained in the room, occasionally bending over Black Otter's injured body with Doc's stethoscope plugged in his ears, listening, wide-eyed, to his chief's heartbeat as Maxwell removed chips of bone from the chief's leg.

The man's presence reassured Black Otter, and for Maxwell that – and the relief in the chief's eyes as the painkiller took hold – was enough. However crude and rudimentary the shaman's knowledge of medicine, the two men shared this patient.

"Your medicine puts him to sleep," Maxwell's barefoot assistant had said, shaking his head in disapproval.

Maxwell nodded. "Sleep is good."

Daybreak brightened the windows at the end of the library before Doc Maxwell finished and they got Black Otter into a bed brought into the library. With a sigh, the doctor straightened up over the chief and rolled his sleeves down.

Maxwell snapped his bag shut and started for the door. As

he did, the shaman slung a white buffalo robe over his shoulders and opened a leather pouch. He sorted through the sacred bundle, preparing for the prayers and rites with which he would heal his chief as soon as the white doctor was gone.

Doc Maxwell smiled and slipped out into the hall.

It seemed all wrong to Emily. The morning after the stampede had dawned with birds chittering and a sky so bright, so blue, it hurt her eyes to look at it. As if nothing had happened, she thought. Life went on.

For hours last night, she'd dozed in Luke's arms on the sofa in the darkened parlor, listening to the serious voices in the hall, and waiting until Doc Maxwell could leave Black Otter and attend to Luke.

Early this morning, she slipped from his arms and stood up. She straightened her clothes and patted her hair, trying to put herself together. Still sleepy, she rubbed her face. Coffee — she needed some coffee to clear her head. Trying not to wake Luke, she left the room quietly and went off to the kitchen.

Alone in the big room, she poked sticks of kindling into the firebox of the stove to start breakfast. No one had slept much the night before, and from the looks of Luke when she left him, he was worn out. It had been a nightmare, beginning the afternoon before, when Luke, New Hope's men, and a dozen Crow Indians rode up with an unconscious Black Otter in a litter.

"Any coffee?"

She smiled, recognizing his voice. "Not yet." She turned.

Still in his bloodstained buckskins, Luke stood in the doorway, his left arm hanging useless in a sling. She glanced away, her eyes filling.

In three steps he was beside her. "Don't do that," he said, his voice husky. "I hate it when you cry."

"I'm sorry. I keep thinking you could've been killed."

"But I wasn't."

"Not this time." She pulled away, filled the big percolator with water, its strainer with ground coffee, and set it on the stove to brew. She didn't know if Indians drank coffee or not, but it would be there if they did.

Luke slid his hand around her waist and turned her to him. For several minutes he wrapped his good arm around her and watched the flames licking the kindling in the stove. The air in the kitchen hung heavy with the familiar smell of woodsmoke.

She sighed and wondered why things happened the way they did. Axel and Clete both killed. "What an awful day," she said, and leaned her face against his shoulder.

Luke nuzzled her ear. "Let's go upstairs to your room. Or mine. I don't care which. I want to be alone with you. We need to talk."

She shook her head against his chest. "We can't. It wouldn't look right."

"After yesterday, I don't care what it looks like or what other people think. I care what you think." The words came out harsh. He was angry and hurting, both inside and out. He paused, took a long breath, then said, "That's what I want to talk to you about. Going upstairs together, I mean. No one would pay any attention to it if we were married."

Emily didn't answer right away, but instead let the words soak in, unsure if she'd heard him right. "But we're not married," she said softly.

A slow smile drifted across Luke's face. "Why don't we change that?" A big warm hand ran up and down her arm, his voice as quiet as hers. He held her away from him and looked down at her, she up at him. "Marry me, before something else goes wrong."

"I'm not sure I know what you're saying," she said.

"I'm saying I love you. What do I have to do—go down on one knee before you understand?"

Emily gave him a wobbly smile. "You'd never do that, not in a million years. Besides, the way you look right now, I don't think you could."

"I might just be able to manage it," he said, backing up a step, as if to show her that he could do it if he had to.

"Don't," she said, alarmed. "You'll never forgive me."

"You're too smart to marry me, but I'm asking, anyway. Will you?"

Emily started to throw her arms around him but remembered the arm in the sling across his chest just in time. She checked herself and hugged him gently instead. "Yes, I will."

He swooped her up with his good arm and swung her feet off the floor. In a hoarse whisper he said, "Yahoo! Thank you, Lord. I must've done something right."

An hour later Doc Maxwell said, "Hold still, Luke. Let me see what we got here." He dug in his bag resting on the table in the kitchen and pulled out several sharp, shiny instruments. "Throw those in that pot of boiling water over there, will you?" he said to Emily, then slowly rotated Luke's wrist and elbow, nodding, making noncommittal doctor sounds in his throat. "Like I said, it's not broke. Just shot clean through. Real nice-looking hole, too."

"Thanks," Luke said dryly.

Emily leaned forward, watching everything Doc did, blanching at the run of fresh blood as Doc started probing around in the hole in Luke's arm.

Across the room, Sheriff Tucker leaned against a cupboard, scribbling in a small notebook.

"What happened to Axel's men?" Luke asked him.

Before Tucker could answer, Doc's scissors snipped out a ragged shred of live flesh still attached somewhere inside. Luke's jaw clamped shut tight, and he set his teeth hard together and swallowed a groan. He scowled at Doc Maxwell. "That hurt."

The sheriff looked up from his notebook. "I already had three of Axel's men in jail," he said, his voice curt and business-like. "Then this morning I woke up to find six of the strangest cowpokes I've ever seen in my life standing inside my office. They had the rest of the drivers of the Parker herd with 'em, trussed up like turkeys. Said they wanted to swear out war-rants against them."

"Let them," Luke said.

"No. Under the law, Haldane and those men ain't done one single thing wrong."

"What?" Disbelieving, Luke looked up.

"Under the law, I said. After all, they were driving their

own cattle, wearing their own brand." The sheriff shook his head. "Six Injuns with tomahawks and guns, dressed like white men – sort of – every one of 'em madder than I've ever seen an Injun. Speaking of which, Doc, how's Black Otter doing?"

Maxwell dusted a powder that stung like a hive of bees into the raw hole in Luke's arm.

"Ye-ow!" His patient leaped off the stool, doubled over, his arm cradled protectively against his chest.

"Sit down, Luke. I'm not done yet." Doc turned back to the sheriff. "The shot busted the chief's leg and messed up an artery. He's in bed in the other room. I expect he'll be all right in a couple months. His people are all riled up, though, and don't know as I blame 'em, either. His medicine man's back there with him now, burning pine needles and rattling bones."

"At least that doesn't hurt," Luke muttered, glaring at Maxwell.

"You're right there." Doc smiled blandly. "Don't work, neither. Sit down, I said."

Sheriff Tucker ignored the exchange and continued. "Well, I wasn't about to argue with six Crows. So I locked Axel's men up for rustling their own cattle. Probably kept them alive, though."

"How's that?"

"The Crows said Haldane got away, escaped when they were bringing him in. Don't know as I believe 'em, though. There was no way to prove he killed Jupiter, and they knew it. I just figure we won't be seeing him again. And if they'd brought him in, I'da had to turn him loose for lack of evidence. At least, that's what the boss says."

Luke's snapped his head up. "What boss?"

Tucker's lips thinned, and his voice went frosty. "The whole Department of Justice, the Attorney General, and the President of these United States, Mr. Sullivan. They are my bosses. And I was wrong when I figured you couldn't do much more in Repton. Before I came out here today, I got a telegram from Washington. Seems a whole lot of folks are upset down there. They say I got a federal treaty violation against the Crow Nation, a shootout between – if you can believe it – two groups of white men on a Indian reservation, and every man-jack of you swearing the Crows weren't involved."

"They weren't," Luke said firmly.

"Then how come I got a Indian chief with a bullet in his leg and a scalping to explain?" He sighed. "I just may have to go to Washington on this myself."

"Sheriff," Luke said slowly, "if you do go to Washington, would you mind taking New Hope's deed with you?"

Tucker's eyes narrowed. "Why?"

"Because it's wrong. Part of New Hope land belongs to Black Otter and his people. The government made a mistake when they drew up the treaty."

Unblinking, Sheriff Tucker stared at Luke for a full minute, his face hardening. Pushing himself away from the table, he gave a disgusted snort. "The U.S. government made a mistake on a treaty, you say? In the middle of all this mess I got, you really expect me to tell Washington that?"

"Please, Sheriff," Emily broke in. "The Crow are good people. They don't deserve this."

Sheriff Tucker started for the door. Hand on the knob, he turned around, as if he'd just remembered something. "By the way, I heard outside in the hall that you and Mr. Sullivan are getting married. Is that a fact?"

"Yes," she said. "Next month. We just decided."

Luke went to Emily and with his good arm pulled her close to him. "In Repton. A big church wedding next month when Molly gets back. You're invited. The whole town's invited."

"Well, well, well. Congratulations! That's mighty nice, Mr. Sullivan. Tell me," he said, smiling, "you plan on having a large family by any chance?"

"Half a dozen," Luke said, beaming at Emily.

Tucker's eyebrows shot up. "Six?"

"At least," Emily said.

Tucker's smile faded. He went out the door and shut it quietly behind him. Outside, he untied his horse and swung himself into the saddle. Halfway back to Repton, he looked at the mass of black clouds piling up on the horizon and churning toward him across the sky. A sobering thought flickered through his mind like the distant lightning.

Six little Sullivans. Six of them. And probably every blasted one a redhead.

Tucker raised his eyes to the rainy skies overhead. "Hey, Sir—if you can hear me up there—any chance you could make 'em all girls?"

A mile-high tree of lightning blazed in the sky, and an instant thunderclap exploded like artillery.

"I was afraid you'd say that," Tucker muttered. "Soon as Luke said he was marrying her in church, everything changed."

ACKNOWLEDGMENTS

To Bob Lemen, "Cowboy Bob" Lemen, a former Minnesota state legislator, writer, amateur historian, and horseman, who helped vet some of the details in this book. His Web site—*www.lemen.com*—has thousands of insights into good horsemanship and Old West history.

To Mary Margret Daughtridge, who was always there and willing to put down her own writing to read for me.

To Ron Kent, my crit partner and head cheerleader, never too busy to brainstorm over coffee.

To Monica Harris, my eagle-eyed sister-in-law and first reader.

To Dr. Rosemary Harris, who made certain the medical history and details were accurate and who inherited her mother's weakness for cowboys.

To Jolie Bosakowski, who dragged her high-stepping grandmother in and out of more horse barns than she cares to count.

To David Long and Luke Hinrichs, two editors this writer was lucky to have in her corner. Their encouragement and support meant so much.

And to Mary Sue Seymour, my agent, for unfailingly good advice.

ABOUT THE AUTHOR

Yvonne Harris earned a Bachelor of Science degree in Education from the University of Hartford and has taught throughout New England and the mid-Atlantic. She lives in Southern New Jersey and teaches writing at a local college. She is a winner and three-time finalist for the Golden Heart Award. *The Vigilante's Bride* was a 2009 finalist and is her first historical romance novel.

She is the author of *Hindu Kush,* a romantic suspense, and *For Honor,* winner of the 2002 EPPIE. Before she turned to fiction, she wrote business articles for magazines.

Though Yvonne and her husband live in New Jersey to be close to family, she was raised in Alabama and considers herself a Southern writer.

If you enjoyed *The Vigilante's Bride,* you may also like…

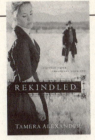

In the late 1860s, three couples carve out a new life in the wild, untamed Colorado Territory. Each person will be called upon to stand on nothing more than faith, risk what is most dear to them, and turn away from the past in order to detect God's plan for the future. By the time Colorado becomes a state, will they be united by love or defeated by adversity?

Fountain Creek Chronicles series by Tamera Alexander
Rekindled, Revealed, Remembered

Nestled beneath the Maroon Bells in the Colorado Rockies is an untamed land that holds the promise of a fresh start. As three women from the East carve out a place for themselves in the community of Timber Ridge, they seek to fulfill their dreams and hopes in a place where love has the power to change lives.

Timber Ridge Reflections series by Tamera Alexander
From a Distance, Beyond This Moment, Within My Heart—**Coming Soon!**